CRESCENDO

by

PHYLLIS BENTLEY

LONDON
VICTOR GOLLANCZ LTD
1958

The lines in italics on page 167 are from
Worry About Money by Kathleen Raine,
which appears in *The Pythoness* published
by Hamish Hamilton Ltd.

*Printed in Great Britain by Richard Clay and Company, Ltd.,
Bungay, Suffolk*

CONTENTS

Part One: IMPULSE

    Peter   9

Part Two: CRESCENDO

  1. Ernest Armley, foreman   15

  2. A. A. J. Barraclough, millowner   37

  3. Richard Cressey, schoolmaster   70

  4. Dorothea Dean, shop assistant   98

  5. Ethel Eastwood, landlady   112

  6. Francis Freeman, stage designer   129

Part Three: COUNTER-IMPULSE

    Gay   173

Part Four: DIMINUENDO

  1. Ethel Eastwood   183

  2. Dorothea Dean   188

  3. Richard Cressey   191

  4. Arnold Barraclough   196

  5. Ernest Armley   213

PART ONE
IMPULSE

PETER

"Every moment of the world's history is a product of all the previous moments," said the old man.

"I don't altogether admit that as far as humanity is concerned," said Peter Trahier, smiling.

He spoke with deference, because there was nobody in the world he respected more than his father-in-law; his very love for his wife, which formed so great and deep a part of his existence, had begun in the look in her eyes, the spring in her step, the note in her voice, the nobility in her nature, which she derived from that powerful, experienced, rather terrifying, still handsome old man, her father. Peter had loved her for that before he had desired her for her beauty. "Every moment is a product of all the *relevant* previous moments," suggested Peter courteously. Much, very much, that he knew and was, though not perhaps as much as he had once thought, reflected Peter, he owed to courteous discussion with his father-in-law.

"All moments are relevant."

"No, sir. Excuse me. Suppose a man dying in a desert. Alone."

"Alone with himself."

"Well, yes. But he's going to die before he makes contact with anyone else. Now suppose that man performs some base act."

"Such as what, for example?"

"Well—suppose he gulps his last mouthful of water greedily, in an impolite and vulgar manner."

"Then he will die less well than if he had drunk politely."

"Granted. But nobody sees him."

"Possibly when his body is discovered, that last crude failure of decency shows in his bodily attitude."

9

"Certainly not," said Peter, laughing. "He's not found till he's become a skeleton. Nothing is deducible from the posture of his bones. Nobody hears of his action, nobody ever knows. How then can his action affect any succeeding moment of the world's history?"

"The history of the world, viewed in its totality, is the blacker for his vulgar action."

"But who is to see that? Who is to know it?"

"A man who believed in God would answer: God," replied the old man. "But I am too doubtful of his existence to give you that answer. Instead I will say: it is worth while acting rightly, simply to make the sum of human activity nobler."

"You must excuse me, sir," said Peter, smiling and moving his neat sandy head sideways with a cheerful, confident, slightly condescending air: "If I say I consider that far-fetched."

"Not nearly as far-fetched as your man in the desert," said his father-in-law, also smiling. "What a long way you had to go to find a human action which could not have a direct result! However, my dear Peter, I ask you to remember that men dying alone in deserts are very rare. Most of us are inextricably entangled with our fellow humans. Our every action has its consequences in their lives."

"Granted again," said Peter. "But life is so complex now-adays, so many factors enter into every situation, that what you call a 'good' action can as easily have bad consequences for some persons, as a 'bad' action."

"True," admitted the old man. "But in that case, if you have acted with all the knowledge, power and goodwill at your disposal, you are not *morally* responsible. If you have not acted to the best of your ability, and evil ensues, you are morally responsible. Suppose, for example, a fire-engine rushing to save your house in response to your call, encounters some accident and a man is killed. If your call was genuine, you have no moral responsibility for the man's death; if your call was deliberately false, I think you have. It is a heavy responsibility. One sometimes finds it hard to bear."

A look of gentle derision crossed Peter's face.

The old man is growing perhaps a little *too* old, he reflected. Out of date. All these ethical categories have long since gone by the board. Still, they do him credit, of course. He wouldn't be so lovable without them. "To return to the beginning of our argument," he said aloud, with an air of returning to reality from illusion: "I still feel that one should subordinate one's means to one's ends. One must keep a sense of proportion. Minute scruples must be waived for the public good."

"There speaks the rising politician," said the old man grimly.

Peter coloured, not altogether with displeasure.

"Let us state the problem in specific terms," said he. ("I enjoy hearing myself talk," he thought: "And why not? I talk well.") "Will you grant that it is for the public good that I should be elected to the Hudley Town Council rather than my opponent in the ward, who is generally admitted to be a mean-minded, uninformed, outdated and not very honest person?"

"I shall vote for you, certainly."

"On the afternoon of this day, Monday June 9th, I saw, through the windows of the Ashworth County Borough Treasurer's Office, where I work, the Alderman who is the head of my party in the Hudley Town Council, passing along the street outside. It was useful to my candidature to see him."

"You mean you wanted the opportunity to ingratiate yourself with him."

"Put it that way if you like, I don't mind. My motives for wishing to be on the Council are above reproach. What shall I get out of it anyway, except a lot of hard unpaid work?"

"Power, perhaps," murmured the old man.

"I desire it only so as to serve the community."

"Well—I grant you that, Peter."

"To leave my work a few minutes early——"

"—was a breach of trust."

"But it was more important for the welfare of the community that I should leave than that I should stay. There was nobody waiting to be attended to, at my counter. Therefore on an impulse I left, and had a most useful and helpful conversation with the Alderman. My contention is that the impulse was justified."

"You put your case well, Peter."

"It was you who taught me to do so, sir."

"But all the same you are wrong. The whole structure of society collapses unless it is supported by its members' good faith."

"I must repeat and insist," said Peter with a slight impatience: "That an action which a man performs alone, which nobody else ever knows or hears of, cannot affect the course of the world's history."

"How is one to know?" said the old man thoughtfully. "In any case, my dear Peter, the action affects the man himself, and therefore affects all his subsequent actions."

Peter's wife came into the room, carrying a loaded tray. Peter went up to her and took the tray from her. Moved, as always, by her radiant serenity, and especially moved now because she was bearing their first child, he kissed her lightly but tenderly on the mouth. He did not wish, now, to appear to be differing seriously from her father.

"All this because I left the office three minutes before the clock struck this afternoon!" said Peter in a tone of affectionate raillery.

"Exactly," murmured the old man.

PART TWO
CRESCENDO

I

ERNEST ARMLEY, FOREMAN

I

ERNEST GAVE A careful, meticulously detailed account of all the defects he had noticed in the cropping-machine he and Mr. Arnold had just inspected together at the maker's with a view to purchase.

"Oh, come, Ernest," said Mr. Arnold, turning the car into the main Ashworth road: "I think you take rather too serious a view, you know. Those are all minor points, mere matters of a screw here and there."

"The bed's that inaccessible, it'll take half an hour to change the cover every day, and half hours cost money," said Ernest gloomily. "But of course that's your affair, Mr. Arnold, not mine."

His tone was offended. He felt vexed because he thought his employer spoke too lightly, was not valuing his opinion at its true worth, and if Mr. Arnold thought he knew more about cropping cloth than Ernest did, he could think again, that's all.

Mr. Arnold began to describe the machine's good points. Ernest listened, nodding gravely from time to time. But while he listened, he pondered. Perhaps he *had* been rather too earnest about that bed cover. Ernest by name and earnest by nature—that had always been Millie's joke, ever since the day he asked her to marry him. But it had begun earlier than that, his earnestness. Ernest knew just when it had begun.

It did not spring from anything in his childhood. True, his

father, a large heavy man who drove a waggon for an Ashworth textile firm, was rather slow in speech and thought; but
he was not bad-tempered or even glum—there was nothing
the boy Ernest enjoyed more than a day out with his father. In
those days the waggons—they were really long flat drays—
were drawn by horses, and required a whole day for a journey
from Ashworth to Leeds and back, a distance of some fifteen
miles. Ernest's father sat on the side of the dray holding the
reins and Ernest sat beside him, and the big solid brown horse
drew them slowly up and down the hills of the West Riding.
The pieces of cloth lay on the waggon covered by a tarpaulin;
if rain or snow fell heavily his father, silent but smiling, would
lift the edge of the tarpaulin and Ernest would creep within;
his father however remained outside, his cap well pulled down,
a sack over his shoulders, heroically impervious to the weather.
When they set out in the early morning the roads were full of
exciting things to look at: people, horses, trams, railways in the
valleys; Ernest's father occasionally explained some of these
sights to Ernest, slowly, in a few mumbled words but under-
standably to his son. Then as they climbed higher the air grew
colder and the traffic rarer, and Ernest's father would point
his whip at distant landmarks and speak their name. The
town again and busy traffic, and a mill with a boiler winking
fiery eyes, and a crust to eat while Ernest's father helped by
one of the mill men carried the pieces in and took on a fresh
load, and then back slowly over the hills, perhaps with dusk
falling and lanterns swinging back and front, to the lighted
streets of Ashworth and the mill, and home. Yes, Ernest loved
a day out with his father; it was not his father who had made
him over-earnest. Nor was it his mother, who though rather
sardonic and trenchant in manner, was thoroughly warmhearted, nor his two younger sisters, of whom he was suitably
fond in a mild way. Of course, being the eldest of the family
and the only boy, Ernest always had a proper sense of responsibility—he could be trusted to take the two younger children

into the park and bring them back dry and in one piece, keeping them from all dangers of pond and steps and mowing-
machine—but it did not weigh him unduly down; they were a
happy family and he took it in his stride. Trouble befell the
Armley family early in Ernest's life, when horse-drawn waggons were superseded by motor lorries, and his father, unable
to learn this new technique, from being the all-powerful driver
became merely the driver's mate. His wages suffered a corre-
sponding decrease and Ernest's mother had a good deal to say
about it, but though the child Ernest was saddened by all this,
in his secret heart he admitted the justice of the demotion, and
he saw that his father admitted it too. No—it was not this
trouble, though of course it gave him much food for serious
thought, which planted the chip on Ernest's shoulder.

The incident which really caused the iron to enter Ernest's
soul, as he preferred to describe it, took place in his teens, at
the mill where his father was employed. Those were the good
days in the wool textile trade, the post-first-world-war boom
days, and Ernest's father had had no difficulty in getting the
boy taken on. The pride and joy with which Ernest set off to
the mill beside his father on that Monday morning, his first
day at his first job, would never be forgotten by Ernest; he
could see yet the happiness which beamed back at him from
his dark brown eyes as he combed his straight dark hair in
front of the mirror by the sink in the living-room downstairs.
Father and son took a tram together through the early morning dark; they met other workers from the mill in the crowded
tram, Ernest was introduced and men nodded kindly to him.
They entered the mill and clocked in, the buzzer sounded,
the machinery stirred; Ernest felt that now he was indeed a
man.

Ernest was bidden to the warehouse, where the pieces of
cloth were packed and despatched, and ordered to assist an old
man who was stitching up bales of cloth with string threaded
through a long thick crooked needle. At this time a tall, weedy

youth with rather large feet and thin though muscular arms, Ernest heaved at the heavy bales and held the coarse sacking in position energetically. Presently a sudden silence, a sudden cessation of all chat, warned him that some boss or other was in the neighbourhood. Out of the corner of his eye he perceived such a one approach: a youngish man in a blue suit, boss's son probably, with a collar and tie. He paused nearby and appeared to watch Ernest. Not unwilling to be commended, Ernest tugged at the heavy wrapper with especial zeal, then turned eagerly towards the next bale. As he had thought, the blue-suited boss was watching him.

"Finding that a bit heavy, eh?" said the boss.

His understanding, sympathetic tone was very agreeable to Ernest; it would be something to tell at home, that the boss had spoken to him so friendly like on his first morning. He felt himself colour with pleasure.

"Aye, just a bit," said Ernest truthfully, nodding.

"You'd better get your cards, then," said the boss, and turned away.

Even now, more than thirty years later, Ernest, sitting at his present boss's side, prosperous, respected, a foreman earning fourteen pounds a week with a television set and a threepiece upholstered suite and an electric washing-machine (all paid for, not bought on the never-never, mind you, Ernest would have none of that, except for Kenneth's motor-bike)—even now he could not think of that awful moment without deep anguish. To be sacked like that on his first morning! Before breakfast! To say he was stunned was altogether below the mark; it almost killed him. His mouth dropped open, his eyes almost fell out of his head; he felt the blood drain away from his cheeks. (And indeed his complexion was never bright-coloured again; from that moment onward—the doctors mightn't be able to explain it, thought Ernest grimly, they could pooh-pooh it as they liked, but it was a fact—his face was colourless.) He stood silent and motionless, swaying on his

18

feet, till some of the men came up to him and with great kindness and sympathy urged him to go home right away. They clapped him on the shoulder, they handed him his cap and coat, they said they'd explain it all to his father when he came in—luckily the lorry had driven off before the incident, for if it had occurred in front of his father, Ernest thought, he would without any doubt have died of shame. He found himself in the open air with his insurance card in his hand; he thrust it into his coat pocket as if it burned him.

His first impulse was to get home and hide himself as quick as he could, but he remembered in time that his two sisters would not have left for school yet, and he did not want to face them. So he walked home taking a long way round. He had sometimes thought since that this was a pity. If he had reached his mother while he was still in a blazing rage, so that he could have stamped and shouted and perhaps even—for he was only a boy after all—given out a sob or two, and received comfort from her, it might have been better for him. As it was, by the time he reached home it was too late for that. His anger had turned cold and hard and lay like a bar of iron—yes, just like iron, the psalmist knew what he was talking about—heavy in his entrails; it would never melt again.

His mother, energetic woman, was standing on tiptoe hanging out the weekly wash on the clothes line stretched across the street, when he arrived. She gazed at him aghast, a clothes peg in one hand, and came down slowly on her heels.

"Ernest! What's matter, love? Are you feeling poorly?"

Ernest could not speak; he raised the sneck of the door-latch and went into the house. His mother followed him.

"What's wrong, love? It's not your father happened an accident?" she said in terror.

"No. I've lost my job."

"Lost your job! Why, you've hardly getten it."

Drily, Ernest related the incident.

"Whatever will your father say!" exclaimed his mother.

She had perceived at once, what Ernest only now understood, that his father's position among his fellow-employees had been compromised by the dismissal of his son. His father would lose face, having a son to be ashamed of. It was an added misery.

"Well, never mind, love," said his mother warmly, putting her arm about Ernest's shoulders. "It wasn't your fault. Don't take on, now."

"I won't," said Ernest grimly.

"I'll make you a cup of tea," said his mother.

He drank it sitting in his coat, with his elbows on the table, then took up his cap.

"Where are you going, love?" said his mother. "Stay home a bit with me."

"I'm going to Labour Exchange," said Ernest.

"Well," said his mother, reluctantly conceding the point.

Luckily those were the good days of the wool textile trade, the post-first-world-war boom days, thought Ernest again—he hadn't realised at the time just how lucky that was, but by God he had realised it later. He got another job by the end of the week, with a bigger firm which owned several mills in different locations around Ashworth, so that outwardly, you might say, the "sympathetic" incident, as Ernest always called it to himself, hadn't done much harm. But inwardly it had made a lasting mark. The wound had never healed, but lay there always ready to suppurate. The bitter disappointment, even the injustice, of the dismissal, might have been endured. The Armleys worked it out among themselves that probably the job given to Ernest was wanted for the son or nephew or friend's son of some person more important to the firm than Ernest's father, and this theory seemed strengthened if not absolutely confirmed by the identity of the lad who held it after Ernest. Then why could they not have said so straight out? (By *they* Ernest meant the boss class.) It would have been unjust to sack Ernest thus, but at least open and honest; it could have been endured. It was the pretence of sympathy which sickened Ernest. Sham! Cant! Humbug! Bunk! Never believe *them* again! Never let *them* take you in by pretending to understand, pretending to be on your side, for it was always lies! Never show a weakness, for *they* would always take advantage! Never! Never again! Never!

It was from the date of the sympathetic incident that Ernest became the over-earnest glum young man whom Millie joked about. He also became a very staunch, steady Trade Unionist and an admirable workman. He'd show 'em!

For the next few years there was nothing, certainly, to cheer him. In 1926 came the General Strike. ("Serve 'em right!" thought Ernest with a sombre joy.) In 1931 came the frightful business recession. The firm his father served collapsed. Ernest was pleased, though for the Armleys it was, of course, a disaster. There were simply no jobs going in the textile trade; the old man got work for a few weeks as a night-watchman on some road repairs, but then the rheumatism which his hours of driving in the rain had started years ago descended on him and crippled him, and Ernest was left as the main financial stay of the family. (His sisters were by now both married, but their husbands were out of work like everybody else and on the dole, and they had children to keep.) An excruciating reorganisation took place in Ernest's firm; for a couple of years nobody ever knew from one week to the next whether they would have a wage-packet to take home or not. Ernest lay awake at night sweating with fear lest he should lose his job. He felt as if he were being buffeted incessantly by stormy seas which threatened to drown him, without being able to do anything to help himself—he had no confidence at all, of course, that *they* would manage to extricate the textile industry from its troubles. However, somehow he kept his job, and somehow —small thanks to *them*, Ernest felt sure—the waves gradually calmèd, though just before they really settled, his father, worn out by it all, developed rheumatic fever and painfully died.

Ernest felt angry about this; it was a shame his father could not see his son's later prosperity.

However, there it was. His mother and Ernest were left alone together. His mother began to tease him about getting married.

"And what would you do if I got wed?" enquired Ernest.

"Go to our Amy's," replied his mother promptly.

Amy was the younger of Ernest's sisters; her husband had turned into an invalid and Amy had to go out to work, so that a grandmother to look after the children would be of real assistance. Ernest pondered. He was now twenty-six, but had never yet seen a girl he had a fancy for. He looked around seriously to see if he could find one. Almost at once his eye fell on Millie. (Or perhaps after all he had noticed her before? He was never quite sure about this, though he often gave serious thought to the matter.) Millie was a mender at Holmelea Mills outside Ashworth where Ernest still worked after all these years; in a large light room opening off his own department she sat before a window, dealing with knots and broken ends in the cloths. Mending was highly skilled work so that menders' wages were relatively good; it was also a craft which mothers often taught their daughters. There were several of Millie's relatives, of different generations, beside herself in the mending-room; in fact, it was quite a family party; they were all large, plump, jolly women, with abundant brownish hair and sparkling grey-blue eyes, much given to laughter. Indeed their favourite beginning to an anecdote—and they told many— was: "It was that laughable . . ."

The gas stove on which the men's lunches and cups of tea were heated stood in the mending-room, and the menders were not averse to "giving an eye" to the food and drink of such of the men as were friendly with them. Ernest never ventured to ask this favour, but listened with interest, even smiling a little, to the repartee freely exchanged around him as he stood by the stove. When he began seriously to consider marriage somehow his thoughts flew at once to Millie, though he had hardly ex-

when he came in. The only time he ever remembered her crying, for example, in all the years of their married life, was when she dropped a dish of dehydrated potatoes which she had just hydrated and heated, during the war. The hot dish slipped from the oven-cloth to the floor and broke, and Millie burst into tears. (He was home on leave, Corporal Armley, at the time; that was when young Iris was started.) Yes, that was the only time he had ever seen his Millie shed tears. Upset because his meal was spoilt. Just like Millie. Always thinking of him and the children, never of herself. So he always took care—Millie called it worrying, he called it taking care—to let her know when he was going to be out late, or come in early. That's why he had been careful to tell her last night, Sunday, after supper, as they all sat round supping a bedtime cup of tea:

"Don't get in a panic now, if I'm late or early back tomorrow—I'm going out to buy a new machine with the boss."

Then what must young Kenneth do but up and ask if Ernest would be passing anywhere near Ashworth Town Hall.

"For if you are, dad," said he, "you might renew my driving licence for me, eh?"

Well, that was the younger generation for you. He'd reminded Kenneth and reminded him, over and over again, that his driving licence—he drove one of those motor-bikes, very unsafe Ernest thought it, particularly when he had his girl Edna planted on the back; the way they swerved round corners was nobody's business—was due on Monday, and with driving licences there were no days of grace allowed. He'd even brought Kenneth the necessary form. But still he hadn't renewed the licence. True, the engineering firm where Kenneth worked stood on a hill a good way out of town, so it wasn't easy for him to get to the Borough Treasurer's office in the Town Hall on a weekday. But there was Saturday morning, as Ernest explained to Kenneth; he could have renewed the licence then.

"The office closes at eleven-thirty on Saturdays, dad," said Kenneth.

Ernest was rather taken aback, but rallied.

"If you young chaps left your beds a little earlier, Ken," he began.

But Iris interrupted.

"Oh, don't be such a Malvolio, dad," she said.

"You have the advantage of me there, Iris," said Ernest seriously. "I don't know what that is."

"Oh, well, never mind, dad. I daresay he wasn't the same at home. Not to worry, as they say," said Iris, dropping a kiss on his bald spot as she passed on her way to the teapot. "Have another cuppa."

"Well, you know your dad," said Millie comfortably, passing Kenneth's licence and form across to Ernest. "Ernest by name and earnest by nature. You can't hardly expect him to change at his time of life."

Ernest, stowing the form and the little red book neatly away in his wallet, had pondered. Not to worry! That was what the doctor had said. But how could he help worrying? There was so much to worry about. He'd always thought so; he'd thought so last night and he certainly hadn't changed his mind today.

"I think I shall buy it, choose how," said Mr. Arnold at this point in a jocular tone. "We need another cropper, you know, Ernest."

There you were, you see! A new machine to be installed! Plenty to worry about, coming up!

"Well—it mightn't be so bad if we altered it a bit to suit us own idea, like. It'll do delicate work and run fast," agreed Ernest grudgingly.

Always new machines, running faster and faster, and complete automation just round the corner. (Ernest spared a thought here for his father the driver, superseded by the motor lorry.) But that was the least of it. If automation came, it came; he could do nothing about it one way or another. It was the things he was so to say responsible for which worried Ernest. Nuclear fission now—these bombs. Should we make them? Should we test them? Was Russia sincere? Was America over-bossy? (The antics of their Trades Unions made Ernest gravely shake his head. As for the Russians, they had no T.U.'s as he understood the term.)

But these things too, troubling though they were, did not worry Ernest as much as economic problems. All his life since the "sympathetic" incident he had been firmly determined, absolutely set, to distribute the wealth of the country more evenly and raise the standard of living for the working classes. Well, they'd done it and he rejoiced in it, and he hoped they'd go on doing it even more. But a whole batch of economic worries seemed to have come in the Welfare State train. Mr. Arnold, for instance, sometimes said that if wages went much higher, England would price herself out of world markets and lose her trade. Ernest listened sceptically. In the view of his party, the bosses never lost from a rise in wages, they always passed the rise straight on to the consumer, and took a little salary rise themselves on the way. On the other hand, in the thirty or so years he had known Mr. Arnold, he had found him on the whole shrewd, and honest within the code of his class; he was not one given to "sympathetic" humbug, he played the game according to the rules. Mr. Arnold said that the very thought of inflation made his hair stand on end; look what happened to the currencies and trade position of countries with inflation! England might quite simply starve, Ernest, he said, and that's flat. The young shop steward at Holmelea on the other hand said the Union didn't mind a spot of inflation as long as wages kept up with it—the worst time the workers had this century he pointed out, was with deflation, in 1931, and Ernest knew this to be true.

So there was much to ponder and worry about. It was all very well Iris saying "not to worry"; somebody had to worry or where would the working class be? These young people nowadays! His mother wouldn't have demeaned herself by entering a public-house, but his daughter Nora thought nothing of it, went regularly for a drink with her husband. And look at Kenneth's wages! And his motor-bicycle and his leather coat and that! The young people nowadays had no ideals, thought Ernest sadly; they couldn't be bothered to attend Union meetings, with them it was all football pools and rock and roll and motor-bikes and the telly. Everything for themselves and let the other fellow go hang.

"A chap's entitled to a bit of fun, dad," said Kenneth once, when Ernest expressed these sentiments.

Entitled? "A chap's not entitled to anything but what he earns, in my view," said Ernest slowly.

"Oh, go on, dad. Don't you want us to enjoy ourselves? Don't you want us to be happy?" said Kenneth, laughing.

Ernest pondered. Yes, he certainly wanted them to be happy. So it was all very perplexing. The rock bottom of it all was, that nowadays Ernest could not rightly see what was right and what was wrong. So how could he help worrying?

"You'll have to try, Mr. Armley," said the doctor.

The doctor. Yes. Because for several weeks this spring Ernest had suffered from pain in his abdomen; nausea, vomiting. But he had concealed his distress, he had fought it down as long as he could. Stay away from work? Show a weakness? Lay himself open to sham sympathy, which would lead in some clever fancy way to the sack? (*Finding the work a bit heavy, eh?*) No fear! Ernest endured in silence as long as he could, till he was hardly able to stand upright between his cropping-machines, then secretly, without a word even to Millie, he visited the doctor. Not that one could be very secret nowadays, under the National Health Service; all those queues! Still, Ernest had managed his various medical visits quite successfully; he set off to go ostensibly to a Union meeting, and dropped in at the tail end of the doctor's evening surgery and hadn't long to wait.

The doctor sent him to be X-rayed and he had to go off work in the middle of the afternoon; he lied at the mill and said the trouble was toothache (a thing that might happen to the healthiest person), not wanting to give himself away.

"You've got yourself a nice little ulcer with your worry, Mr. Armley," said the doctor, holding a set of nasty cloudy photographs up to the light. "You'll have to knock off work for a few weeks and stay in bed, drink milk every four hours and forget your worries, or you'll be in for an operation."

"And what do I use for money meanwhile, eh?" said Ernest grimly.

"Talk sense, man," said the doctor. "You'll have your National Health benefit."

"And suppose I don't lay off work, what'll happen?"

"The ulcer will get rapidly worse," said the doctor shortly.

"I shall worry far more lying at home in bed than standing about at the mill," said Ernest.

"Rubbish," said the doctor.

They argued the matter back and forth for some time.

"Well, if you want to be a fool in your own way, of course you can," said the doctor at length. "But don't say I didn't warn you."

He prescribed a diet, medicine, as much rest as possible, and repeated strongly his injunctions that Ernest should not allow himself to be irritated, should avoid sudden shocks and angers, and above all should not worry.

"I'm not given to bursts of temper," said Ernest stiffly, offended.

"No? Well, that's all to the good," said the doctor.

He clapped Ernest on the shoulder and pushed him gently out of the consulting-room. "Come in to see me every week, keep to a milk diet and don't get worked up about anything, and you may get rid of it without our having to do anything drastic."

In point of fact, now that Ernest knew what the trouble was

and what had to be done to cure it, he felt much better. He obeyed the doctor's orders with his usual meticulous care. He told Millie that his stomach was a trifle out of order and she gave him his milk punctiliously; he went to bed early and rested all day on Saturdays and Sundays; above all, when he felt vexation rising in him he subdued it and tried to think of something else—his newest grandson, a charming infant in white creepers, was very useful in this respect. As a result, he had had no severe attack of pain in the last five weeks, and the doctor was pleased with his progress.

"The ulcer's quiescent," he said.

"Isn't it going away?" demanded Ernest, disappointed.

"Possibly," said the doctor. "Yes, possibly it may be diminishing. On the whole I believe it is. You may be going to escape more lightly than you deserve."

Ernest grinned, well satisfied. Nobody except the doctor and himself had ever heard the word ulcer mentioned in connection with Ernest—certainly Mr. Arnold, sitting so bland at his side and thinking about the new machine, knew nothing of his foreman's ailment, and if Ernest had his way, never would.

They had now reached Ashworth. Mr. Arnold glanced at his watch.

"There's no point in your going on to the mill now, Ernest. You'd hardly get there before it was time to turn round and come back."

Ernest looked up at the Town Hall clock. It was ten minutes to five.

"That's right," he agreed. "I gave the lads full instructions for the work this afternoon, before I came out," he added virtuously.

"Shall I run you up home? It's still Walker Street, isn't it?"

There was just time to get Kenneth's licence before the Borough Treasurer's Office closed.

"No—I'll just get out here, if it's same to you."

The car drew up beyond the corner.

On the one hand, Ernest was quite glad that the business of the licence forbade his acceptance of his employer's offer, for he liked to keep his independence, he wanted no sympathetic humbug from anyone. On the other hand, he couldn't help regretting it. The June day was hot and he was tired, and the buses up Walker Street would be full when the buzzers sounded in a few minutes' time. However, it was worth a sacrifice to save the boy from possible trouble with the police. He got out of the car, shut the door carefully, gave his usual rather dour smile in farewell, and turned along the street towards Ashworth Town Hall.

2

Sunshine blazed on the windows of the Borough Treasurer's Office, and a wave of warm stale air puffed into Ernest's face as he pushed open one of the heavy swing doors. He entered and stood for a moment gazing seriously about him, taking in the appearance of the place, which he had not before visited.

It was a long room divided by a high wooden counter on which wire netting still further cut off the clerks from the pub-lic—like a post office, decided Ernest, reassured. Signs directed where one should go in and out and transact various kinds of business—it's everywhere the same nowadays, re-flected Ernest; can't stir a step without a notice. Still, on the whole he approved. It made for dignity and order, and gave everyone his proper turn, his rightful due. The place was al-most empty; no queues anywhere, probably because it's near on closing time, thought Ernest; just a woman or two paying rates (as Millie paid theirs) and a young man in a sports coat discussing some problem about a printed form, with a clerk at a PAY HERE sign. Driving licences, it appeared, were dealt with at the far corner. There was nobody waiting at that section of the counter at all; a young clerk with sandy hair very neatly brushed stood there unoccupied, gazing dreamily out of the window.

Pleased, Ernest made his way with his usual dignified step down the length of the room, planted himself in front of the driving licence position and thrusting his hand into the inner pocket of his coat, withdrew Ken's licence and the printed form, which Ken, to give him his due, had filled in very neatly. He laid these on the counter, hauled the necessary silver from his trousers pocket and pushed the whole paraphernalia under the brass netting towards the sandy-haired clerk.

The sandy-haired clerk, however, was not there.

Ernest gaped. At what point in Ernest's progress down the room had the lad vanished? It was impossible to say. But vanished he certainly had; he was not visible, either at the counter or amongst the rows of high desks in the back portion of the room. It was keenly disappointing. Ernest leaned against the counter and waited.

"He'll be back," he told himself.

He waited.

The hand of an electric clock on the wall moved with an emphatic tick.

Ernest started, and shifted his position so that he could look up at the clock. The time was now two minutes to five.

"He'll be back," Ernest told himself uneasily.

He waited.

One of the rate-paying women gathered up her change and left.

Ernest began to feel hot and cross.

The clock gave forth another tick.

Ernest seized one of Kenneth's halfcrowns and beat a strong tattoo with it on the counter.

The nearest clerk, who was still engaged in serious discussion with the young man in the sports coat, raised his head and called:

"He'll be back in a minute."

A minute's going to be too long, thought Ernest grimly.

He waited.

The young man in the sports coat and the clerk arrived at some mutually satisfactory conclusion; the young man offered pound notes and the clerk began to make out a receipt.

Far above Ernest's head the Town Hall clock began to strike five. Behind the counter a bustle of preparations for door-locking and home-going began.

Ernest lost his temper.

"Here I've given up the chance of a lift home and I'll have to stand in a crowded bus and I'm dead tired already and I haven't got Kenneth's licence all because this little whipper-snapper isn't at his post!" he shouted to himself.

He snatched up his property from the counter; his hand, trembling with rage, crumpled the application form and sent one of the coins bouncing to the ground. In an access of fury Ernest kicked it viciously; it shot across the tiled floor and hid itself behind the dusty heating pipes. Ernest felt his body suddenly flood with hot violent anger; it pounded in his head, tingled in his wrists, then stabbed unexpectedly into his stomach. Astonished, a little afraid, he left the halfcrown where it lay and stalked off towards the exit, but by the time he reached the heavy doors the pain in his abdomen was already so severe that he had to hunch himself into a crouching position before he could even try to open one. Luckily the young man in the sports coat came up briskly behind him and gave the other door a good strong push and Ernest was able to wriggle through before it swung back, but even this effort was quite agonising. As he emerged into the hot sunshine Ernest remembered the doctor's injunction to eschew painful excitement.

"Damn that sandy-haired lad!" he thought, almost weeping. "It's all his fault! Damn him!"

The journey home was a nightmare, and when Millie saw him she exclaimed.

"It's the heat's upset me," said Ernest testily. "My stomach's a bit out of order. I shall be all right tomorrow."

He could not eat, but took a cup of milk; then was ordered off to bed by Millie. To lie quietly there was bliss; but of course in a household presided over by Millie, quiet was not easily come by. Kenneth came in and had to be told about the licence fiasco. Ernest trembled with anger again as he related the story, though Kenneth took it calmly.

"Well, never mind, dad, never mind," he said soothingly. "I'll get it myself tomorrow."

"Take the money," said Ernest, pointing a quivering finger at the coins which, as was his nightly custom, he had emptied from his pockets on to the dressing-table.

Unluckily the exact change which Kenneth had given him was not to be found there, owing to the loss of the kicked half-crown, and it was clear that Kenneth found this odd and unlike his father. He looked at Ernest curiously.

"You don't look too good to me, dad," he said. "You'll have to take it easy."

"I shall be all right tomorrow," said Ernest crossly.

Nora and the new grandson were the next visitors to Ernest's bedside. The child, sitting on his mother's arm, spruce and cool in a summer suit of blue, surveyed Ernest with grave curiosity but seemed disinclined to kiss him, which wounded Ernest. (As if he were an invalid already, no longer Ernie's playmate grandfather.)

"You must take care of yourself, dad," said Nora seriously.

"I shall be all right tomorrow," repeated Ernest, vexed.

"Not you," said Iris, bouncing in with a cup of milk. "Stay at home and let them do without you for a bit, that's what I say."

Various other relatives and friends came to the house that evening, but did not visit Ernest, contenting themselves with friendly messages called up from the foot of the stairs—Ernest suspected that Nora, who had more of his own serious disposition than his other two children, was keeping them away. Accordingly he dropped asleep and enjoyed a refreshing nap, so that when Millie came up at last to bed she told him he looked a lot better already, which pleased him.

But perhaps the nap was a mistake after all, for he woke in the middle of the night and of course began to worry. He thought about Millie and Nora and Iris in their smart flowered frocks, Kenneth in his silk sports shirt, little Ernie in his clean neat suit. In a way they all hung on him. Ken wasn't quite out of his apprenticeship, Iris had a very long way to go before she could keep herself. Nora's husband was a nice willing lad, and learning fast, but compared to Ernest he knew nothing about cropping cloth, absolutely nothing. If Ernest were to be ill, really ill, ill for a long time; if his £14 weekly wage dropped to £4.15.0 sickness benefit, thought Ernest, rapidly totting up what would be due for a man, his wife and one dependent child, they would all suffer. Millie was always helping the children, giving them this, that and the other; they would miss all these little presents very seriously if she became unable to make them. And suppose he actually lost his job! Unemployment benefit after £14 a week! He lay beside the sleeping Millie and worried.

He lay and worried, and the ulcer gnawed. At one point nausea overtook him, and he was obliged to slide out of bed and crawl towards the chamber-pot which, with "outdoor sanitation" by the back door, was the only facility for sickness Walker Street houses offered. Once there, however, his sickness deserted him; but for some time he could not make himself stand upright in order to climb into bed. (His position, on hands and knees on his own bedroom floor, afforded Ernest a certain sardonic amusement.) At last the pain eased a little

35

and he was able to grasp the bedclothes and heave himself into bed. But immediately his weight depressed the mattress Millie awoke.

"What's matter, love? Are you poorly, eh?"

"No," lied Ernest firmly. "I just thought I'd get myself a drink of milk."

"I never did meet anyone like you, Ernest Armley," laughed Millie, throwing back the clothes. "Couldn't you have asked me, you silly lad?"

She fetched warmed milk and Ernest drank it gratefully and was soothed and slept.

In the mornings, the men of the family were supposed to clean out the hearth, lay the fire and make the cups of tea, but it was too often Ernest who performed all these duties, for Kenneth slept the sleep of the young, and Ernest simply had not the heart to wake him till the last minute, though in the evenings he grumbled and threatened about this matter a good deal. This morning, however, when the alarm clock woke Ernest, he could hear Kenneth already downstairs, banging about at the fireplace with the clumsy vigour of youth. Ernest was pleased by this thoughtful behaviour on his son's part, and still more so when the lad soon ran up with a cup of tea in each hand. It was lucky, it really was, that Ken had had this good idea, for Ernest found he could move only very slowly if he were not to start the pain. Still, he could manage. He'd carry on. He'd get to the mill as usual. He wouldn't show any sign of illness there. (*Finding the work a bit heavy, eh?*)

"Don't go, Ernest," said Millie.

"Don't go, dad," said Kenneth. (Iris was still in bed.)

"You're wasting your breath," said Ernest, frowning.

Kenneth shrugged and went out at the back and rushed off on his motor-cycle, and Ernest slowly opened the front door and slowly closed it behind him and slowly walked towards the bus-stop.

It was a lovely summer morning, quiet and sunny, and

Ernest felt almost happy as he trailed along down the street. If once he could get to the mill he would be all right; he'd let himself off easy, sit around a bit, give instructions and let Nora's husband, young Clifford, do the work. If once he could get to the bus, he'd be all right. But could he get to the bus? He saw that other men in the street, with whom he usually travelled, were many yards ahead of him. He was alarmed. The bus service down to Ashworth was frequent, but from Ashworth out to Holmelea, much less so. If he missed this bus, he would be very seriously late at the mill. His department would have to begin without him. He must hurry. He quickened his step.

At once an acute spasm of pain seized him. He sank down in agony on the nearest doorstep.

The bus rushed cheerfully past the end of the street.

"Missed it! Well, I shall be late," thought Ernest, almost weeping. "I've never been late before in forty years. But I shall be late now, choose how."

He dragged himself up and walked on slowly, carefully, towards the end of the street.

II

A. A. J. BARRACLOUGH, MILLOWNER

I

THE LIGHTS TURNED green, and Arnold swung the Jaguar swiftly round the corner into Mill Lane.

At once Holmelea Mills came into view fifty yards away down the hill: a solid compact building in good repair, its many windows all unbroken, its white paint gleaming, its tall round chimney well pointed, emitting a neat though not excessive wisp of smoke, A. & J. Barraclough, 1815, inscribed in handsome green letters across the façade.

To see it always gave Arnold a feeling of pride and satisfaction. He'd saved Holmelea Mills; he, A. A. J. Barraclough, alone. True, in the old days, his grandfather's days, the entry of BARRACLOUGH, AMOS and JANNA, in the Yorkshire Textile Industry directory, had given the names of three mills under their control and stated proudly: *35,000 spindles, 600 looms, dyeing and finishing plant for own use only,* whereas now Messrs. Amos & Janna Barraclough neither spun yarn nor wove cloth nor owned three mills. All that was left to them was the original Holmelea property where Arnold's great-great-grandfather had started the business with his brother in 1815, and the dyeing & finishing plant was very much for others' use and not their own. But to have retained even so much had meant a tough, hard, protracted struggle, after the debacle of 1931; in fact it had meant pretty well all Arnold's life to date. The sleeve of his elegant charcoal grey worsted suit, the cuffs of his admirable white silk shirt with the platinum links which Meg had given him last Christmas, his strong square hands skilfully handling the Jaguar's wheel, all pleased him as he eyed them now, not for themselves but as symbols of his triumph over catastrophe. For catastrophe it certainly had been, that morning in 1931.

To understand how peculiarly awful it had been to be woken from a drunken sleep by his mother in hysterics and told that his father had shot himself during the night and the Barracloughs were ruined, it was necessary to remember not only Arnold's life until that moment, but the history of Messrs. A. & J. Barraclough for the last hundred years. The original brothers had prospered exceedingly and presently built solid Victorian mansions for themselves and rows of Victorian cottages for their workpeople and sustained the village of Holmelea by their charitable donations and bequests; indeed the Barracloughs had quite simply *been* the village of Holmelea for the last hundred years. By 1931 they had long been county gentry, with public school educations and admirable accents. One branch of the family always named its heir apparent (so to speak) Amos, the other Janna; this Biblical nomenclature no doubt dated from way back in the 18th century during the Wesleyan Methodist movement, or perhaps even further to the days of the Civil War, when the West Riding towns took the Parliamentarian, Puritanic side in the struggle. But the Barracloughs had long forgotten this and could not now imagine themselves as ever having been other than good Church-and-State Tories. The Janna Barraclough of Arnold's father's day was killed in the first World War; Arnold's father (Gervase Amos) married Janna's sister and called his son Arnold Amos Janna. It was therefore clear that Arnold would inherit from his parents the whole of the might, majesty and wealth of Messrs. A. & J. Barraclough, and Arnold's life was arranged on that assumption.

He went to a good public school and enjoyed himself there, being of a strong and handsome physique, broad-shouldered though stocky, spirited, daring and generous, quick-tempered when roused but pleasant and easy enough among his equals when decently treated. He was good at games though not superlative, and had enough native shrewdness to rub along in his lessons without appearing too much of a fool, though he never did any work if he could help it. He had no desire whatever to proceed to a university, and was relieved, though a little surprised, when his father did not press this.

He came back to the West Riding and found Holmelea Mills an awful bore. He supposed he should have to settle down to them some day, and he had an idea that when he did he might want to alter quite a bit of the organisation there. His father, grey-haired with a silky moustache, struck him as being just a trifle too soft and yielding to the heads of the various departments, for Arnold's liking. But meanwhile, all this fuss about shades and patterns and finish was immensely tedious and—

39

Arnold could not help thinking—rather low. He couldn't help regretting that his family were engaged in trade. Of course, there it was and one must face it squarely and not pretend that it was otherwise, and the Barracloughs of Holmelea were undoubtedly important people in the West Riding. But it was far more enjoyable, more in his line, to ride, to rush about the country in his sports car, to dance, to drink, to pursue a few hot little girls here and there, than to sit at a desk and cope with tops and noils. It was understood that when Arnold became twenty-one he was to be made a director of the firm, and he perceived that it might probably be the decent thing for him to settle down then. He grimaced when he thought of it; he had never really known what unhappiness was and did not intend to, but as far as he allowed himself to indulge in such feelings, he experienced a repugnance to the prospect.

Accordingly he made up his mind that his twenty-first birthday celebrations should make a riotous finish. The family dinner was dullish but tolerable, the ball which followed went with a bang; then when all the guests had left but a few chosen friends of the male persuasion, Arnold went off with them to a place or two they knew where they could get liquor out of hours. They carried off bottles of whisky and some girls of the less reputable kind who had certainly not been invited to the ball, drove up to a place in Wharfedale where one could swim, and fooled about between girls and river until a young man drunker than the rest fell into the pool and was only rescued with some difficulty. This sobered them a little, though they staggered about for some minutes roaring with laughter at his dripping hair and the back of Arnold's new dress suit which he had slit pulling the lad out of the river. They tore at the slit, Arnold joining in the joke lightheartedly, until the coat parted, when Arnold tore off the two halves and flung them separately into the river. He now found he was cold, and set off home with some determination. The others followed, but as they neared Ashworth and turned off towards their respective homes, they all drove up to Arnold's car with much hooting, and insisted on sharing a farewell drink with him. He was thus decidedly muzzy when at last he used his new latchkey on the large door of Holmelea Hall and staggered up the stairs. In his bedroom he managed to tear off his collar but could not cope with the studs of his starched shirt front. The struggle to wrench them out made him violently sick; he vomited all over the carpet, threw himself on his bed still half clothed, filthy and sweating, and fell heavily asleep.

It was thus his mother found him when she ran in next morning. She cried: "Arnold! Arnold!" threw herself on her knees beside her son and beat at him with her fists. Arnold awoke to find his pretty, conventional, rather silly but lovable mother stretched across his body, looking like a harridan, some mad woman off the streets, with her greying hair dishevelled, her mouth a gaping circle of horror and her pretty face blanched and contorted almost out of recognition. A continuous thin scream shrilled out of her throat in an oddly mechanical way, as if she were not responsible for its production.

"Mother!" exclaimed Arnold, struggling to a sitting position.

"Your father's killed himself, Arnold!" cried Mrs. Barraclough.

"No, no! There must be some mistake," said Arnold soothingly.

His mother, gazing at him from very widely-opened eyes, fell silent and slightly shook her head. "I've seen him," she whispered.

"But good God! Why?" exclaimed Arnold, clambering out of bed.

"We're ruined. It's the slump. It's been coming on for a long time, but your father didn't want you to know till after your birthday party," said Mrs. Barraclough, sitting back on her heels and passing a shaking hand over her eyes.

This succinct statement proved to be the exact truth, to which the interviews of the next few wretched days merely added elaborations. Lawyers, accountants, bank managers, works managers, doctors, police inspectors, made the details clearer, but the main outline never changed: the Barracloughs were on the verge of going bankrupt to the tune of a couple of hundred thousand pounds, and Gervase Barraclough had shot himself because he couldn't face it.

So now the whole complex towering structure of the Barraclough affairs fell with a crash on Arnold's shoulders.

He was conscious from the beginning, and the impression continually deepened, that the Barraclough disaster was not viewed with very great sympathy in the West Riding. At the inquest Mrs. Barraclough's statement, taken down at her bedside (for she collapsed of course) and read in court, of her husband's recent insomnia under the pressure of his agonising anxieties, gave sufficient excuse for the inclusion in the verdict of the mitigating words *while the balance of his mind was disturbed,* and enabled Gervase Amos Barraclough to receive Christian burial, and public opinion approved of this—after all, he was a Holmelea Barraclough, it was more decent so. But Gervase Barraclough, with his rather over-gentle manner and his lisp and his silky moustache, had not, it appeared, been very popular with his textile colleagues. They impugned his textile knowledge in the familiar West Riding joke.

"Doesn't know woollen from worsted and never did."

"Nay, that's going a bit far. But he hasn't run A. & J. Barraclough himself for years—left it all to managers. We all know what that means."

"Aye, we do. He should have given up earlier, however. Banked when he could still pay twenty shillings in the pound."

"It's a difficult decision to take, is yon."

"It is *that,*" agreed men whose own positions in that terrible year 1931 were too shaky for them to consider any question concerning bankruptcy without discomfort.

Owing to this general insecurity and anxiety, the heroic gesture of the birthday ball was sourly received by the Holmelea creditors, who were deprived by it of a few hundreds of pounds which might have gone towards paying the Holmelea debts. On the other hand, the story of the "drunken orgy" of Arnold and his cronies on the very night of his father's suicide spread rapidly through the West Riding, and excited a natural resentment against Arnold on his father's behalf.

"Young wastrel," was the general comment. "His father didn't get much comfort from *him*."

But this did not improve the general view of the Barraclough disaster. The West Riding contrived to dislike both Arnold and his father by saying that the whole Barraclough family was in decay. Burned itself out. Exhausted.

"They've had more than their three generations and it's time they went."

"The industry's better off without them, I say."

"That's right."

Arnold was therefore somewhat chillingly handled. The manner of the family physician, Dr. Avery, when he offered the young man remedies for his aching head revealed that he knew and despised its origin only too well. The bank manager, to whom the Barraclough crash was a disaster for which he would pay dearly to his head office, remarked with a surface politeness which did not conceal his real contempt:

"I believe you knew nothing of all this?"

The department heads and works managers and foremen who attempted to explain to Arnold the complicated economic blizzard which had blown down A. & J. Barraclough broke off in the middle and concluded irritably:

"Well—you wouldn't understand, Mr. Arnold."

Wretched enough for any young man, to a fortune's favourite such as Arnold had been this treatment was so utterly foreign to his experience that he simply did not know how to behave under it.

Worst of all was the funeral. The workpeople of Messrs. A. & J. Barraclough lined the streets and crowded the church. Arnold's mother, though she seemed barely conscious and hardly able to move, insisted on being present. Arnold had almost to carry her up the church aisle, and down again when the service was over; there was a moment when her head seemed to loll towards his shoulder. This would have been bad enough before a sympathetic audience, but Arnold felt, in all the eyes so avidly fixed upon him, a terrible anxiety, an angry reproach—was not the whole livelihood of Holmelea village being buried, queried these eyes, in Gervase Barraclough's coffin? In this atmosphere of barely suppressed hostility, of agonised suspense, Mrs. Barraclough dragging heavily on Arnold's arm, the cortège (as they say) stumbled through the long grass to the Barraclough family vault and arranged itself round the open grave. It was here that the incident occurred which was to shape Arnold Barraclough's life.

During the last few tragic days Arnold had been vaguely conscious of a soothing presence about his mother. A girl about his own age, with large quiet brown eyes, well-marked fair eyebrows and thick straight fair hair, she spoke very rarely; when she did so her voice was soft, quiet and slow. His mother clung to her and seemed to find her few words comforting. It became apparent to Arnold that Dr. Avery was not too pleased by the girl's presence and made one or two attempts to secure a trained nurse for Mrs. Barraclough, which however came to nothing; it seemed the girl was the doctor's daughter Margaret, who in his view was far too young for such a task and had nothing to do with the ill-fated Barracloughs anyway. Of course, remembered Arnold casually, he knew Meg; she was on the fringe of his circle of friends, had been present at the birthday ball; he had danced with her occasionally in the last couple of years, played tennis with her once or twice. But though she was well thought of by those who knew her well, she was not, he seemed to remember, beautiful enough or elegant enough or witty enough, did not drink enough or racket about enough, in a word did not glitter enough, to be in Arnold's intimate group. She was just a nice ordinary girl who wore ordinary clothes, managed her father's household—he was a widower and there were younger children—with quiet ordinary competence, and would doubtless presently marry some dull ordinary man. Meanwhile Arnold was grateful for her presence at the Hall, and it was a great relief now when she quietly stepped up and took Mrs. Barraclough's other arm. Thus they stood at the graveside with Mrs. Barraclough drooping between them, and the Holmelea vicar began pronouncing the solemn sentences of committal.

The Barraclough vault was near the churchyard wall, and the wall was thickly lined with Holmelea villagers, who indeed filled all the lane beyond, silent and watchful.

"Forasmuch as it hath pleased Almighty God of his great mercy to take unto himself the soul of our dear brother here departed," said the vicar.

A voice from the crowd rang out:

"He were a flipping coward!"

"Shame!" cried other voices immediately, while others again cried: "Nay, he's right!" A rippling movement was set up in the crowd, as people turned about to see where the various voices came from. But the vicar, professionally accustomed to public crises, went on smoothly with the burial service, and after a moment the crowd subsided again into the decorum it thought proper to a funeral.

The blood rushed into Arnold's face. Between shame, sorrow and anger he simply didn't know what to do, and had the greatest difficulty in restraining himself from rushing into the crowd and striking out right and left at those hostile faces. He raised his head to glare defiantly at them, and met Meg's eyes. They were great, glowing eyes, he found, which were fixed upon him in a passion of feeling.

Arnold Barraclough was not usually a particularly sensitive

or perceptive person, but his present great trouble had stripped away from him many layers of protective conceit and left him vulnerable, open to impressions. He looked into Meg's eyes and at once knew all about her. She loved Arnold, she had long loved him, she would love him for always; she had come to Holmelea Hall to help Mrs. Barraclough because Mrs. Barraclough was Arnold's mother. She agreed with the voices which condemned Arnold's father as a coward, she desired with all her heart and soul that Arnold should not show himself such a coward, she had faith in him that he would not do so. Everything in his situation was all at once perfectly clear to Arnold Barraclough, and he knew exactly what he had to do. The scarlet cleared from his face and he held his head up and stood straight and still till the service ended, and then put his arm about his mother's waist and held her firmly and conveyed her to the waiting car without any real difficulty. His face now looked pale, grave and stern. The crowd probably did not formulate to itself the idea that the lad had grown into a man in the last few minutes at his father's grave, but it felt differently towards him and cast down its eyes with decent propriety as he passed.

Back at the Hall, there was a bustle of luncheon preparations, for suicide and bankruptcy notwithstanding, distant relatives had to be entertained. Mrs. Barraclough was entrusted to sympathetic aunts and cousins. Dr. Avery rather sharply declined to stay for the meal.

"We will go now, Meg," he said, frowning.

"Yes, father," said Meg in her slow equable tones.

"I'll fetch the car. Wait here."

"Yes."

Luckily the doctor's modest car was entangled in a group of others at the side of the house.

"Meg," said Arnold.

He threw open the door of a small breakfast room. The wreaths had been received and listed there that morning, and

46

crushed leaves and dropped petals and pieces of florists' wire lay about the floor. Meg passed silently in and turned towards him.

"Meg," said Arnold again.

The next moment, in the midst of all these wretched and sordid circumstances, with Arnold disgraced, ruined and despised, they were in each other's arms, gripping each other fiercely, passionately, with all their strength, as if they wished to crush each other's bones. They kissed and kissed again. It was not in the least like the other kisses Arnold had lightheartedly enjoyed, nor did he wish it to be so. It was entirely different; it was Meg; it was his whole life.

Dr. Avery could now be heard in the hall, enquiring rather crossly for his daughter. Meg withdrew quietly from Arnold's embrace. She smiled at him. Without a word they parted. Henceforward Arnold Barraclough's life ran on clearly determined lines.

His first task was to reduce the affairs of Messrs. A. & J. Barraclough to something like order by selling off everything he could sell and discharging the firm's debts. This was not easy. The year being 1931 and the West Riding in the depths of one of the severest depressions it had ever known, textile mills and textile machinery were drugs on the market. The considerable Barraclough properties began to melt away for the price of a song. The whole lot would have gone if Arnold had not developed an immovable obstinacy about Holmelea. Whether it was because his ancestors had founded the firm there, or because he lived there, or because Meg lived there, or because of those hostile faces, those contemptuous cries, at his father's funeral, Arnold could hardly say: but he dug in his toes about Holmelea Mills and stuck to them through thick and thin. He sold the other two mills, he mortgaged the Hall, he threw in all his father's outside investments, his mother's settlement, everything he could lay hands on; he argued with creditors, he shouted at accountants, he was rude to bank managers. He also gave up drinking and sold his sports car. In a word, he saved Holmelea Mills out of the Barraclough debacle, and eventually Holmelea Hall as well.

The next item on his programme was to marry Meg, and this proved not as easy as could have been desired, for Dr. Avery disliked the idea heartily. Not only was the doctor deeply devoted to his daughter and not at all eager to part from her, but he regarded Arnold as a callous, dissipated, spoiled young playboy, thoroughly unreliable and not fit to be trusted with any woman's happiness. Accordingly he used Arnold's deplorable financial situation as a lever to keep the pair apart. Gradually, however, Meg's calm, quiet certainty wore him down, and as Arnold's new steadiness confirmed itself the doctor began to like him better, though never regarding him as the ideal husband for his beloved daughter. But at last Arnold and Meg married.

It was not so much a question of mere happiness with them as of being whole together where they were incomplete, lacking each other, before. Then there was Meg's miscarriage. But she recovered well and bore Arnold a son, Gervase Amos Janna, a delightful healthy fair-haired boy. Then there was the war—but Arnold survived it. Then there was the peace and the Welfare State—but Arnold survived those too. Mrs. Barraclough and Dr. Avery presently died off, after being carefully and affectionately tended throughout by Meg. So here was Arnold Amos Janna Barraclough in the summer of 1957, arriving at his solid, reputable, well-equipped mill, without a debt in the world, perfectly happy in his marriage, and except for the inevitable chances and changes of this mortal life, one would think no longer seriously vulnerable at all.

"Here we are," said Arnold to the guest beside him.

But on the contrary, reflected Arnold grimly, twisting the wheel to take the Jaguar neatly into the mill yard, A. A. J. Barraclough is very vulnerable indeed. He is vulnerable through his affections. He is vulnerable through the third passenger in the car, the handsome lad in the back seat, Jerry, otherwise Gervase Amos Janna Barraclough, his seventeen-year-old son.

It had been a mistake, perhaps, to call him Gervase. Perhaps it was a calm defiance of public opinion, to call the boy after his unfortunate grandfather? Or perhaps a desire to retrieve, to justify, to ennoble the name? It was Meg's doing; Arnold had been away in the Army when the boy was born. Meg was always quiet and reserved, not given (perhaps not able) to express her feelings much in words, and she had not expatiated on her reasons for naming the boy so, to her husband. But Arnold relied always on the essential rightness of Meg's feelings; he had relied on them on the day of his father's funeral and every day afterwards, and had never found cause to think his trust mistaken. Besides, the boy knew nothing of his grandfather; it was absurd, it was mere superstition, to imagine that the mere giving of a name could influence a character or a destiny. All the same, Arnold rather wished that his son was not called Gervase.

As a child Jerry—for this was the suitable, less high-flown, modern version of his name—had been everything a man could wish for a son: fair and healthy and merry, with plenty of friends always about him; equable in disposition, he betrayed none of the more disagreeable faults one had to watch for in little boys, for he was neither a bully nor a coward, did not cheat or lie, showed no excessive greed, could win without jubilation and lose without resentment. That the boy had never displayed any special brilliance in lessons did not worry Arnold. His own performances at school had been mediocre; of course he hadn't tried very hard, but he knew quite well that he couldn't have done much better if he *had* tried. Meg on the other hand had tried quite hard, but had not been brilliant either. They were ordinary people, with no special claims to intelligence but shrewd enough to hold their own; all they asked of their son was similar common sense and

49

decent behaviour. Arnold therefore made no grumble when Jerry's end of term reports, whether at the little private day school, or the "prep" and public school whose bills Arnold winced at but paid manfully, showed only a moderate level of attainment. He was a little surprised perhaps that Jerry seemed rather worse at mathematics and science than at literature and history, but there was not enough difference in the marks Jerry gained in any of these subjects to excite comment. The boy was not good at football, and this was indeed something of a disappointment to Arnold, who had been a scrum half of some fierceness in his day; but on the other hand Jerry wielded a graceful bat and played very successfully for his school at a surprisingly early age. At seventeen he was a quiet, gentlemanly lad, with a pleasant young face, fair smooth hair and serious grey eyes; he was devoted to his mother (which was very proper), took Holmelea and his position therein for granted (knowing nothing of his father's struggles and his grandfather's defeat), showed a little carelessness about money but nothing to speak of, and altogether was a highly satisfactory and much beloved son. Arnold did not know him very well nowadays, of course; Jerry had been away at school so much these last years, and in any case had a rather reserved disposition, like his mother, so that it was rather difficult to tell what he was thinking. But he was clearly a thoroughly good lad, whom Arnold looked forward to introducing with pride into Holmelea Mills when he left school.

And then suddenly everything changed. It changed in the Easter holidays of this year, after Jerry had been away to stay with a friend in London. The boy's reserve seemed to have grown upon him unduly; he appeared positively morose, strolled about by himself with his head bent, kicking stones, for hours on end, spent days alone out on the moors, and so contrived engagements and excuses that, as Arnold realised when it was too late, he never once set foot in the mill. Even so, Arnold had not attached much importance to all this. Lads

50

had their private disappointments and worries, just as men had, one should not intrude, one should let them live their own lives. Jerry's moodiness would pass.

But it had not passed, and presently its cause had been made clear. On the last day of Jerry's Easter holidays, the day before he was to return to school for his last term, Meg rushed out of the house to meet her husband the moment the car reached the top of the Hall drive at the end of the afternoon, and drew him through the open French windows into a small room known as the library—not that anyone ever read in it. Her eyes were wide with distress.

"What's wrong, love?" said Arnold, kissing her.

"Arnold, I'm afraid this is going to be a great disappointment to you," said Meg, her hands against his breast. "It's Jerry. He asked me to tell you. He says he doesn't want to go into the mill."

It was certainly a blow. For a moment Arnold's long hard struggle seemed a useless waste of time. His world seemed to crumble beneath his feet. Yes, for a moment he certainly felt daunted. He sat down heavily. Meg sat down beside him and took his hand.

"But why didn't Jerry tell me himself?" said Arnold at length, perplexed.

"I think he's a little afraid of you, darling," said Meg.

"Afraid of *me*?" exclaimed Arnold, astounded. "What on earth for? Has he been getting himself into a scrape of some kind?"

"No. He's just a little afraid of you. You can be rather fierce at times, you know, darling," said Meg with a smile.

"Can I?" wondered Arnold.

He considered himself for a moment. Possibly his long years of struggle had in fact made him a trifle tough. But that his son, Meg's son, should be so afraid of him as not to venture to tell him his ambitions, wounded him deeply. It was so unnecessary too. He voiced his views.

"He'd no need to worry," he said, a trifle drily. "God knows I don't want to force anybody into textiles if they don't want to go. I've had too much trouble in them myself. I didn't particularly want to go into them as a lad, so I could hardly blame Jerry for feeling the same. Besides, it may be better for the boy not to have all his eggs in one basket. He can earn an income outside Holmelea, and still draw the interest from his Holmelea shares."

"Holmelea shares?" said Meg, wondering.

"After I'm dead, I mean," said Arnold irritably.

"You're so good, Arnold," said Meg.

As always during the last twenty-six years, Arnold felt soothed, strengthened, supported, by Meg's love.

"Well, what does Jerry want to do, then?" he said in a cheerful, sensible tone. "Some profession? Medicine, like your father?"

He gave a mental grimace as he contemplated the further long years of fee-paying which in that case lay ahead, but did not blench.

"No. Oh, no," said Meg.

"Law, then?"

Like most business men, Arnold detested the legal profession as an establishment devised on purpose to prevent business men from doing sensible things, but he admitted that one had to employ lawyers in order to keep out of trouble from silly regulations, and lawyers always seemed to flourish.

"No." Meg hesitated. "It seems to be something to do with literature and the arts," she said at length.

"Literature and the arts!" exclaimed Arnold in capital letters. "But has Jerry shown any talent for that sort of thing?"

Meg said nothing.

"But, Meg, he hasn't. You know he hasn't," said Arnold, now really troubled. "I mean to say—look at his reports! That fellow what's-his-name, that play-writer, you know, was at school with me and you could see at once that he was out of the ordinary. Always at the top in English, and writing poems for the school magazine, and so on. A perfect fool in everything else, of course. Jerry hasn't done anything of that kind! Or has he?" he added, suddenly remembering how little he really knew about his son.

Meg shook her head. Slowly and reluctantly, with head averted, she brought out that there was some young man whom Jerry had met in London while staying with his school friend there, who was engaged in doing everything that Jerry wanted to do, and Jerry wanted to go off to London with him and do it too.

"But good lord!" exclaimed Arnold, aghast. "*What* is it he wants to do?"

"I don't know," said Meg.

She turned towards her husband, and Arnold saw that tears stood in her eyes and her lips were trembling. Arnold had seen tears in his wife's eyes on only one occasion before in their life, namely when they lost their first hope of a child some twenty years ago. (One of the good things about his wife, Arnold had often reflected, was that she was not given to frequent tears—unlike his mother.) He was thus very much upset to see Meg's tears now, and put his arm round her protectively. His wife buried her face in his shoulder and quietly, without any fuss, in her own reserved and undemanding manner, wept as though her heart would break.

"Jerry says he feels at ease with this man Chillie—Chillie's the only person in the world he feels at ease with. Why doesn't he feel at ease with us any more, Arnold? We all love each other."

"Parents and children," said Arnold gruffly. "When the children grow up they have to leave the nest, you know. Jerry'll come round to us again when he gets a bit older."

"It's hard, Arnold," said Meg.

"Yes, it's hard," agreed Arnold.

He felt sore all over. But the boy had a right to choose his own career. Men should do the work they wanted and marry the girls they wanted and pay the necessary prices for their choice, in Arnold's opinion.

"Don't worry, Meg. We'll sort it out somehow. It's a disappointment, but it's not the end of the world. I'll talk to Jerry," he said staunchly. "If he really wants that kind of career, he'll have to go to a university. I'm ready to start the boy off properly in any profession he chooses."

Meg gave him one of those looks of trust and love on which his whole life had been founded, and he felt that this difficulty too he could conquer for her sake, as he had conquered all the rest.

The interview with his son, however, which he undertook that same evening, did not go off quite as well as he had hoped. Jerry stated with something like horror in his tone that he did not wish to go to a university.

"Very well, don't," said Arnold. "But what *do* you want, Jerry? I only want to help you do what you want, you know."

Jerry, frowning and hanging his head, muttered that he wanted to go to London and live with Chillie.

"But what does this Charlie *do*?" persisted Arnold.

At this Jerry threw up his head and announced sharply, his fair face flushed:

"It's not Charlie. His name is John. Chillie is a nickname."

"Oh," said Arnold. His tone was dry; with his practical, realistic view of life he tended to dislike nicknames, and why a man should abandon a decent solid name like John for a sloppy address like Chillie passed his comprehension. However, it was clear that Jerry thought Chillie extremely *chic*. Arnold experienced a pang of tenderness for his son's youth.

"What does—he—do for a living?" pursued Arnold, not quite able all the same to utter the appellation.

"He writes and paints. He has a small private income, of course," muttered Jerry, hanging his head again.

54

It was at this moment that Arnold began to wish his son was not called Gervase. The boy's reserve, which Arnold had hitherto regarded as an inheritance from Meg, the mistrust of himself which he had been ready to regard as his own fault, now struck him as the kind of weak inability to face up to life he had known in his own father, which had contributed so greatly to the Holmelea misfortunes. Jerry's obvious predilection for an unearned private income also struck him unpleasantly as resembling the conduct of the elder Gervase, who had maintained the standards of Barraclough gentility far longer than honesty dictated.

"Well, Jerry, I'm afraid I can't provide you with a private, that is an unearned, income," he said gravely. "You'll have to work for your living."

"Oh, of course. I thought perhaps just for a year or two—until I found my feet—it wouldn't cost as much as going to Oxford," said Jerry.

"Found your feet at what?"

"And perhaps to travel a little," said Jerry.

Arnold sighed. He jingled the coins in his pocket thoughtfully.

"Look," he said: "How would it be, Jerry, if you asked this friend of yours to come and stay at Holmelea?"

The sudden flash of happiness in his son's face hurt Arnold more than anything in the last twenty years. How unhappy the boy must be at home, to take such joy in the anticipated visit of a stranger!

"Well, then, ask him for your long half-term weekend in June. Your mother and I only want your happiness, Jerry."

"I know, dad."

"We shan't stand in your light."

And so, last Friday afternoon Arnold came home from the mill to find that the guest had arrived. (Jerry having risen at the crack of dawn had contrived to reach home for lunch.) A shabby and bulging suitcase stood in the hall, and sounds of animated conversation came from the drawing-room. Arnold, feeling nervous, settled his tie and went in.

Meg, Jerry and Chillie were still at tea. Meg was pouring into one of the best Rockingham cups, Jerry stood attentively at her side waiting to hand it to his friend, Chillie with his arm stretched across the back of Jerry's chair was gazing up at the tall fair boy.

Arnold was instantly and irrevocably convinced that the man Chillie was a sexual pervert. He was dark, bearded and though somewhat slovenly in dress not ill-looking, but Arnold had not spent a rather dissipated youth and several years in the army for nothing; he knew the signs.

He closed the door behind him; at the noise Chillie looked up and their eyes met, and Arnold knew that Chillie knew he knew. The whole affair was perfectly clear. In Chillie's eyes Jerry was not only handsome but rich, and he intended to live for a few years, while the infatuation lasted, on an allowance provided by Jerry's father. Arnold had the disgust for sexual abnormality often felt by strongly virile men of instinctive, unthinking disposition, and such a rage possessed him at the thought that Meg's son should be mixed up with this dirty fellow that he could hardly contain himself; it was all he could do not to rush at Chillie and batter him with his fists.

"Well," said Arnold. "Our guest has arrived, I see."

Introductions were effected. Arnold sat down and declined tea. His manner was so grim that it was impossible not to notice it. Meg glanced at him beseechingly, Jerry with astonishment. The boy's young face showed that he was completely unaware of the true nature of Chillie's feeling for him. Arnold saw this with a thankfulness which left him weak. Arnold fixed his gaze on Chillie and kept it there. After a moment or two of this the man shifted about in discomfort, and at last said lightly:

"I'm afraid I'm not quite the friend you expected for Gervase, Mr. Barraclough?"

His tone, smooth, liquid, assured, was yet impertinent.

"He thinks he's got such a tight hold on Jerry he needn't trouble to be polite to me," thought Arnold. Aloud he said roughly: "Well, I hadn't expected a beard."

"Arnold, dear!" Meg rebuked him.

Jerry coloured and said quickly:

"In Yorkshire that sort of personal remark is considered friendly and forthright, Chillie."

He gave his father an angry glance. A satisfied smile gleamed for a moment on Chillie's lips. For a moment Arnold was at a loss to interpret this sign of triumph, then he understood. "It's his game to set Jerry against his parents," he thought. "Once he gets the boy to London with him, he knows we shan't let him starve." Clearly it was Arnold's line to combat this by being as pleasant, friendly and agreeable as possible. He smiled and said in a cheerful, kindly tone:

"Sorry if I was a trifle heavy-handed. It's as Jerry says, in Yorkshire we pride ourselves overmuch on speaking our mind. Did you point out the mill to your friend as you passed, Jerry?"

Jerry frowned a little and said shortly: "Yes."

"It wasn't as large as you had expected, perhaps?" said Arnold mildly, turning to Chillie.

He saw at once, by a disagreeable flash in the man's eyes, that he had hit the mark. Jerry's calm assumption that the world was the oyster of any Barraclough of Holmelea had deceived Chillie into crediting the Barracloughs with a higher status than they now possessed. Chillie had let his disillusion show a trifle at the sight of the mill, and Jerry had seen it and been a trifle vexed. Arnold was pleased. The battle was joined. It was the greatest battle of his life, more important even than that earlier battle he had fought to save the Barraclough honour, and he meant to win. The great thing was to keep Jerry's affection and trust, so that when the revelation about Chillie was finally made to him by his father, he would believe it.

"I'm afraid I know absolutely nothing about dark satanic mills, textile or otherwise," said Chillie crossly.

"Well, we can soon cure that. If you wish, of course. Bring your friend down to the mill any time you like, Jerry. But only if it wouldn't bore him. Each man to his trade, you know."

"My father knows a great deal about cloth," offered Jerry.

"Indeed?" said Chillie with an air of ineffable boredom.

"As much as you know about pictures, I dare say," said Arnold cheerfully. "Or is it books?"

Chillie coloured and seemed a little uncomfortable. Suddenly he took a corner of his loose jacket between his fingers and offered it to Arnold.

"Is this good cloth, Mr. Barraclough?"

He meant to provoke Jerry's father into a jeering "Yorkshire" answer which would shame Jerry. Arnold, who of course had perceived the poor quality of the stuff the moment he entered the room, bent forward and felt the jacket with a serious air.

"I'm afraid not," he said pleasantly. "We could fit you up with something better than that at Holmelea, if you cared for it. You must come down some morning and we'll see what we can find."

"But wouldn't that be damaged cloth, Arnold?" said Meg. "Sent back to you by the manufacturers?"

"A damaged piece isn't damaged in every yard," explained Arnold. "We could find a suit length of good stuff, I'm sure."

"Is trade unionism strong in your mill, Mr. Barraclough?" demanded Chillie abruptly.

"Of course," said Arnold impatiently. "I don't employ any non-union labour. Who does, these days?"

The battle continued through the weekend. Chillie had a melodious voice, a fluent ease of speech, an admirable diction, and he gave these weapons the fullest possible play. His aim throughout was to make Arnold appear a mercenary, vulgar, greedy, bourgeois capitalist, an exploiter of his employees, a reactionary, a cumberer of the earth, a stupid ignoramus on all artistic matters; altogether unworthy, therefore, of his son's love.

Arnold did not find these insinuations quite as difficult to counter as Chillie had evidently expected. He was not especially enamoured of the capitalist system, merely preferring it to any of the alternatives which had yet been suggested, and he was quite ready to discuss these alternatives in an unheated style. In matters of art he yielded gracefully to Chillie's superior knowledge, contriving however to put a few questions of a probing kind which revealed to Arnold and Meg, if not perhaps as yet to Jerry, that Chillie had never done a hand's turn of real work in any art whatever, in his life. To the anxious enquiries by Meg, in the privacy of their bedroom, as to what Arnold thought of Chillie, Arnold replied briefly that he was a bad lot, and must be prevented at all costs from carrying off Jerry.

"We'll send the boy to a university," said Arnold. "At a university he'll meet men who really know what's what in these matters, and then he'll see what a phony poser this chap Chillie is."

Arnold did not, however, as yet tell his wife the whole truth about Chillie and the nature of his designs on their son. The knowledge would upset Meg terribly, it would break her innocent heart in pieces—he felt he must save her from it if he possibly could. Besides, it would be so embarrassing for Jerry. Far better that the matter should remain quietly private between his son and himself. At the bottom of his heart Arnold knew that he was keeping Meg in reserve. If all else failed, he would have to tell her; her anguished outburst of grief would convince Jerry if nothing else could. But sons were apt to resent the frustration of their wishes by a parent's grief. No, he would try not to tell Meg. He would be perfectly polite and

59

considerate to Chillie as long as he was in the house, and the moment he was gone he would tell Jerry his suspicions. But the boy's trust and affection must be retained, repeated Arnold to himself, so that Jerry would believe him.

Arnold had a great desire to take Jerry and Chillie down to Holmelea Mills together, so that they might see in each other's company that the place was not in the least dark or satanic, but on the contrary extremely well-lighted and comfortable. The windows were large, the power mainly electric, the lighting fluorescent; the machines gleamed with speed and newness—he was always on the look-out for new machines, had bought another only yesterday; pieces of cloth were shot down slippery slides or wheeled about in neat trolley-carts, no man ever having to carry the weight of one on his shoulder. In fact, Arnold set such store on this visit to the mill that he made up his mind to insist on it if necessary. But no insistence was necessary; Chillie's greed supplied the impetus. Arnold observed with sardonic amusement that Chillie wanted very much to come down to the mill and be fitted up with a suit length, while Jerry was ashamed of his father's ham-handed generosity, as he regarded it, and took Chillie for walks on the moors instead. It was Chillie's greed, too, which prevented any show-down taking place about Jerry's project of living with Chillie in London. The boy often approached the subject but Chillie as often headed him off. Chillie had had second thoughts, Arnold surmised, and wanted the cloth and the comfortable weekend's accommodation before he had to quarrel with his hosts.

Tuesday morning, the last of Chillie's stay, was thus reached without the mill visit having been paid, and Arnold was afraid that he would be obliged to exert pressure to assure it, when at the breakfast table Chillie suddenly said in a petulant tone:

"I must see the Barraclough mills before I go."

"There's scarcely time before your train," began Jerry, but Arnold interrupted.

"Come down with me," he said. "I'm always there by nine. Bring your case—you can go on afterwards to Ashworth station. I'll drive you. I have to call on some customers in that direction, some time today."

"We needn't trouble you, Mr. Barraclough. We can go by bus," said Chillie, intending as usual to show his high-minded contempt for every luxury.

"Well, we can settle that later," said Arnold impatiently. "I've picked out a few lengths, Jerry, for your friend to see." (He could not bring himself to use the man's absurd nickname, and Chillie's real surname escaped his recollection.) He rose from the table, saying: "Get the car out, Jerry. Come along."

So now the three of them were turning into the yard of Holmelea Mills.

"Here we are," said Arnold again to Chillie, who sat beside him.

2

The moment Arnold entered Holmelea Mills he felt happy and at ease. This was his own stamping-ground; here he was appreciated and needed. He had hardly entered his private office—bright and sunny, with large windows overlooking the valley, and admirable modern appointments—before he was in the thick of business; his secretary presented him with a mass of opened letters, the telephone rang, the works manager came in, queries of every kind seemed to pour in upon Arnold, who answered them with ease and decision. During these first minutes Jerry and Chillie stood about the office in a rather hangdog style, very much in the way of the various people who hurried in and out and clearly feeling unwanted and insignificant. Between telephone calls, while he changed into his mill coat, Arnold urged them to sit down; Chillie took a chair and Jerry balanced himself on the end of his father's desk, his fair head drooping disconsolately.

"Now!" said Arnold at length briskly: "We'll go up and see what we can find in the way of a suit-length."

He led the way to the lift. It was in motion, descending; it drew up and out stepped young Clifford from the cropping department.

"I was coming to fetch you, Mr. Barraclough," said he in a serious tone. "Ernest says, could you come up to the cropping-room for a minute?"

"Something wrong, Cliff?" said Arnold.

Clifford coloured and muttered.

The four men crowded into the lift and Arnold pressed the button for the floor which held the cropping department. The lift drew up; Arnold pushed back the gates and strode ahead.

He saw at once that something was seriously wrong.

It was not only that Ernest Armley, his foreman cropper, stood by with a face as long as a grave-digger's. Croppers as a category were often moody and difficult, and Arnold for one did not blame them. Their machines ran fast, and new ones ran faster every year. The process of shearing the surface of cloth to make it smooth always presented a difficult problem requiring skilled judgment; crop too little and the surface remained rough; crop too close and the fabric's coherence was shorn away. A cropping-machine must be watched every minute of the eight-hour day; the cropper couldn't ever relax and discuss last Saturday's football match with the chap working next to him. Ernest was a particularly skilful, reliable and conscientious cropper; a glum look from Ernest was accordingly normal. But this morning all the cropping-machines stood motionless; the men stood round looking helpless and upset, and the gaze of all seemed to be centred upon some pieces of bright brown cloth with self-coloured raised stripes, which had just come through the newest cropping-machine and lay in loose folds (*in cuttle* was the technical term) in the cart at the far end.

"Well, Ernest? Something wrong?" said Arnold cheerfully.

"Mr. Arnold," began Ernest in a solemn tone. (This form of address revealed Ernest's length of service with the firm, reflected Arnold; he had worked at Holmelea Mills when *Mr. Barraclough* meant Arnold's father. "I'm afraid there's been a very serious mistake made here this morning."

"Oh?"

"I'm afraid so. These Bedford cords here."

"Well?"

"They have to be cropped very delicately, you see."

"Of course."

"Well, they've been cropped ordinary. The machines were set in the ordinary way, and it's cropped them too clean. Too close, like."

With a horrid sinking at his heart, Arnold strode round the machine and stooping down lifted an edge of the brown cloth. Ernest followed.

"It's made them tender," said Ernest, bending beside him.

Arnold took the cloth in both hands and pressed his thumbs down strongly. The cloth split by the cord stripe.

"Good lord!" exclaimed Arnold. "It's as tender as tissue paper."

"Aye, it's a bad business," said Ernest mournfully.

"The cloth can't be worn. It's useless. The manufacturer will invoice it up to us," said Arnold.

"He will," agreed Ernest.

His sad eyes roved, and Arnold perceived, what he had not before noticed, that every piece in the cart was brown, while heaps of other similar pieces occupied other trolleys at the side of the room.

"How many of these Bedfords are there?" he demanded.

"Thirteen."

"And how many have you cropped too close, eh?"

There was an awful hush for a moment, then Ernest replied: "All t'lot."

"Good God!" exploded Arnold, violently losing his temper.

"They'll cost me sixty pounds a piece! Nigh on eight hundred pounds! Do you think I've got money to throw away? Do you think I've got eight hundred pounds to throw down the drain?" (The money was just the cost of keeping Jerry at a university for a couple of years, he reflected furiously.) "How did it happen? Who set the machines?" he raged. "Don't you know enough about cropping after all these years not to set the gauge too close, for cords? Ernest? Eh? I'm talking to you."

"I weren't here," said Ernest sadly.

"Not here!" bellowed Arnold. The enormity of it suddenly struck him speechless.

"I missed my bus," said Ernest in his heavy pompous tones, "and came late to mill. The lads here didn't think on cords had to be treated special like, you see, so they just set to and cropped 'em ordinary."

"I don't know what you think, Ernest, but I think it's about time we had a foreman cropper at Holmelea who's on the job when he's supposed to be," said Arnold. He spoke savagely, fast and furious, and threw the end of the unlucky cord violently away from him. "Well! Whose are the pieces, eh?"

Ernest muttered the name of an old and valued Ashworth customer.

"I thought as much. Be a long time before he sends us any more. Give me the numbers, then. I'd better telephone him right away. May as well make a clean breast of it."

Ernest withdrew a stump of pencil from behind his ear and began slowly and clumsily to write down on the back of an old label the reference numbers stitched into the end of each piece. The younger men, awed by the magnitude of the row, silently shifted the pieces about and turned up the head ends to help him. Arnold stood by, fuming. At length Ernest proffered him the list, saying heavily:

"I don't suppose it's much use, Mr. Arnold, to say I'm sorry."

"I don't suppose it is," snapped Arnold. "A. & J. Barraclough have lost eight hundred pounds and a good customer, and you say you're sorry."

He stamped out of the department. He would liked to have slammed the door, but it was not of the slamming kind, being a heavy old swinging door, with a leather strap to keep it close where the years of use had worn it away. Lacking this means of expression, Arnold needed another so badly that he disregarded the lift, the gates of which Clifford was holding open with a subdued and deprecating air, and rushed down the stairs and into his office as hard as he could go. One or two workmen he met as he passed stared at his scarlet face in astonishment and grinned a little, backing up against the wall to get out of his way.

"They'll grin on the other side of their faces when they hear what's happened," thought Arnold furiously, for it was not only the loss of the money but the slur on Holmelea's reputation which wounded him deeply.

He strode into his office, snatched up the telephone and got at once into communication with the manufacturer of the unlucky cords.

"We've had an accident with them and they're useless," he explained. "No use blinking it."

"It's a nuisance. They were due to go to the States next week. How did it happen?" said the manufacturer, curious.

Arnold went into technical details. "The foreman was away and the men set the machines too close."

"Well, we shall have to invoice them to you, Arnold."

"I know. You'll have to debit them to our account."

"I'm sorry, but there it is."

"I'm not trying to get out of it."

"If you're coming round this way today, Arnold, you might bring one of them with you. I'd like to see it—see the effect too close cropping has, you know."

"I'll do that," said Arnold pleasantly, perceiving that he was being let off lightly.

"Right. Well, don't take it too much to heart."

"I reckon I shall take it several hundred pounds to heart," said Arnold grimly, putting on a Yorkshire accent to carry off his loss as a joke.

"I reckon you will," said the manufacturer in the same tone.

Arnold put down the receiver and sat still for a moment, cooling down. Ernest of all people to do a thing like that! The solemn, serious, reliable Ernest! Well, you never knew! Poor old Ernest!

"It's the only mistake he's made in all his time as foreman," reflected Arnold. "But by God it's a big one when it comes. I must say I'd rather he'd made a small one every year."

He gave an exasperated sigh. I suppose I shall have to go up and have a word with him presently, he thought, but I'll let them all stew a bit first. Now, let's see; what was I doing before this happened?

Good God, he remembered suddenly, he'd been taking Jerry and that ghastly homo round the mill. He was on his way to the top room to find a suit-length for Chillie. He looked up in alarm at the office clock; well, there was plenty of time yet before the man's train, fortunately. He sprang to his feet. But where were Jerry and Chillie? Had they stayed upstairs on the cropping floor, he wondered? Were they perhaps waiting for him there? He hurried out into the general office, calling for his secretary. She came towards him rather nervously, and said at once:

"Mr. Jerry and his friend have gone to the station."

"Gone to the station?" said Arnold blankly.

"Yes. They went by bus."

"There was no need for that," exclaimed Arnold, wounded in his hospitality. "I meant to drive them—there's plenty of time."

"I said so to Mr. Jerry, but he was determined to go," said the girl.

Arnold walked back thoughtfully into his private office and

66

sat down at his desk. He looked out of the window, considering, and slowly the full enormity of what had happened flooded his mind. That he had promised Jerry's friend a suit-length and failed to keep his promise was bad enough, but the real trouble was his explosion of wrath against that daft-head Ernest. He had shouted, he had sworn, he had not condescended to ask for an explanation of Ernest's bus-missing; he had bellowed and stamped as if a few hundred pounds were all he cared about in the world. (He had unfortunately never mentioned the damage to Holmelea's reputation, which would have appealed to Jerry's young idealism as a more legitimate cause for wrath.) In a word, he had behaved exactly and precisely like the vulgar, mercenary, exploiting, capitalist boss which Chillie had spent the weekend trying to make him out to be, in the eyes of his son. Chillie must have been delighted.

It came to Arnold suddenly that he had a picture in his mind of Chillie looking delighted, smirking venomously all over his sly face, with Jerry beside him, white and contemptuous and horror-stricken. Was this picture a remembrance of reality, or an invention of fear? It was real, thought Arnold, wincing; he remembered seeing the two faces in the background during that very unfortunate speech in which he practically threatened to give Ernest the sack. Of course he hadn't the least intention of giving Ernest the sack, but he had felt savagely angry and had meant to wound. He had felt so angry that for a moment he had forgotten Jerry, Chillie and Ernest's long service, and in so doing he had, he now saw, lost the game for his son's affection.

Arnold sat for some minutes by the window, his strong square hands, loosely clenched, lying on his desk. They were loosely clenched because he could not see how to continue fighting; he was defeated. His heart felt heavy and cold. He had failed Jerry. He had failed Meg. Of course he could probably manage to keep his son out of Chillie's clutches, for the present at any rate. Jerry was under age and had no money of his own; short of very violent rebellion the boy would be obliged to obey his father if Arnold forbade him to join his friend, and a lack of money would be strongly operative in any case as regards Chillie's willingness to receive him. But if Arnold exercised the rights of parentage and the power of money in this way, he would completely forfeit his son's trust and affection. The only hope of retaining that affection was to convince Jerry that Chillie was worthless, that his father was a better man, more worthy of trust, than Chillie, and this hope Arnold had in the last hour destroyed. He struck his fist savagely on the desk and cursed Ernest; why the hell did he have to make an appalling mistake, the only one of his working life, on this particular day? Those confounded spoiled cords had hamstrung Arnold in his fight for his son's future.

3

After a time Arnold roused himself with a sigh. He chose a handsome suit-length for Chillie and had it parcelled. He could not bring himself to go up and speak a soothing word to Ernest—indeed, if he saw Ernest while he was feeling as he did about Jerry, the word he spoke would probably not be at all soothing—but he sent a message for one of the cord pieces to be brought down. He drove into Ashworth with it in the back of the Jaguar, and discussed the details of the disaster in a light-hearted manner with its owner, though he felt all the time as if he could choke. He had a luncheon engagement with another customer at a hotel in Bradford, and kept it. But in the middle of the meal he felt he could bear his anxiety no longer; he excused himself and rose from the table and telephoned Holmelea Hall to find out whether Jerry was there. To his relief the boy was at the Hall, but Meg did not sound happy as she announced this. Arnold asked to speak to his son. There was a rather long pause, then Jerry's young voice said crossly:

"Yes, father?"

"I'm sorry your friend went off without his suit-length," began Arnold in his kindest tone.

"It's of no consequence."

"I've chosen out a good one for him," continued Arnold, describing it in technical terms. "Now if you'll just give me his address I'll have it sent on to him at once."

"I haven't his address with me at the moment."

"Then perhaps you'll telephone it to the mill office this afternoon," said Arnold. "Or give it to me tonight."

"Please don't trouble either way," said Jerry shortly. "I don't suppose Chillie really wants the cloth."

"I do," said Arnold.

"Well, that's where we differ," said Jerry. "Goodbye, father."

He rang off. *Father* was not the fashionable word for a male parent these days, and Arnold had rarely heard it from his son, who usually addressed him by the more childish but agreeable appellations of *daddy* or *dad*. This change of address confirmed all Arnold's fears. He went back to the table feeling more wretched than he had done since the morning of his father's death, twenty-six years before. To conceal this from his customer he put on a jaunty air and drank a little more than usual.

This forced conviviality protracted their meal, and Arnold left Bradford a trifle late. He pushed the Jaguar hard whenever the traffic gave him a chance, and arrived at his next appointment on time but in a rush; hot, a trifle over-stimulated by whisky, profoundly uneasy and furiously angry with the whole universe, especially pseudo-artists.

RICHARD CRESSEY, SCHOOLMASTER

I

Richard Cressey was six years old when, putting out a hand to prevent his younger brother from falling down the cellar steps of the Wesleyan manse which was their parents' home, he overbalanced, fell down the steps himself and slightly damaged his spine. The damage was not terribly serious, though perhaps it might have been thought so if examined by methods available in more recent times—the year of the accident was 1926, so that he was now thirty-seven. Nothing was broken; no distortion of any kind was visible; Richard had no limp (or very little); he suffered no regular or persistent pain; he could walk quite well and endure fatigue as well as the next boy, up to a point. There was just some slight displacement which made it difficult for him to hit or kick really hard and straight, or balance with complete steadiness. At first this not very obvious disability was attributed not to his accident but to general weakness, for he was not very tall, and somewhat slight in frame. But one day in his early teens the truth broke upon him.

It was winter; a bright, cold, hard, sparkling winter's day in the Christmas holidays. A light coating of snow covered the ground, and the outlines of the interlocking West Riding hills made a delicious white pattern against the clear blue sky. Richard and Edward were given sandwiches and sent off for the day to the field down beside the mill in the valley, which was flooded when the weather made skating seem probable. For the first time in some years the field was now a vast expanse of ice, on which experienced skaters were already drawing beautiful figures-of-eight. The two Cressey boys were so excited when they saw this novel spectacle from the hill that they both broke into a run, slipping and sliding down the slope and hurrying under the railway arch without a thought for its dark charms, which usually intrigued them greatly. A stall for buns and tea had been set up beside the gate of the field; there were skates for hire and rough wooden benches on which to sit to put them on. Richard as the elder had been entrusted with the funds for the expedition; he laid them out carefully, studying the various types of skates and watching to see that Edward's were securely clamped to his boots.

Edward tottered impetuously over the rough frozen hummocks of grass to the ice, struck out, flailed his arms, fell heavily, rose laughing, repeated this performance several times, was lost to view amid other skaters and presently reappeared skating about at a great pace in a crouching attitude, which though not very elegant was undoubtedly effective. His cheeks were red, he laughed aloud in the joy of the swift motion. Richard reached the ice with less abandon than his brother, struck out with his left foot and enjoyed for a moment the exquisite sensation of smooth gliding. He then attempted to strike out with his right foot. But somehow his right foot could not be persuaded into smooth gliding; it proceeded only for a few inches, in a sideways direction, and then halted, while his right ankle wobbled painfully. He struck out again with the left foot; the right foot trailed behind.

Seriously, conscientiously, trying with all his might and main to skate in a proper fashion, Richard proceeded slowly round the field. Presently Edward came up at a great rate and circled round his brother. (Edward and Richard were devoted friends.) He stood still and watched Richard's efforts soberly.

"Let's try together," he said then, ranging himself at Richard's side.

With hands criss-crossed they struck out down the field. On the left foot the action was superb. On the right foot, Richard clung desperately to Edward (the taller of the pair); his right ankle quavered, he acted as a brake to Edward and eventually brought him down.

"Tell you what," said Edward when this had happened twice or thrice: "That right skate of yours needs tightening."

They repaired to the bank. The skate was tightened. For a few moments Richard's skating improved, then the right foot dragged again. At noon, when they ate their sandwiches, this had happened several times, and Richard gratefully accepted the advice of the skate-man, who suggested he might do better on old-fashioned wooden skates, they being, as he said, so much nearer the ground. Edward scowled a little at the thought of his brother wearing old-fashioned girls' skates, but the change seemed to bring Richard some relief. The brothers continued as before, Edward flying around, Richard soberly struggling, every so often the two joining for a few moments of joyous motion before Richard brought the pair to the ground.

It was afternoon, and the sun was sinking in a red glow behind the hills, when this happened for the last time. As the brothers rose, dusting the snow from their jackets, Richard remarked in a regretful but untroubled tone:

"Don't bother with me any more, Ted. I can't do it."

"But why not?" said Edward, his cheerful round face puzzled.

"My right foot just won't go."

"But why won't it?"

"I really don't know," said Richard, gazing down at the offending ankle thoughtfully.

Then, suddenly, he knew. For suddenly there rose up in his mind, apparently without reason, a picture of bare white-washed walls and a stone floor with a pool of milk lying across it. The walls were cellar walls, the milk had just been spilt by his mother in the alarm caused by his fall. He looked again at the mental picture; yes, there in the middle distance behind the milk rose a flight of white-stoned steps. He knew.

"See you later!" he cried, striking out on his left foot with all his force.

He went off behind an island formed amid the ice by a

grassy ridge topped by thorn bushes, and standing quite still in the shadow, argued the matter out with himself.

What pierced his heart and almost bore him to the ground was the fact that his disability had been imposed on him because he had engaged in a good action. If he had not stretched out his arm to prevent Edward from falling down the stairs, he would not have fallen down the stairs himself and thrown his vertebrae slightly out of true. Or so it seemed. Did he, then, wish that Edward had been hurt instead of himself? No! But what kind of God was it who posed such awful questions?

For a moment Richard Cressey almost rejected God altogether. Then something strong and passionate rose up in a great flood within him, saying: *I will not be defeated*. Whether this great impulse came to him from his father, that warmhearted, sweet-tempered lover of the good, or from his mother, sandy-haired and freckled and upright, with Scottish Covenanters in her ancestry, he did not know; perhaps indeed it came from neither, but from something he had read in the books he devoured: some Roman conception of virtue, some idea of nobility gleaned from the poets. But there it was; he made up his mind that he would not allow himself to be defeated by this accident and its circumstances. He would be defeated if he abandoned God; he would be defeated if Edward ever knew that his brother's effort to save him had damaged his brother; he would be defeated if anyone ever pitied him. Therefore none of these things should be allowed to happen.

He came to himself and found that his teeth were chattering with cold, and saw Edward in the distance skating about with an anxious look, evidently searching for him. It was now quite dark. Richard skated vigorously round the island (on his left foot) and fell two or three times, in order to gain warmth and an appearance of animation, before joining his brother.

As they trudged up the long snowbound slope together towards Ashworth, Richard was silent, burdened with too many thoughts.

73

"Are you tired, Richard?" enquired Edward. (Edward had always a slight trace of Yorkshire accent which Richard, who had none, found endearing.)

"Yes and no."

"I don't see why your right foot won't skate properly."

"It's just that you skate better than I do—you play all games better than I do. Games come more naturally to some people than to others," said Richard lightly.

"You're better at lessons than I am," said Edward in his staunch Yorkshire tones.

"True," said Richard, nodding.

It was indeed true, and the remembrance of its truth brought a touch of warmth and ease to Richard's ravaged heart.

Next day, the ice held and skating continued to be possible. Richard, who woke early, saw that it would be so by the appearance of the icicles depending from the wooden canopy above the bedroom window. They were hard and firm and cold—as hard as the decision which he had to make, as cold as the world in which he had to make it. That he meant to be a scholar, a learned man, was already settled in his mind. But was he to be one of those arid, dried-up, half-atrophied scholars who took no part in ordinary life? The kind of scholar known as *swot* and *sap* in old-fashioned school stories? Was he to run away from all physical effort, escape from life into books, shelter from participation in the sweat and tussle of ordinary men behind the plea of mental superiority? That would be altogether too easy, reflected Richard; that would be defeat in its most dishonourable because most unacknowledged form. He declined to be defeated. The question lay right before him for a decision, for he had to make up his mind at once whether to stay at home and read all day, or go out skating with Edward, knowing that he was inferior to his younger brother on the ice. He went to the skating field and spent quite a happy day there.

From that time onward Richard played all games with a

74

cheerful mediocrity, while Edward excelled. In cricket, for example, Richard became one of those useful persons who stay in for a very long time, making almost no score, while brilliant batsmen at the other end pile up large totals and go quickly out. Thus, although he was undoubtedly a scholar ("too brainy for words" was Edward's description), of slight physique and mildly plain—his school nickname was *Tadpole*, which he thought justifiable, his grey eyes being somewhat too large for his face—he retained the respect and affection of his school-fellows, and though he was not made head boy during his last year when he might have expected this honour, he acted as prefect with sufficient success. An agreeable feature of his schooldays, which of course were spent at various schools as his father moved round the circuit, was the complete mutual affection and respect felt by the Cressey brothers. They were entirely loyal; no wedge could ever be driven between them. They closed their schooldays in a blaze of different glories; Edward as captain of everything and *victor ludorum*, and Richard by winning a desirable scholarship to Oxford.

In Oxford Richard thought that he was now entitled to let games drop. He was a reading man among other reading men and there was nothing weak or cowardly in that. This was a relief; but his previous participation in games enabled him to take an intelligent interest when they were spoken of, and thus to share the interests of many of his fellows; he thought this a gain.

The second world war supervened, and here for the first time his physical disability gave Richard an advantage, for which he was heartily sorry. The whole thing was rather a muddle as far as he was concerned; there were periods when he was allowed to stay in his university—during these he contrived to take a good degree; periods when he was in the army, and periods when he was encouraged and even commanded to fol-low his wish and enter the teaching profession. In the army he found himself handing out stores. Here he invented one small but very effective improvement in the method of record-keeping. (His superior officer gained a decoration as a result.) Richard often chuckled to himself when he thought of the brass-hats solemnly adopting this detail originating in the brain of a C3 highbrow whom they would have scorned to speak to in regimental life. Meanwhile Edward entered the R.A.F. and presently became a squadron-leader with a decoration. The service he rendered his country was great, and nobody was prouder of this, or respected Edward more, than Richard. A lucky crash threw Edward into hospital for a few months and saved his life.

At the end of the war Edward went into business with a Scottish relative, and did well—he was always a pleasant, capable, active fellow. He married an agreeable Scottish girl and they had several delightful children, to whom Richard was an affectionate and well-thought-of uncle. He enjoyed his visits to them very much—although occasionally, in this as in other experiences of Richard's life, his enjoyment was streaked with pain and wistfulness. (His equable manner, his affable tone were the results of continued victory in struggle, not easy acceptance.) He envied with all his heart Edward's happiness as a husband and father. He wished with all his heart that he could have such happiness himself. He was not unsusceptible to feminine charm nor devoid of the ordinary instincts of a man, and he often saw pretty and intelligent women whom he could imagine himself loving—he had a fund of tenderness, he reflected sometimes wistfully, which it seemed a pity not to use. Women liked him, too; they trusted him and gave him confidences. But that, he told himself sternly, occurred only because they felt safe with him; they knew they would feel for him only as a friend, never as a lover. How could they do otherwise, thought Richard, comparing his insignificant person with the tall, broad Edward's virile and handsome figure. No! Love and marriage were not for him; he must content himself with what was after all, he assured himself, his deepest love, his profession.

For he was an excellent teacher. He had, of course, an excellent knowledge of literature, which was his "subject," but nobody knew better than Richard Cressey that knowledge, though necessary, did not necessarily bear with it good teaching. There was something else one had to have, and to his grateful joy, Richard turned out to have it. It was not just sympathy—boys were apt to resent too much sympathy. It was not merely the power of interesting exposition, though Richard in a modest way could claim that. Charlotte Brontë's M. Heger had called it *dévoue absolu*, reflected Richard, and certainly one must be able to detach oneself from one's own interest, one's own ambition, and devote oneself to those of one's pupils, at any rate while one was teaching them. (It was not difficult for Richard to detach himself from his private interests, reflected Richard, because apart from a genuine interest, such as all good citizens should take, in politics, art, music, literature and culture generally, he really had no private interest of his own. As to ambition, he would like to try his hand as a headmaster, naturally, for then he could work out some ideas of his own for the boys' welfare.) But on the whole, Richard liked to think that his ability to teach came from his long struggle to disregard his physical disability.

Presently a post as Senior English Master offered itself in Ashworth. Richard had not been to Ashworth for a long time, but suddenly he felt drawn to the place. Several years of his childhood had been spent there, and the skating field, scene of the most profound and formative experience of his life, lay in one of Ashworth's many valleys. He examined himself carefully to discover whether any morbidity, any self-pity or self-admiration, lay at the root of his desire for these scenes of his youth; on the whole he thought he was innocent in these respects.

He obtained the post in the Ashworth Grammar School, and at once felt at home again in the West Riding; its dramatic industrial landscapes, its significant sociological history, the independent, efficient and stubborn character of its people, their love of music and football, their rough sardonic manners, even their very accent, found their way straight to his heart; he felt for them a strong if amused affection. He adapted himself to their customs, and would sometimes employ their mode of intercourse to keep his end up. For example, about a month after his arrival, one of the lads in his class said to him, as they were walking back from the football field together after watching a school match:

"We weren't sure we were going to like you when you first came, you know."

"Suspension of judgment about a newly made acquaintance is natural and proper," said Richard mildly. He spoke thus far with perfect sincerity and ease, but then added in what he called his Yorkshire style: "I felt the same about you."

The boy gave him a startled look, then grinned and drawled: "But now we're fairly sure we do."

"The feeling is mutual," responded Richard without emphasis.

Naturally the bookshops of the town, and its municipal library, soon became familiar haunts to him, and it was in the best furnished of these bookshops that he met Dorothea.

"What a radiant creature!" thought Richard, as she advanced smiling towards him and enquired his needs.

She was taller than Richard, with a shapely not too slender figure, a rich carmine cheek, fine dark eyes, thick arched eyebrows and a mass of short, curly, glossy black hair; she held herself superbly and walked with vigorous grace. She was not pretty, handsome or beautiful, for her features were irregular, but the rich vitality, the glowing life, which her personality radiated around her had the same effect on Richard as some magnificent painting or master symphony. Her age, he guessed, was twenty-two or three. Her eyes were kind and her speech, though faintly Yorkshire, was accurate and pleasing, her voice being a rich contralto; she attended intelligently to

Richard's requirements and took pains to see that he got exactly what he wanted.

"Yes, a radiant creature," thought Richard as he stepped out of the shop with a couple of books under his arm.

Really it was a pleasure to see such a radiant creature! Especially as in dress she was always extremely fresh and crisp and had an air of style about her which Richard recognised though he could not define. In his subsequent visits to the bookshop, which owing to the nature of his profession and interests were many, he always sought her out and presently by chance learned her name. Soon he was known there as her customer.

"Miss Dean won't be a minute, Mr. Cressey," said other assistants and even the proprietor, apologetically, as they passed by.

Miss Dean was very quick in the uptake—to use a West Riding phrase. She soon understood that Richard liked to carry books away loose under his arm, not hidden away and constrained by string in a brown paper parcel. Richard had hardly known before that he had this predilection, but now he realised that he had, and it was pleasant to have it as a quiet little joke between himself and Miss Dean. He noticed too that if he mentioned a book which had been reviewed in the Sunday newspapers, she often knew of it; an intelligent girl, he thought approvingly.

Then came the day when they met in the municipal library. Richard, emerging from the reference room, found himself unexpectedly involved in the mêlée round the trolley of new novels which one of the assistants had just wheeled in. It was the habit of almost every reader in the library to rush upon this trolley when it appeared, with a Yorkshire determination not to be outdone, to get their fair (or possibly just a little more than their fair) share of whatever new books rested on it. In the resulting scramble, a girl on the fringe of the crowd was pushed back sharply, almost into Richard's arms.

"I beg your pardon," said Richard politely, withdrawing.

"I'm so sorry," began Miss Dean.

They recognised each other and smiled. Miss Dean's rich colour deepened, really very beautifully. She was carrying a large open leatherette bag, typical of the period as Richard reflected, and this bag was full of books of a by no means frivolous kind. (It was impossible to deceive Richard's eye about the nature of a book.)

"Ah!" exclaimed Richard, pleased. "A little heavy reading for the weekend."

"A busman's holiday," said Miss Dean, blushing still deeper. "I read too much."

"Nobody can read too much," said Richard, smiling.

They walked out of the library and through the park, together.

After that Richard did not hesitate to ask her help, in the bookshop, in tracking down any obscure or little-advertised volume he required, because he felt that she enjoyed the task. They pored together over catalogues, and formal postcards in Miss Dean's hand announcing the arrival of some long-sought second-hand purchase from time to time reached Richard at the Grammar School. Her handwriting was firm and clear, pleasantly influenced by the prevailing cult for cursive script. Of course when Richard required maps and guide-books for his projected Easter holiday exploration of the Yorkshire dales, it was Miss Dean who sold them to him.

He was coming down a moorland road from a high fell on the afternoon of Easter Saturday when at the small gate beside the cattle grid he overtook Miss Dean. The catch of the gate was a little awkward if one did not know its secret; Richard opened it for the girl without quite realising who she was—he was busy thinking up arguments with which to persuade his headmaster to allow the fifth to take the new Oxford General Literature syllabus next year. Then as she passed through and round the gate, she faced him; he recognised her and exclaimed.

"Miss Dean! What a pleasure to see you in such——"

He was about to say "suitable surroundings", but decided he was not entitled to make such a personal comment, and suppressed the adjective. But indeed, against the vast widespread panorama of hill and dale, moor and fell, with the sun on her cheek and the wind in her hair, her splendid vitality shone as if enhanced by its proper setting.

They walked on down the hill together, in silence. Richard was a trifle perplexed. His companion seemed greatly embarrassed. To ease the situation Richard began to talk, lightly and affably as was his way. He told her where he was staying, and described some of the walks he had already performed. In an uncertain tone, holding down her head, Miss Dean volunteered the information that she was staying in the next village. There was a pause.

"What you said about the dales when you bought the maps —interested me so much—I thought I would like to see them," said the girl suddenly, as if in explanation.

Her voice was, again, panting and uncertain, her cheek the colour of a clove carnation; Richard was still more perplexed.

"Naturally you wish to know the beauties of your own county," he said in soothing agreement.

But the tension between them did not seem to ease. Then a car came racing down the road, Richard put his hand beneath the girl's elbow and drew her quickly into safety. The action brought them face to face, and he saw the look she gave him from her fine dark eyes. Richard was no fool, he had been about the world and mingled with many different kinds of people, he knew the look. It was a look of love.

He felt the shock through his whole body, and stood still, amazed. Could it really be possible that this radiant young creature should feel love for him? Could it really be true that through her love he would enter, warmly and fully, the main stream of life? Not be alone any more? Such a gush of tenderness filled his heart at the thought that he felt quite weak. But no, no! It was probably only pity that she felt. Still—surely he was entitled to probe the matter further? Mere courtesy to her seemed to demand it. When the car had passed he said, striving to give his speech its usual lightness and ease:

"Since we find ourselves so happily on the same square of the map, so to speak, could we not join in some expedition together?"

She murmured: "Yes."

"I ought to explain," said Richard—it was the thousandth time he had forced himself to similar statements, but he had never found it more difficult to sustain a light unemphatic utterance—"that it is not within my power to cover very great distances. I could not attempt more than, say, seven miles."

"Seven will be ample," said the girl, smiling.

They spent the next two days—the last of Dorothea's holiday —together. In the sun and the wind, over the sweeping fells, soft turf or craggy rock beneath their feet, with the larks singing overhead, the lapwings turning and calling, and the great velvet cloud-shadows trailing majestically across the hillsides, they were happy together. They became, at Richard's request, Dorothea and Richard to each other, and found that their views on all the important matters in life—religion, politics, human relations—were basically at one. Dorothea of course did not know as many facts about all these matters as Richard, but she seemed to listen avidly to what he had to tell, and for his part he had never talked so well or felt so much at ease.

On the following morning he rose early, met her outside her inn, carried her suitcase to the bus stop and stood there, making a smiling sign of farewell as she was borne away.

Term began again and the schoolmaster returned to Ashworth. Now that Richard and Dorothea were friends, his visits to the bookseller's became a curious mixture of joy and embarrassment to him. Joy because he would see Dorothea, and draw immense stimulus and refreshment from that radiant sight; embarrassment because somehow he felt that it was not quite right for him to be served now by her—it did not represent their true relationship and therefore was a kind of falsity, a kind of deception, foreign to his nature. For now they often went out in the evening and at the weekend together. To concerts, to foreign films, to art exhibitions, to theatres, whether in Ashworth, Hudley or even Bradford, they travelled by bus together—Richard had no car; on Sundays they quite often made expeditions together to old houses and other places noted for beauty or some historical incident. Richard's whole life seemed to have bloomed, like a desert after rain. Far from detracting from his teaching ability, moreover, this wonderful new interest seemed positively to have increased his understanding of his pupils. He began to think seriously of marriage.

There was one material difficulty in the way of this, which however was slight compared to the immense barrier of his own diffidence. His father, who had married late so that he was an older man than Richard's age would lead one to expect, had had a stroke a couple of years ago and been obliged to retire from his ministry. His pension was small, and naturally Richard and Edward contributed to the support of their parents. They had discussed thoroughly the amount of this support and its just division between them.

"I earn more than you, Richard," said Edward.

"True. Suppose we each contribute the same percentage of our respective incomes?" suggested Richard.

"Well, yes. But five per cent off a small income hits harder than five per cent off a large one," said Edward shrewdly.

"True," said Richard again. "But you have a wife and children, Edward."

"Well, yes," said Edward.

The matter was therefore thus arranged. The Rev. Mr. Cressey and his wife were comfortably settled in a small terrace house in a southern seaside resort, and Richard and Edward cheerfully supplemented their pension, making besides such Christmas gifts of small luxuries as seemed necessary and

83

suitable. Richard also, as being the nearer and the less domestically encumbered of the two brothers—he lodged in a pair of small though decent rooms near the Ashworth Grammar School—visited his parents regularly. The distance was considerable and the visits cost money. Although, therefore, as a single man his circumstances were not too uncomfortable, he felt he had little to offer to a wife. Dorothea no doubt earned a good wage, and had nobody to spend it on but herself, for as he understood she was parted from her family, and she lived as he did, in rooms. (Her landlady, by the way, was something of an interfering old dragon; Richard had had to speak to her once rather sharply.) To ask Dorothea to give up her independence and her solid salary, and live with him on the somewhat meagre provision which was all he had to offer, seemed to him a piece of impertinent presumption. For it was not as though he had much to give in other respects. He was fifteen years older than Dorothea, and owned (he reflected) no physical charms. So he hesitated to put his fortune to the test.

Then something happened which made everything seem different. The headmastership of the Holmelea Grammar School was advertised, and there seemed no reason why Richard Cressey should not apply for the job.

Holmelea Grammar School had a reputation far beyond that its situation might lead one to expect. Holmelea was a high windy village outside Ashworth, one of those old townships which in the West Riding are to be found up on the hillsides, built safely above the steep and once scrubby banks of the streams. The school was an old foundation; its original single chamber and fine rose window dated from Elizabeth I, Richard had discovered; in past centuries it had flourished under some notable headmasters and had acquired good new buildings. Today its numbers were between three and four hundred, its scholastic successes numerous, its sixth form intellectually strong. It had made that compromise with the 1944 Education Act which results in the category of *voluntary aided school,* its governors being equally divided between local notabilities and County Education Authority appointees, but it would doubtless fall more and more into the hands of the West Riding Education Authority, as time went on. Richard, who believed passionately in a great deal of education for every child, viewed this situation with equanimity, not to say pleasure. Very tentatively and diffidently he mentioned the matter to his present headmaster. The man scowled.

"So I'm going to lose you, am I?" he said in a vexed tone.

"That depends on the Governors of Holmelea Grammar School," Richard pointed out. "They will have many applicants. They may not appoint me."

"Of course they'll appoint you," said his headmaster gruffly. "They'll be lucky to get you. I'll give you a rousing testimonial."

Thus fortified, Richard sent in an application. He was placed on the short list.

Almost he asked Dorothea then to marry him, but he held himself firmly back from doing so. It would be presumptuous, it would be taking too much for granted, it would be contrary to all the ethical canons by which he had so scrupulously lived. He had already, however, as it chanced, invited Dorothea to dine with him at the White Hart, Ashworth's newly decorated hostelry, and accompany him to a film, on the very day when he was to be interviewed at Holmelea in the afternoon. He let the invitation stand. He had not told Dorothea yet anything of the Holmelea project, but he thought that on Tuesday evening after the meeting he might perhaps do so. If by any chance —if, if, repeated Richard to himself firmly—the omens seemed favourable (for he supposed one could usually tell from the Governors' manner), he thought he might allow himself to make a proposal. Seeing her in the bookseller's on Saturday morning, he could not quite keep all the excitement from his voice when he mentioned their appointment for next Tuesday.

Tuesday morning passed off extremely well. The six candidates spent it all at Holmelea Grammar School with the present headmaster, who was leaving because he had obtained an admirable post at a much larger school. Richard liked him and liked what he was doing with the school; he also liked immensely the school buildings, new and old. There was a delightful headmaster's house attached, a plain compact not-too-large affair of early nineteenth-century date, with a superb view over rolling Pennines. Could it really be possible that he and Dorothea should inhabit this agreeable house together, gaze out side by side on that harsh but exciting panorama? He subdued the thought sternly, but it recurred with increasing frequency, encouraged not only by his opinion of the other applicants, who though in their different ways all suitable enough were not outstanding, but by the headmaster's attitude to him, which was undoubtedly very favourable. As the man showed them round the school and gave the necessary explanations, he seemed more and more to address himself to Richard.

The candidates parted for lunch and returned in ample time for their interviews, which had all been set for three o'clock. They were shown into the school library, where they were joined by the seventh applicant, the present second master of the Holmelea school. Richard studied Mr. Piers searchingly, fearing to find a more formidable opponent than those of the morning. He saw a tallish, large, handsome, greying, elderly man, with a sallow complexion, dark blazing eyes, a sharp nose and a firm narrow-lipped mouth. His conversation revealed him as an extremely experienced teacher of the classics, and he was probably an able administrator into the bargain, thought Richard. In addition he had a mellifluous voice and a neat turn of phrase; altogether he was a highly capable person. But there was something bitter and disdainful about the man; had his been the choice, Richard would not have entrusted any boy's future to Mr. Piers' care.

The applicants were now wandering about nervously, standing and sitting and standing again in the attempt to conceal their agitation. Richard went over to a window and stood looking at the view; Piers came to his side and directed his attention to the foreground of the landscape, the main school entrance where the Governors who were to decide their fate were now arriving. Piers knew and named them all, adding comments which Richard thought witty but unkind and probably unfair.

There was a stooping, white-haired man with fine features blurred by age.

"Chairman," said Piers. "Well-meaning, but still living in 1910."

There was a forceful-looking woman, thin, beak-nosed, well-tailored.

"Former headmistress. Acid as an unripe apple."

There was a fiery eager youngish man whose politics bristled from every angle of his personality.

"Our left-winger."

There were a couple of thin capable-looking persons with brief-cases, obviously official nominees—"They're the ones for the tricky questions"—and there were several large florid balding burghers whose Yorkshire voices rose in stubborn though not unfriendly argument to the window above.

"Mostly Old Boys. No real knowledge of what they're trying to appoint, of course. They are mere cloth manufacturers, as devoid of sensibility as their own looms."

"Well, it's an industrial community," said Richard mildly.

Lastly there came ripping up the drive a large and gleaming blue and white car, which turned and parked with such skilful swiftness that the gravel flew up in all directions. A good-looking solid Yorkshireman in middle life sprang out and ran up the school steps energetically.

"That's the boy you've got to watch," said Piers. "Mr. Arnold Amos Janna Barraclough of Holmelea Mills and Holmelea Hall, no less. He's the V.I.P. round here. His grandfather gave the land on which the new school buildings were erected, so there's always a Barraclough on the Board of Governors."

He looked at Richard expectantly, obviously anticipating questions. Richard, disliking his tone, was rather markedly silent.

"No doubt he's a good man of business," continued Piers as before: "But he knows nothing of education. I shouldn't suppose he ever takes a book in his hand."

"Let us hope he is a good judge of character," said Richard lightly, turning away.

"Yes—let us hope so," said Piers, grim.

"Is there any set order in which we are likely to be interviewed?" asked Richard, speaking pleasantly to mitigate his previous snub.

"They usually interview in alphabetical order unless there is some special reason against it."

"I shall come second, then," thought Richard, at the same time perceiving that Piers had revealed an all too familiar acquaintance with candidate procedure—he had applied, and failed, many times.

The Clerk to the Governors—a local solicitor, Piers had informed him—came in, and took the first candidate, whose name began with the second letter of the alphabet, away. The young man was not absent very long.

"They've soon finished with *him*," murmured Piers to Richard with satisfaction.

"Is that a bad sign or a good one?"

"Usually bad."

The candidate certainly looked chilled and crestfallen.

"One can always tell," murmured Piers as before.

"Mr. Richard Cressey, please," said the clerk.

Richard's pulse leaped and he smiled nervously, but his hopes were high as he followed the Clerk into the next room. He disliked accepting any indication from Piers, but the way the man had sought Richard's company seemed to show that

88

he had privately tipped off Richard as his probable Head. A sounder basis was the kindness the Holmelea headmaster had shown Richard that morning. Yes, Richard's hopes were high.

2

He found himself in an armchair at the foot of a long polished table, with the Chairman facing him at the other end and the Governors clustered at the sides. On either hand of the Chairman sat the Clerk and the schoolmistress; then on Richard's left came a couple of official nominees and the left-winger, with one of the men Piers had designated as Old Boys looking rather uncomfortable, between; while on his right sat three Old Boys and Mr. Barraclough.

"Mr. Richard Cressey," began the Clerk.

There was a general greeting to which Richard replied, then the Clerk read out Richard's academic qualifications and the course of his career hitherto, from the top paper of a pile in front of him. Similar piles lay in front of every Governor, and they all perused the top paper carefully. At this Richard's heart warmed to them. He thought them an admirable cross-section of a modern industrial community, all on different social levels of wealth, speech and dress, but all honest persons, trying to do their duty to the school according to their several lights.

"I shall only deserve to get this job," thought Richard, "if I answer the questions with the most careful honesty, so as to reveal myself as I really am."

Immediately he felt calm and even happy, rather as he did when he sat down to write a necessary letter to a pupil's parent, something important and difficult but useful and well within his powers. All he had to do was to think as hard as he could and translate his thought accurately into simple words. These people would understand him.

"Well now, Mr. Cressey," began the Chairman in the thin

voice of old age: "This is a very glowing testimonial about you that we've had from your present headmaster."

Richard coloured with pleasure.

"It seems you like teaching."

"Yes, sir," said Richard.

"We all have some questions we should like to ask Mr. Cressey, no doubt," continued the Chairman, looking interrogatively round the table.

"Yes, I have one!" cried the left-winger immediately, his long nose quivering, his fanatical eyes flashing, as he bent forward. "Why are you applying for this post, Mr. Cressey?"

"I should very much like to be headmaster of a school of this kind," said Richard thoughtfully. "There is much useful work to be done through such schools, and I should like to have a hand in it."

"And you'd like the increase in salary too, no doubt?" cried the left-winger.

"That too would be agreeable," said Richard, smiling.

The left-winger snorted but subsided.

"Why did you come to these parts at all, Mr. Cressey?" said the Old Boy on his left. "You're not a native of these parts, you see, are you? Why did you come to Ashworth Grammar School, eh?"

"I lived here as a child when my father was a minister in Ashworth," explained Richard. "I felt an inclination to return to the West Riding."

"And how do you like it now you've got here, eh?"

"It interests me keenly," said Richard.

"What do you think about our dialect here, then?" said an Old Boy from across the table.

"Historically it is a fascinating study," began Richard. "It is a survival of old speech, as you know, not a modern corruption."

"Aye, but what about the boys using it?"

"I should not tolerate any grammatical errors in their

90

speech," said Richard, considering. "A Yorkshire intonation is perfectly natural and permissible, of course, but it might militate against their success in certain professional spheres. I think probably it is best to put that point to them clearly. I ought perhaps to say," he added, smiling, "that I am all on the side of good manners. I very much dislike rudeness masquerading as sincerity."

"Well—you've got your work cut out with these lads," returned the Old Boy sharply. He grinned, however, and Richard did not feel him to be unfriendly.

"Your subject is English," began one of the official nominees in a prim, precise style. "How will that influence your allocation of time in the school?"

"I should like to give a good deal of time to teaching," said Richard frankly. "But I'm fully aware of the importance of administration in a school, and I should put my duties as headmaster first."

"How many hours a week are you prepared to devote to the job?" snapped the left-winger.

"As many as are necessary for the proper conduct of the school," snapped back Richard with a smile.

"Have you ever had any trouble with discipline, Mr. Cressey?" said the second official nominee.

"No," said Richard laconically.

"Would you insist on the boys wearing their school caps out of school?" said the Old Boy on the left.

"Yes."

"What would you do if they disobeyed, eh?"

"I should take all the usual disciplinary steps—and," said Richard, looking round at them sternly: "I should expect support from my Governors."

There was a pause. The Governors exchanged glances—Richard thought, of a not unfavourable kind.

"Mr. Cressey," said the Chairman in his thin old tones: "You are thirty-seven. If you were appointed headmaster here, you would find on your staff one or two men over sixty years old. How would you tackle that problem?"

"With consideration, I hope," said Richard. "I would discuss any alterations I proposed making, thoroughly with all the staff, before I took action. But the headmaster's decision must be final, since the responsibility is his."

The Chairman nodded thoughtfully.

"Mr. Cressey," broke in the former schoolmistress in deep Oxfordian tones: "Do you enjoy good health?"

Ah, trust a woman's eye on a physical question, thought Richard with a pang. For the thousandth time he wished that his large grey eyes, his clear pale cheek, could be metamorphosed into a beefy stare, a florid tan. He considered. Of course he lacked the animal vigour of, say, the man Barraclough. On the other hand, he was rarely ill.

"Yes," he said at length, "I do." Seeing that his hesitation had produced a look of doubt on the faces round the table, he felt himself entitled to add: "It is certainly seven years since I had to consult a doctor."

The faces brightened.

"And what was the diagnosis then, Mr. Cressey?"

"Just a touch of influenza," said Richard.

The faces brightened still further.

"May I ask what your hobbies are, Mr. Cressey?" bayed the former schoolmistress in a friendly tone.

"Oh, all the arts," said Richard. "Music, drama, painting, films. And to a certain extent, walking. I take my longer holidays as far as possible abroad."

The schoolmistress nodded, smiling.

"Mr. Cressey," said Arnold Barraclough suddenly in a very loud tone: "What would you do if——"

Richard turned to him. To his astonishment he saw that the man was furiously angry. His shrewd kindly face was crimson, his heavy nostrils dilated; the square hands protruding from the sleeves of his admirably cut grey suit and fine white shirt were screwing up the sheet of paper which held Richard's qualifications, with savage strength.

"What would you do if you found a boy or group of boys in the school encouraging improper behaviour?" he shouted.

Richard was annoyed. He hated being shouted at and particularly disliked any illiberal frenzy on sexual questions.

"I should certainly never dramatise the matter," he said coldly. "These things are normal in small boys during a certain phase."

"Oh, you'd take it lightly," said Barraclough grimly. His eyes were positively red and sparkling with rage, Richard noticed; really they looked quite extraordinary.

"No, I should not," began Richard, still more annoyed. "But——"

"Have you ever played any games, Mr. Cressey?" said Barraclough, still in the same loud, brutal tone.

"I have played almost every game in my time," said Richard stiffly. "Except golf and squash."

"Ever do any good by it?"

"In what sense?"

"Ever play for your house, or your school or your university?"

"No."

"You're not married, I believe, Mr. Cressey?"

"No," said Richard. He hesitated, wondering whether he might perhaps venture to say: "Not yet," but decided against it—he had no right to presuppose Dorothea's consent.

"Have you any intention of marrying?"

There was a movement of protest round the table.

"Mr. Chairman, I hardly think——" objected the schoolmistress.

The Chairman, coughing, began: "Perhaps, Mr. Barraclough, that hardly comes within our——"

Richard interrupted. He was extremely angry and had turned very pale.

"Nothing is settled yet," he said.

"I thought not," muttered Barraclough. He glared directly into Richard's eyes, his whole face expressing contempt and hate.

The tenour of the last few questions seemed clear to Richard; they were meant to show him as feeble, sapless, morally effete, and therefore quite unsuited to be in charge of boys. He resented these insulting implications strongly, and debated with himself whether or not to voice his resentment. But after all, he had come to this interview to be questioned. His habitual fairness and modesty restrained him; he remained silent, but looked round urgently at the other Governors, hoping for a decent question to which he could give an honourable reply and thus reinstate himself in their good opinion. But some of the Governors returned his glance doubtfully, while others looked down in an embarrassed way and doodled on their notes. The Chairman coughed, looked around and collected his colleagues' glances.

"Well, thank you very much, Mr. Cressey," he said in a dismissing tone.

Richard rose, gave a quick formal bow, and left the room.

"They gave you a good long dose," said Piers enviously when he returned to the library.

"You need not be troubled," said Richard coldly. "They will not appoint me."

"Really? I'm surprised. I thought you had it in the bag. But you can usually tell how the interview's going, I agree. Turned against you, did they? Any tips you can give me?" said Piers with unconcealed relief.

Richard was silent.

For the next hour he would not allow himself to think about his disappointment; he concentrated on maintaining a decent appearance of composure. He sat in an armchair in a relaxed attitude, and turned the leaves of the week's *Times Literary Supplement*, which he had read before, with a nonchalant air while the other candidates came and went between study and library. He presumed that Piers would now receive the appointment—certainly he himself had lost it. All the same his heart beat fast and he had difficulty in remaining in his chair when the Clerk at length entered the room. To whom would he turn?

The Clerk looked towards one of the younger men and said: "The Governors would like to see Mr. Seldon again, gentlemen."

3

The hand-shaking, the goodbyes, the playful mutual commiserations, the walk to the bus and the journey back to Ashworth with some of his colleagues were really torture. The younger applicants took their rejection philosophically; they would apply again elsewhere, they had time before them. Piers was extremely, almost uncontrollably, angry and disappointed; like Richard he had thought himself sure of the job once Richard was rejected. Richard could not help remembering their conversation before the interviews, when he had voiced the hope that Arnold Barraclough would prove a good judge of character. An unfriendly observer, he thought sardonically, might consider that Barraclough had proved too good a judge for the pair of them. Naturally he kept this thought to himself.

At last he was alone in his rooms and able to allow his disappointment expression. He paced up and down with his light, slightly uneven step, turning quickly in the confined space, while an immense flood of bitterness rolled agonisingly through his body. He found the situation too painful to be borne with any pretence of equanimity. The man the Governors had chosen was, perhaps, the best of the younger bunch—on that point Richard was prepared to grant him the benefit of the doubt. But he was younger than Richard, with far less teaching experience and a much inferior degree. If the Governors had chosen Piers their choice would have been less of a personal slight to Richard. Piers' degree was good; his knowledge of the school of course much more extensive, his teaching experience longer, than Richard's. The choice of such a man, though it would have been a serious mistake in Richard's view because of Piers' cynical and ambiguous character, would have been a natural mistake, a justifiable choice, for which many reasons could be offered. But to choose young Seldon!

"I ought to be glad for the boys' sake, that they'll have a cheerful honest young man instead of Piers who is tainted by defeat," thought Richard.

He made one of his customary mental efforts, tried to compel himself to feel the decent gladness he postulated. But he failed. To be rejected for that insignificant, inexperienced lad, who had hardly been distinguishable from the other three young candidates! What on earth would Richard's present headmaster think? Only some prejudice against his person could have rejected Richard in favour of young Seldon. And of course, thought Richard angrily, it was clear what that prejudice was. The unlucky question of the schoolmistress about his health had brought it on the *tapis*, he supposed, and the Barraclough man, hearty well-fed animal that he was, had picked it up and high-lighted it and tossed it round the table, and the Governors had made the usual conventional response. Once again Richard was turned down, rejected, because he had prevented his baby brother from falling downstairs and spoiled his own spine in doing so.

"It's been the same tune all the time," said Richard to himself in anguish.

He had heard this phrase in a wartime revue and always remembered it because it seemed so relevant to his case, but never had it seemed so bitterly, terribly relevant as today.

For today, for the first time, the disadvantage of his physique had invaded his own chosen, intellectual sphere. *From him that hath not, shall be taken even that which he hath*, remembered Richard bitterly. It could be borne that he was a mediocre performer in the physical world, it could be borne that he was slight and plain; it could be borne, though Richard winced at the thought, that he was not even considered as an entrant in the lists of love. But that his professional standing should also be adversely affected was not to be endured. His innermost stronghold, his ultimate hope and confidence, his pride and joy in his good brain, his soundly based learning, his rational powers, his professional ability—all this was pierced, broken, tumbled. It was too much. What was the use of his long years of cheerful outward acceptance? (The struggles to maintain which had in early life been so painfully severe.) His so-to-say "sporting" behaviour? His firm rejection of all jealousy and resentment? His victory over all the envious impulses of his baser self? All useless; such moral victories counted for nothing beside a florid cheek, a straight spine. Why try any more? Why not let himself slip into the jaundiced envy which—with, Richard felt sure, much less cause—Piers showed? Headmasterships and marriage were clearly not for Richard Cressey; they were mere castles in the air for him, groundless as a rainbow and as evanescent. He must return to reality, content himself with a lonely, sterile life, an undistinguished and merely moderately useful career. But he could not so content himself. He could not! He struck his fist hard into the palm of his other hand, beside himself with grief and rage.

As he wheeled angrily about the room, the clock on the mantelpiece caught his eyes and reminded him of his engagement with Dorothea. They were to dine early, he remembered, so as to catch the opening sequences of a film.

For a moment he laid his hand on the telephone. He was no fit companion for any woman that evening; like a wounded animal he wished only to lick his sores alone in the obscurity of his lair; besides, all that notion of love and marriage was nonsense, nonsense! He coloured with shame to think that he had ever for a moment entertained such a preposterous, such a presumptuous, such a really wrong, idea.

But presently he took his hand from the instrument again. It was not in his nature deliberately to cause humiliation to any living being, he hoped, especially not to a woman, especially not to a woman for whom he had experienced such tender and protective feelings as he had for Dorothea. Besides, the only telephone in the house where Dorothea lived was her landlady's telephone; it stood downstairs in the hall, and when Mrs. Eastwood had summoned her guest to the instrument, she was apt to hang around in the middle distance, pretending not to listen to the conversation and hoping to be told about it in full when it closed. No, Richard could not subject Dorothea to the humiliation of such a public cancellation by her escort.

With angry, jerky movements he shaved and dressed; he was, he felt, defeated by life, but he would pretend not to be, he would keep up these minor defiances, these minor outposts against despair, as long as he could. He hurried off to the bus; by swift walking at either end of the journey, he contrived to reach the Hart just as the Town Hall clock struck the hour; he was not late.

IV

DOROTHEA DEAN, SHOP ASSISTANT

I

ALL THE DEAN family were tall, healthy, determined, unsentimental people, reflected Dorothea, gazing with eager question into the rather spotty mirror which was all that Mrs. Eastwood provided.

Her own back was as straight as a ramrod, her head was

always high, she walked down the Ashworth streets with a brisk decided step which set her skirts swinging as rhythmically as if she were marching to a band; her skin was clear, her teeth white, her flesh warm and firm; she enjoyed every minute of life, she was never tired.

Her father, whose enlarged photograph, in dress uniform with medals, hung on the wall beside the mirror, had been a "regular" soldier, sergeant-major in his Yorkshire regiment, killed marshalling his men on the beach at Dunkirk when his youngest child was only five; but though Dorothea did not remember him, he looked to her every inch a fine stalwart sergeant-major, with all that rank implies of disciplinary capacity in his large stern features. His close-cut hair betrayed the merest hint of the crisp dark curls which Dorothea had inherited from him.

Dorothea's mother, of whom no photograph existed for she saw no sense in wasting money on photographs, remained in Dorothea's memory also as tall, dark-haired, robust, honest as the day and devoted to her children in the Yorkshire fashion, that is cooking and cleaning and sewing and ironing for them with boundless energy and attending to their morals and manners with unfailing vigour, but not expressing her love much in words—or, as she would have put it, not fussing over them, not indulging in any sloppy nonsense. Everything in the Dean household was perfectly clean, perfectly respectable, perfectly decent, but there were, again as Mrs. Dean would put it, no fancy frills there. Left a widow with three children to bring up on an army pension, Mrs. Dean had taken over the small corner shop previously kept by her father at the end of Naseby Terrace and ran it extremely well. She sold newspapers and cigarettes and chocolates, string and pencils and notepaper and a few toys. The shop window was cleaned rigorously every week and the stock was always good and fresh, but it was set out in plain symmetrical rows, arranged for usefulness, easy access, rather than beauty.

The children in their young days helped occasionally in the shop, but were soon sent out to other work so that the Dean eggs should not be all in one basket: Kathy to a large Ashworth haberdashery establishment, Tom as an engineering apprentice, Dorothea when she presently left school to a stationer's shop, as she had always been, in Mrs. Dean's phrase, "fond of books and such."

Kathy, who was tall and bouncing, with lots of dark hair very neatly brushed, a bright complexion, a loud voice, a hearty laugh and a big bust, did extremely well in the drapery store; she became particularly skilled in corsetry—the difficulties of her own ample figure inclining her to knowledgeable treatment of customers' problems—and received steady promotion.

Tom grew up before the war was over and entered his father's regiment, but luckily the fighting was over before he could get to the front. When he came back from the occupation forces in Germany he very soon went off, capable and energetic, to Canada, prospered and presently married very suitably there. Mrs. Dean of course missed him, but never thought of objecting to his departure—she would have regarded any such objection as "standing in his light" and altogether "silly work." She wrote to him regularly once a month, just two sheets of a lined writing pad, signing her letters *your affectionate mother* in a sensible unfussing fashion.

Yes, they were a strong, sensible, healthy family, deeply attached to each other without making any fuss about it. Dorothea as the youngest perhaps received more outward show of affection than the rest. Ten years younger than Tom, eleven years younger than Kathy, she was always something of a pet and a plaything to her brother and sister. They cared a great deal for their little sister, and had a feeling that there was a kind of grace about her which was lacking in themselves. But this did not incline them to be possessive or selfish with Dorothea, and certainly they would never dream of "standing in her light."

Accordingly when Mrs. Dean a couple of years ago suddenly died of 'flu, and her daughters' first grief was over and plans had to be made, there were no floods of tears, no outraged protests, on Kathy's part at Dorothea's announcement that she wanted to remain in Ashworth and continue in her present work, though Kathy had decided to move to Scarborough and take up a better job she had been offered there. True, Kathy looked disappointed; true, she pointed out the economic advantages of living together and the beauties of the seaside resort; true, she threw out a blunt word on the dangers of a young girl's living alone. At this Dorothea quietly laughed. Her sister joined in the laughter.

"But why do you want to stay behind, Dot?" she asked in a sensible, friendly tone.

Dorothea hesitated, for in truth she hardly knew.

"I want to be on my own for a while," she said at length.

"Well, you do right to say what you want," said Kathy approvingly, and she made no further attempt to prevent Dorothea from having her own way.

The house and shop were sold advantageously and the money divided between the three Dean children; the furniture was stored; a room for Dorothea was taken with Mrs. Eastwood at the other end of Naseby Terrace, and Kathy departed cheerfully for Scarborough, stipulating only that the separation should be regarded as temporary and reconsidered after a year, and that the sisters should meet at least three times meanwhile.

Towards the end of that period Kathy heard of a highly suitable flat which was to fall vacant on the outskirts of Scarborough in a few months—suitable, that is, if Dorothea came and joined her; it was too costly for her to rent alone. At first Dorothea regarded this plan without disfavour if without enthusiasm. She was by now tired of Mrs. Eastwood; she found herself a trifle lonely in Ashworth without her family; she was fond of her sister and willing to oblige Kathy now that she had lived alone and managed her own affairs long enough to have established an independent status; she could not altogether disregard the financial benefits which would accrue from shared expenses; she had no fears about getting a good job in Scarborough, and being young she liked the idea of a change of scene. She therefore replied in a temporising but not rejecting sense to Kathy, and the plan was discussed in some detail and communicated—as was only fair—to Mrs. Eastwood, who laid down the principle that a fortnight's notice must be given of Dorothea's departure.

But the next time the sisters met—Dorothea had taken a Sunday coach trip to Scarborough—and Kathy announced eagerly that she had arranged that Dorothea should see the flat, Dorothea, looking aside, said firmly:

"Kathy, I'm terribly sorry, but I don't want to come to Scarborough after all."

"You don't want to come!" exclaimed Kathy incredulously. "But, Dot, you said in your letter——"

"I know," said Dorothea, colouring. "And I'm sorry, Kathy. Truly sorry. But I've changed my mind."

"Is it because you don't want to come to Scarborough, or because you don't want to leave Ashworth?" asked Kathy shrewdly.

"I don't want to leave Ashworth," said Dorothea, looking aside.

There was a pause.

"Is it a boy-friend, love?" asked Kathy in her kindest tone.

Dorothea coloured deeply and made no reply.

"Do I know him, eh?" pressed Kathy.

"No. And perhaps you never will," said Dorothea.

"Oh, it's like that, is it? Uncertain, is he?" said Kathy, tossing her head. "Thinks himself too good for you, does he? Or what?"

"He *is* too good for me," said Dorothea simply. "He's a truly good man, Kathy. We're friends, but I don't really know whether it's anything more, with him. It hardly seems likely, to me."

"What does he do for a living, then?"

"He's a schoolmaster at the Grammar School. He's been to Oxford and all that."

Her sister was silent for a moment, in spite of herself impressed. Then with the usual Dean mixture of warm kindness and practical good sense, she said shrewdly:

"Well, stay on in Ashworth for a bit, then. Give yourself a chance. Only don't be too long about it, Dot. I shall have to give a firm answer at the end of the season, you know."

"You're very good about it all—the flat and everything, Kathy," said Dorothea.

"Oh, rubbish!" said Kathy, laughing, embarrassed by this expression of feeling.

She had, of course, with the customary Dean shrewdness, hit the nail on the head, for between Dorothea's letter and her visit to Scarborough, the Easter holiday had occurred, and Dorothea's feeling for Richard Cressey, from being a mere wistful daydream, had seemed to take on reality and hope.

Was it too soon yet, wondered Dorothea, turning from the mirror, to put on the brilliant summer frock which she had washed and ironed at the weekend for this dinner with Richard? Yes, it was too soon, for its spotless freshness must not be marred. She threw a towel over her strong young shoulders and sat down—carefully so as not to crease the new lingerie she had bought especially for this occasion. It was the first time Richard had asked her to dine, and she wanted to feel that everything was perfect for him. Fastidious herself, she felt an even more sensitive fastidiousness in Richard, and was determined that in that way at least she would live up to his highest expectations.

It was indeed for this fastidiousness, this delicacy, this refinement of spirit, that she loved him.

The first time he came into the shop she was struck at once by his kind, pleasant, friendly manner. No, it was more than that; quite a few customers had kind, pleasant, friendly manners, but Mr. Cressey had something more. He had what she meant by the phrase, *the flower of courtesy*. There was something polished, something truly civilised, in his ways. Then he spoke so well, using such elegant words, so neatly turned—nothing at all pedantic or high-flown, just simple and clear, but simple as a beautifully curved line, clear as crystal. It was a pleasure to serve him. She had to climb a ladder to reach the book he wanted; turning at the top to enquire which edition he preferred, she found he was holding the ladder steady for her. Many customers would have done the same, of course, but what she particularly appreciated was that when she descended the ladder far enough for safety, he released it, so that there was no question of her hands or body touching his. Nor did he mention the ladder, or show any awareness of it in his speech or look; he did not expect thanks, and would indeed, Dorothea felt sure, have frowned if offered them.

After that he came in often, and Dorothea always felt happy when he entered the shop; his visit made her day. She was puzzled at first because sometimes he seemed to wish his purchases to be thickly packed, and sometimes liked to tuck them loose under his arm; but she soon made out the reason—books were things he cherished; when the weather was wet they must be most carefully protected, but when it was safe to carry them unpacked, he liked the feel of them under his arm. In fact, decided Dorothea, books were almost like living things to him; he disliked wrapping their identity away in brown paper almost as much she would have disliked doing this to a child. When he perceived she understood this, he joked pleasantly about the weather: "Yes, showery, I'm afraid," he said as Dorothea turned to the roll of wrapping paper. Dorothea liked this devotion to books. She liked it just because it was so unpractical and excessive, what the Dean family called silly

104

work. It was something poetic and beautiful, quite outside the prosaic Dean world.

She began to listen to everything Mr. Cressey said, and remember it carefully. Laughing at herself, she actually took to buying one of the dignified Sunday newspapers he mentioned —she concealed this from Mrs. Eastwood at first but of course the landlady found it out presently and said: "Well, well!" in a disagreeable tone. By chance one day Dorothea encountered in the Ashworth Municipal Library one of the books Mr. Cressey had bought recently. She took it home. It was rather hard and dull, she thought, but for some reason it gave her great pleasure to be reading the same words as he had read. She began to seek out these books regularly; many were quite beyond her, she was silly to waste her time thus, she told herself, but all the same she continued to find pleasure in doing so.

Then came the day when she met him in the library. His charming courtesy shone out in strong contrast to the crass bustling self-aggrandisement around as he apologised for what was the others' fault; his hand just touched Dorothea's elbow as he prevented her from falling in the crush. Suddenly she loved him; she loved his fine slender hands, his large grey eyes which often had the pleasantest sparkle of interest or amusement, his well-shaped head, his large but most agreeably chiselled mouth. Yes, after that meeting she quite frankly admitted to herself that she loved him. It was quite absurd, of course, on her part; she took pains to ascertain that he was not married nor apparently engaged with any woman, but all the same it was absurd to love him, he would never look at her. Still, there was something noble, something beautiful, about loving him; something finer and as it were freer than she had ever done before. She awoke every day longing for him to come into the shop.

As to their meeting at Easter, Dorothea was really ashamed. Unfamiliar with large-scale maps and not in any sense a country girl—Ashworth lay in the very heart of the West Riding conurbation—she had no idea that the village she had chosen to visit would prove to be so close to Mr. Cressey's. She had simply wished to see the kind of country he liked to see. When they met at the cattle grid she was overwhelmed with mortification: he would imagine she had followed him! The burning blush which rose uncontrollably to her cheek made it all worse. She gave him a deprecating look, a look which acknowledged a fault and implored forgiveness; she throbbed in every nerve with anguish lest she should have forfeited his good opinion. When he suggested they should make some expedition together, all this anguish turned instantly into ecstasy.

It seemed that seven miles' walking really tired him.

At this Dorothea was racked by protective tenderness and a strange sweet joy; there was something she could give him, something in which she was stronger than he. She longed to cherish him and nourish him, take small physical chores off his shoulders, see that he was warm or cool as the season required, always comfortable, always well fed. He actually rose early and came to her door to escort her to the bus! A piece of delicate consideration and courtesy, just like Richard.

Back in Ashworth, their friendship did not wither, as Dorothea had feared, but grew stronger; they went out a great deal together. Once when she was unable to accompany him on the following Sunday because she must go to Scarborough, she took the opportunity of telling him about her sister. She brought out the matter of the corsets firmly, because she was determined he should know all the prosaic elements in her situation.

"A carver of curves," said Richard, smiling.

It chanced that he was escorting her home to Naseby Terrace for the first time that day.

"This," said Dorothea as they approached the corner where Naseby Terrace turned off from the busy main road, "is the shop my mother used to keep. I was brought up here."

"Really!" exclaimed Richard.

He bounded across the pavement and gazed into the shop

window, glanced sharply from side to side, observed everything in it and asked some highly sensible questions about how one ran a shop. He was genuinely interested. Dorothea perceived with amazement that all those "liberal" remarks of his about a classless society and so on were not merely theoretical chatter; he really meant what he said. That was the greatness in Richard, thought Dorothea; he lived what he professed.

He was extremely interested, too, in Naseby Terrace, asking if she knew who had built and named it, which of course she did not. He had noticed, he said, that the streets in the neighbourhood all had Puritan, Parliamentary, anti-Charles I names: Cromwell, Milton, Hampden, Marston, Naseby— heroes and battles, he explained, of the Commonwealth and the Civil War. The buildings dated, he supposed, said Richard, gazing up at their smoke-blackened but highly respectable rows, from the 1850's or thereabouts. Somebody must have felt very strongly about a struggle two hundred years old, to have named his property thus. Why, he wondered? What upbringing, what passion, had moulded his motives so powerfully? This was typical of outings with Richard, thought Dorothea; he never in the least lectured or preached or appeared to instruct, but something interesting, something new to her, something which made the world a more exciting place, was always dropping casually from his lips. Who would have thought that Ashworth was such an interesting place? Full of history, full of sad old human stories?

Yes, their friendship flourished; but was it only friendship? On Dorothea's side, she knew more and more clearly as the weeks went by, it was definitely love. All other men began to appear coarse and vulgar to her, and any thought of love-making with them seemed positively obscene. It was only Richard she wanted; if he could ever condescend to desire her body, her life would be fulfilled and she would ask no more. But how was it on Richard's side? She wished sometimes she knew how to do something positive to attract him, and considered wistfully the various methods of doing so which she had observed, about her in real life, or on the stage or screen. But she rejected them all; they seemed vulgar and dishonest when considered in relation to Richard Cressey. She just went on loving him and hoping for the best.

And one day at last it seemed as though she were to have her reward. Richard had asked her to dine with him—that in itself was hopeful enough—and on Saturday morning when he referred to this Tuesday appointment again, there was a subdued excitement in his manner. He looked at her and looked away again, seemed about to make some important remark and then decided not to make it. He smiled, he looked happy, he coloured slightly and appeared pleasurably embarrassed. Suddenly Dorothea experienced the certainty—exquisite, delicious, flooding mind and body with quivering joy—that on Tuesday he meant to ask her to marry him.

Could it really be so? Her joy was followed by a moment of panic; she could never do it, she was too inferior to him in mind and manners, she would never be able to keep up with him and make him happy. But why not try, after all? Why always be unsentimental, practical, blunt, prosaic? Why stay down to earth? Why not enter this lovely world which Richard knew, full of music and poetry and art? Why not allow herself to feel all she was capable of feeling, to express her feeling in all its depth and truth? She smiled at him frankly, intending that all the sweetness she felt towards him should be in her smile. And now here she was, about to meet him, having done everything in her power to make herself worthy of the greatest moment of her life.

She threw her frock over her head and pleasurably drew the zip; its bold pattern of deep rose on turquoise blue heightened the rich colour of her cheek, the close-fitting bodice agreeably emphasised the taut curves of her full young breast. She recombed her hair—luckily there was never any trouble about her glossy, tightly-curling hair—picked up her handbag (scrupulously washed and polished the previous day) and trembling a little with happiness ran out of her room and down the stairs.

At the sound of her step Mrs. Eastwood came out from her lair in the kitchen, and stood watching as Dorothea fumbled with the latch of the door. Her shrewd little eyes took in every detail of Dorothea's appearance.

"Going out with Mr. Cressey, love?" said Mrs. Eastwood.

"Yes," said Dorothea. She resented the landlady's question, but answered with proud frankness.

"Well, good luck," said Mrs. Eastwood sardonically. "I hope it comes right for you tonight, love, I'm sure."

Dorothea, vexed, but at the same time secretly unable to be displeased by the discovery that somebody beside herself believed Richard about to make a proposal, gave a final tug at the door. It flew open; sunlight poured in; Dorothea in her fine firm stride swung down the steps and along Naseby Terrace, smiling happily.

2

She turned the corner by the White Hart and saw Richard hurrying towards her from the other end of the street.

A very slight chill seemed to mist her joy at this sight, for hitherto he had always chivalrously preceded her at their rendezvous. But there were a thousand reasons why so important a person as Richard should be late, she reminded herself; she must grow accustomed to accept the delays and disappointments incident to his profession with loving calm, for his sake.

They met exactly at the foot of the White Hart steps.

"Well, here we are!" said Richard. "On the stroke of the clock."

He gesticulated in a friendly fashion, his right hand indicating the steps, the left hovering towards Dorothea as though to encourage her to enter the hotel.

Radiant with joyous anticipation, Dorothea took his left hand in hers and swung it slightly. Richard started back and withdrew his hand.

Instantly Dorothea's happiness fell in ruins. Everything was over. She knew Richard so well, she understood his every movement; she knew that in that instinctive start away, that slight unintended frown, he had rejected her. How could she ever have imagined it would be otherwise? Pain filled her from head to foot; under the sudden shock of the blow she could hardly stand upright.

"Well, shall we go in?" said Richard, again waving her on.

Dorothea bowed her head and climbed the steps. They seemed interminable; she could hardly put one foot in front of the other.

In the dining-room, Richard behaved with his usual courtesy, but tonight for the first time in their acquaintance it seemed to Dorothea artificial, insincere. He looked pale and ill, too, Dorothea noticed. In a word, he was unhappy. He did not wish to be with her. Without once looking at her, he poured out a stream of bright chatter, to which Dorothea at intervals forced herself to utter dull and monosyllabic replies. Before this miserable evening, Dorothea had sometimes feared lest she should make some social error, the White Hart being a more expensive and stylish restaurant than she was accustomed to frequent, and she had promised herself to remain alert and watch Richard's behaviour; now she could not constrain herself to take any interest in manners and customs, but drearily chose what Richard chose and picked up eating tools at random. So inattentive was she that she forgot to drink her coffee, and Richard was obliged gently to remind her.

"We should be leaving soon if we are to catch the opening moments of the film," he said, with as much urgency as he allowed himself in speaking to a guest.

"Richard," said the wretched Dorothea, "would you mind very much if I didn't go to the cinema tonight? I have such a bad headache."

"A headache!" exclaimed Richard, distressed.

He began at once to suggest remedies: aspirins, more coffee, tea, a taxi home, a day's absence from the bookseller's. His solicitude was genuine, and this showed up all the more clearly the factitious character of his previous gaiety. Moreover, as Dorothea perceived only too clearly, he was sorry about her headache but not sorry about her defection from the cinema.

"We should leave now if you're to be in time," she said, gathering her bag.

"Oh, I shan't go without you," said Richard.

This too had a ring of truth, and for a moment Dorothea allowed herself to hope that his behaviour arose because he was experiencing in reality the physical malaise she had invented.

"If he names another night for the cinema," she thought as they descended the hotel steps together, "then perhaps we shall come together again."

But he did not. He did not even make a vague suggestion that they should go to the film on some other, unspecified, evening. He was very urgent that she should take a taxi home, a suggestion she as firmly declined, but his words of farewell, his look as he uttered them, struck Dorothea as final. He did not appear happy in their parting, Dorothea thought, but he had made up his mind that they should part.

3

She hurried home. She tried to hold her head high and swing along as usual, but it was beyond her powers to maintain this nonchalant appearance consistently; from time to time her shoulders drooped, her head sank, her gait stumbled. Then she proudly lengthened her step and jerked herself upright again. But whenever this happened she felt that everyone was looking at her, everyone was deriding her, everyone was saying: *That girl's unhappy. That girl's been jilted.* It was not bearable. She must go away. She must hide herself. Why not withdraw to Kathy's shelter? Why not take the opportunity of diminishing one's expenses? For why not be prosaic, why not be practical? Her attempt to live a nobler, finer, more responsive life had been most cruelly rebuffed. Give it up. Forget it. Retreat. Withdraw.

V

ETHEL EASTWOOD, LANDLADY

I

EVERYONE'S ENTITLED TO what they can get, was Ethel Eastwood's motto. Always had been. It was the only sensible way of looking at things, after all. Nobody was going to give *you* anything on a plate, you had to look out for yourself or you'd have a thin time of it and serve you right. Anyone who thought different was soft, and Ethel didn't mind telling them so. Soft. That's all there was to it. She'd seen that very early on in life. Charlie Martin was soft. He'd never have got anywhere, never, even if he hadn't lost half his arm in world war one. Of course they'd had a nice bit of fun together, she wouldn't say no to that; walking along in the dark with Charlie's arm round her waist, stopping to kiss in every archway, it had been pleasant enough, she could still remember the feel of it. But all that, as she often said to Mrs. Clapham next door, all that sex stuff, to call it by its proper name, it doesn't last. It soon dies off. And while it lasts, what is it? For a man, perhaps—they make such fools of themselves over it, it must take them bad. But for a woman, it's something and nothing. Anyway, if you ask me, it's more a question of how than who. And as I say, it doesn't last. Nothing really matters except a roof over your head and something to eat. You'd have thought

Charlie Martin would have understood that, but no! The way he carried on! The way he created, when he came back from the war and found Ethel had married Mr. Fred Eastwood while he was in hospital!

"That pompous old bastard!" Charlie shouted.

He shouted quite loud; you could hear him all down the terrace. Not that Ethel minded, really; she wasn't afraid of Charlie; let him shout his head off. The neighbours would be sure to tell Mr. Eastwood, of course; but what of that? She could handle Fred. In those days she had everything a man wanted; fair and bosomy, with fine firm thighs—an old man like Fred would put up with a lot to get her. She'd seen at once, when he came collecting his rents that night and she'd fetched the card and the money to the door, her mother being poorly, that he was taken with her, so the next rent-day she went to the door without the money and had to turn and pretend to look for it in the dresser, and of course it was natural to ask him in while he waited, and that was how it all began. To do Fred justice, he was a kind, decent old chap enough; before he ever so much as asked her to marry him, he said, looking at her meaningly like:

"I hear Charlie Martin's in hospital, like to lose his arm."

"There's nothing between me and Charlie Martin," said Ethel firmly. "He might have stolen a kiss or two now and again, like some others I could mention, but that's all."

That disposed of Charlie Martin all right, put him in the place where he belonged. Also, Ethel saw with sardonic amusement, the mention of kisses had stirred old Fred up. His eyes quite shone and he came out promptly with a proposal of marriage, and Ethel accepted him on the spot, before he could change his mind. Seeing that her mother was ill and her father had deserted them long ago, and the war was coming to an end and there would be no more high wages for munition workers, she was only too glad of the chance. Playing around with Charlie was fun, but this was serious business, this was real life.

She married old Fred and he made a will in her favour and explained all his property to her: houses it was chiefly, scattered about in Ashworth and all around, places he'd picked up here and there as chance offered, for he had a keen eye for a bargain, had Fred. Ethel soon took it all in and was able to help him with his accounts, and they enjoyed making up the books and balancing the cash and that together. She was sharp in all that kind of thing.

"You've the makings of a good business woman, Ethel," Fred often said admiringly.

Then Charlie came home and went straight to her mother's house, looking for Ethel, and her mother, lying bedridden downstairs by the kitchen hearth, sent him straight down to Naseby Terrace.

"You'd have done better to keep him away from me, mother," said Ethel later.

Her mother said nothing but gave her a grim smile with a tinge of triumph in it; there was no love lost between Ethel and her mother.

So Charlie came to Naseby Terrace and shouted at her. He was a smallish fellow, slight and dark, and with half his right arm off didn't look much of a man. He quivered in his rage, too, which seemed childish to Ethel. But how his eyes flashed! And the abuse he poured out on Fred and herself! Really it was surprising where he found all those words—in the army, Ethel shouldn't wonder. Ethel was not at all upset by his ravings, however; indeed in a way she rather enjoyed them. It wasn't unpleasant to know he had wanted her so much, and on the other hand, it was most satisfying to know that she had married Fred, and had all his property safely behind her. Charlie would leave soon and she and Fred would be comfortable together. And so it proved. After a last wild tirade against Ethel's treachery and cold-heartedness, Charlie had suddenly burst out sobbing; the tears lay quite thick on his cheeks as he turned and staggered from the house.

"I've had Charlie Martin here this afternoon," said Ethel to her husband when he came in for his tea. (It was better to tell him, as an insurance against the neighbours' talk, thought Ethel sensibly; she was always sensible.) "He seemed in quite a taking because I'd married you."

"I'm sorry about his arm," said Fred, frowning a little. After a moment he said: "Shall I give him a job rent-collecting, eh?"

"Better not," said Ethel sensibly.

"Just as you like, love," said Fred.

Ethel never saw Charlie again. She heard about him from time to time, naturally, him being a local boy as you might say. He lived rather a wild life for a few months, getting drunk and being unemployed and that, and then suddenly he married some girl or other and got a caretaker job over Bradford way. Ethel, as she always said, did not mind Charlie getting married; it was the sensible thing for him to do, after all, and at that time she was expecting a child and hadn't much time for thoughts of Charlie. Her child was stillborn, and in any case its poor little body was so malformed and puny that perhaps living would have been a crueller fate for it. And after all, what did she and Fred want with a child, said Ethel sensibly. They were perfectly comfortable and well satisfied as they were. (Fred, however, seemed disappointed.) But what was so maddening to Ethel was the feckless, the improvident, the extravagant, the disgracefully prodigal way in which Charlie and his wife set to work to have children. Four! Four, no less! With Charlie always in and out of jobs, his gratuity long since spent, his wife scrubbing floors to keep them, often nothing else coming in but his pension, and still they went on having children! It was really disgusting. Some people have no sense of decency, said Ethel.

Meanwhile her own life went comfortably on. Her mother at long last died, which was a satisfaction to Ethel, and almost immediately afterwards she received a formal notification, as next of kin, of the death of her father in some far-off south-country poor-law hospital—they weren't called poor-law hospitals now, but that's what they were, of course; might as well face facts, thought Ethel sensibly. She went off down south with Fred's full approval and gave her father a decent burial. It was very satisfactory to have both her tiresome parents so well settled.

Then presently Fred fell ill—after all, he was now well on in the seventies. It was a stroke. But contrary to the general expectation he lived a long time bedridden. Ethel nursed him well and faithfully, as she often told herself and others. She kept him clean and comfortable, served him good meals and administered with reasonable regularity most of the medicines prescribed for him. Of course she was obliged to leave him alone a good deal—there was the shopping to do, and anyway you couldn't be expected to sit hours on end in a cold bedroom, talking to somebody who could only make noises at you in return. At one time the old man, during one of his better periods, took to wandering about the house while she was out; but fortunately there was a lock on the bedroom door, so she was able to lock him in.

At last he died. It was certainly a relief, and of course all the property being her own now was a satisfaction. There were two houses in Naseby Terrace, five up and down the main Ashworth to Hudley Road, six scattered about the lower parts of Ashworth near the railway station, a lock-up shop near Holmelea way, and High Royd, a sort of old farmstead without any land attached, up on Blackstalls Brow. Ethel, a buxom widow who looked very well in her black, settled down to a comfortable life alone. She was a good cook and always made nice meals for herself, she kept her house spotless; she went to chapel often enough to be respectable, and occasionally came out with a rather handsome donation to some charity to keep up her standing, but she did not engage herself deeply in any cause, social, religious, political or charitable, because in her

116

experience they cost more than they were worth. Nor did she bother herself overmuch with friends. She had plenty of acquaintances, and they were all she needed, really; friends were apt to be a trouble and an expense.

It was during this most prosperous period of Ethel's life that Charlie Martin died, and his widow, encumbered with debt and with four children to feed, none of them as yet earning, turned up one afternoon in Naseby Terrace and begged Ethel's help. This wife of Charlie's had been a pretty girl once, thought Ethel shrewdly, gazing in silence at the haggard, weeping, shabby woman. She had had to bring the two youngest children with her, having nobody to leave them with at home—if they had a home. They were ill-brought-up children, with grubby hands and running noses, whom their mother continually had to reprove and slap for climbing or kicking Ethel's well polished and thickly upholstered chairs.

"They don't take after Charlie in looks, do they?" said Ethel in her firm, sensible tones.

The children fixed dark inimical eyes on her, and Charlie's widow sobbed. It seemed that the dying Charlie had been terribly distressed to leave his wife and children in their unprovided state.

"Who will look after you? How will you manage?" he moaned. "I've been a bad husband to you, Gladys." His wife denying this strenuously, he muttered, turning his head away: "Well—I did my best." There was a long pause, then he said suddenly: "You'd best go to Ethel. Yes, tell Ethel," he repeated: "She won't see you starve."

"He was right, of course," said Ethel, preening herself. "You can count on me, Mrs. Martin. Charlie and I were old flames, Mrs. Martin—it was long before he met you, of course. Don't give all that another thought, of course," said Ethel, giving Charlie's widow a full account of how Charlie and she were engaged and then she met Mr. Eastwood and married him. "How Charlie did carry on, to be sure, when he came back and found me married! But that's all water under the bridge now, Mrs. Martin. Don't give it another thought."

"It's Charlie's children I'm thinking of, Mrs. Eastwood," said Charlie's widow, not without dignity.

"Well, you've so many, haven't you?" said Ethel. "But let me see now. What can I do to help you, eh?"

She probed every detail of the unhappy widow's situation.

"You must excuse me asking all these questions, Mrs. Martin, but I'm a business woman, you see, and I like to know how I stand."

Eventually, declining the i.o.u. which she herself was the first to mention, she lent the Martins five pounds, extracting the money from her handbag before their eyes and counting it over several times.

"Now if you need any more, be sure to come and tell me, Mrs. Martin," she said cheerfully as she showed them all out of the front door.

She spoke in her usual loud tones—why not?—and one or two passers-by, who could not but overhear, turned an enquiring glance in her direction, while Mrs. Martin hung her head and seemed overpowered with shame.

This incident had occurred near Christmas—there was a mess of dirty melted snow on the ground—and when the following Christmas brought much the same weather, Ethel bethought herself of the Martin children (if indeed she had ever forgotten them) and wondered whether their shoes were good enough to keep out the snow-broth. She sent Gladys Martin five pound notes in a registered envelope. These were acknowledged in a grateful scrawl. She sent the same next Christmas, and again the next, but now the acknowledgment came in a much firmer handwriting and was signed by Charles M. Martin, who stated that, as his mother's eldest son, he hoped to repay Mrs. Eastwood's kind loans shortly. Ethel was vexed; she had enjoyed being generous to Charlie's widow and telling anyone who would listen about her generosity.

"Repay, indeed! I'd like to see them repay a farthing. I shall believe it when I see it. There's not much chance of Charlie Martin's widow ever being able to repay anything, I can tell you," said Ethel.

However, in the following autumn, who should turn up in Naseby Terrace but Charles M. Martin, dressed in khaki if you please, a young man of nearly nineteen, enlisted for this Hitler's war which had just begun. He resembled his father now quite closely, having sparkling dark eyes just like those Charlie had turned on Ethel before he went off to world war one. Taller than his father, though, and more of a man than Ethel remembered Charlie to have been. For a moment Ethel's heart quite turned over, and she invited the lad into the house in quite a flutter. But he would not come in further than the hall. Standing there stiffly, with his heels together, and speaking with a kind of anger in his tone which was really *quite* uncalled for in the circumstances, thought Ethel, he offered her first four five-pound notes to repay the debt, and then two pounds twelve shillings and fivepence in small change by way of compound interest. Ethel was quite taken aback as he stood there counting pennies into her hand. She accepted the five-pound notes, naturally, but suggested the lad should retain the rest for himself, as he was going off to the war and everything. He refused, very sharply as Ethel thought.

"He'll change his mind if he comes back only half a man, like his father," she said on a grumbling note to Mrs. Clapham.

(Mrs. Clapham, her next-door neighbour and tenant, being the wife of a man who for health reasons had been demoted to a part-time job, could be patronised, and thus was a useful listener.)

However, none of the Martin children were killed or maimed in Hitler's war. The two boys came home safely and got good jobs, one in engineering and the other in textiles, and the two girls both married quite well and rather young, and they all had lots of children. It was really disgusting, as Ethel said, how many children those Martins had. Showed you what kind of people they were at bottom. But what did it matter to Ethel Eastwood? She had her property; she prospered.

It was after the war was over that things began to go not quite so well with Ethel.

Fred Eastwood's property was old. One or two of the houses stood in slum property scheduled for clearance—they had been scheduled thus for so many years that Ethel had come to view the likelihood of anything happening to them with derisive disbelief; but now they were duly requisitioned and pulled down. Ethel received compensation, of course, and obtained good advice on how to reinvest the money; but it was not the same. Meagre dividend cheques with enormous income tax sums deducted, were not the same to Ethel as the solid cash she had taken week by week from tenants' hands. Income Tax you could fiddle a bit under those conditions, but when it was taken off before you started, as you might say, where were you? And living expenses going up and up, all the time. Because of some stupid law she could not put up her tenants' rents; yet all the time they were asking for outside paint, and roof repairs, and new sinks, and pipes repaired, and pointing. Pointing! Her own house, the house she lived in, stood at the end of Naseby Terrace. At one time she had been proud of the extra size and distinction which this position conferred, but now she was maddened by the area of that exposed side wall. It was horribly beaten upon by the wind and rain which came sweeping from the west across Ashworth Municipal Park. Yes, that wall would need to be pointed soon, as sure as fate. And its size! And the amount workpeople charged nowadays! Outrageous! It wasn't as if they worked hard, either; their working day was nothing but talk and tea. Taking one thing with another, she was quite glad to take the Dean girl as lodger—it was a kind act, as she explained to Mrs. Clapham, and the girl was well-behaved if a little hoity-toity, and punctual on the dot with her rent. Of course Ethel wouldn't have kept her a week if she hadn't been punctual with her rent—"not a week," she told Mrs. Clapham emphatically. Mrs. Clapham believed her.

Of course Ethel saw at once what was up when Dot Dean began going out with that Mr. Cressey.

"She's head over heels for him," she said to Mrs. Clapham with relish, laughing her coarse loud laugh. "Yes, head over heels. Though I'm sure I can't tell you why. I don't think much to him myself, and that's a fact. He's nothing much to look at, and these schoolmasters don't get much pay."

Mrs. Clapham opined that Mr. Cressey was always very kind and polite.

"Well, yes, though he was very sharp with me once when I asked Dot what film they were going to. There was a rather hot one on, I'd been told, and I gave her a hint not to go. 'That is for Miss Dean to decide,' he said. Such airs and graces! And what is he, after all? *I* don't think much to him. He's lame, you know. He limps. Oh, not much, I grant you; it doesn't show much, I daresay he takes pains enough for that, he doesn't do it always, it's more a sort of a pause than a limp, but there it is."

Mrs. Clapham thought that Mr. Cressey might be one of those who had been ill in childhood; they called them spastics.

"Spastics!" exclaimed Ethel scornfully. "Such fancy names! Why don't they call them cripples outright and be done with it? Cripples, that's what they are. I like to give things their proper names," she concluded virtuously.

All the same, when there was this talk of Dot Dean's leaving Ashworth and going to her sister in Scarborough, Ethel was vexed, for the girl was well-behaved and punctual with her rent and always looked clean and smart, quite a credit to her landlady. Besides, who would Ethel get as a tenant, in her place? As things stood nowadays, she couldn't afford to be without a lodger in the house. It was really a very great relief when after the Easter holidays Dot seemed to change her mind and decide to remain in Ashworth.

"It's that Mr. Cressey," said Ethel shrewdly. "Though what

she can see in him! And it'll never come to anything, you know. Mark my words, it'll never come to anything. It'll just go on and on, you know, without ever coming to anything. But why should I worry? She won't give up hope easily, Dot won't. She'll stay on, hoping against hope, as they say," said Ethel, laughing heartily.

Mrs. Clapham said she thought there was a possibility that Dorothea and Mr. Cressey might get engaged.

"He's not the kind to do anything wrong," she suggested.

"Oh, there'll be nothing *wrong*," said Ethel with crushing emphasis. "Not in my house, I can tell you. No, there'll be nothing wrong. But if they did by some strange chance get engaged, it'd be years before they could marry—schoolmasters don't get much pay, you know. Why should they? Their year's work is half holiday. But *I* don't think they'll get engaged. Still, they might. There's no telling what foolishness folks will get up to when they think they're in love. But I shall be surprised if it comes to anything."

As the weeks went on, however, she somewhat modified this view.

"You might be right about our Dot and that Cressey," she told Mrs. Clapham, nodding confidentially. "They're still going strong."

"Well, I hope he does and I hope she's happy," said Mrs. Clapham with an air of defiance.

Mrs. Eastwood snorted.

There came a sunny evening when Ethel, hearing steps on the stairs, heaved herself quickly out of her chair—she had grown bulky and heavy of late, though still a fresh-cheeked, well-looking woman—and hurried out to intercept her lodger. She returned to Mrs. Clapham, who was having a cuppa with her to pass the time till her husband came home, chuckling sardonically.

"Yes, I think you're going to be right," she said. "Madam's just gone out dressed up to the nines, everything clean on her.

122

I will say that for Dot, she's always spruce and clean. But such a look on her face! She's right down besotted with him." She chuckled. "I wished her luck," she said.

"You shouldn't have done that, Ethel," said Mrs. Clapham. "Young folk don't like having these things touched on."

Mrs. Eastwood laughed.

"What will you do for a lodger if she gets engaged?" said Mrs. Clapham.

"I shall have plenty of time to find somebody else, before it comes to a wedding," said Ethel with confidence.

"Well, I must be off and get my old man his tea," said Mrs. Clapham, rising.

"It's awkward for you, him coming in at such awkward times," said Ethel.

Her voice oozed sympathy, but under its cover she was really giving Mrs. Clapham a little dig about her husband's inferior job, in return for Mrs. Clapham's uncalled-for comment about her good wishes to Dot Dean. Ethel was skilful at thus planting a barb under the pretence of defending its recipient—she prided herself on giving, as she said, as good as she got, always. Mrs. Clapham, fully aware of her hostess's intention, coloured a little as she wished her cheeribye and slipped out by the back door, which stood open.

2

It was not much more than an hour later that Ethel to her surprise heard the front door latch turn. Who could it be? She heaved herself up quickly and hurried out into the hall, alert to defend her property. She had not been quite quick enough to intercept the intruder, however, for her lodger was already halfway up the stairs.

"Dot! Is that you? You're home early," exclaimed Ethel.

"Am I?" said Dot in a spiritless tone. She stood with her back to Ethel, not moving, one hand resting on the banisters.

At once Ethel knew what was the matter. *She* knew. *She* guessed. You couldn't deceive Ethel.

"I knew it in a flash," she heard herself saying to Mrs. Clapham. "That Cressey hasn't come up to scratch. He's disappointed her. He's made it clear he doesn't intend matrimony, and wasn't Madam Dot disappointed! I've always been pretty quick in the uptake, you know, and I guessed it as soon as I saw her. Talk about drooping! She looked right down wilted! Or perhaps I'd better say jilted!"

She could not help grinning.

Dot turned towards her.

"By the way, Mrs. Eastwood," she said in a high uneven tone: "I was going to tell you on Friday, but I may as well mention it now. Will you take a fortnight's notice from Friday, please? I've decided to join my sister in Scarborough immediately."

She ran up the stairs and into her room and bolted the door behind her.

Ethel stood gaping. Then a gust of anger swept over her. Who did Dot Dean think she was, giving Mrs. Ethel Eastwood notice in an offhand way like that? Standing halfway up the stairs! Throwing it out without any reason given, as cool as a cucumber.

"No reason given," she heard herself explaining to Mrs. Clapham. "Not a single word of any reason. That's what annoyed me, Mrs. Clapham. Not a word of excuse or reason. Of course it was all due to that Cressey you're so fond of—he's let her down. But that doesn't excuse her throwing me off like that, does it? 'Join my sister in Scarborough immediately.' Hoity-toity! After all I've done for her, too. These young people nowadays have no gratitude, Mrs. Clapham, no decent feeling at all. Look at those Martins! And now Dot Dean. No consideration for me, having to get another lodger at short notice, no consideration at all."

At this her anger suddenly fell from her, and fear took its place. The money, crisp new notes, which Dot had paid her so regularly every week for the last two years, would cease in a couple of weeks. Its absence would leave a terrible gap in Ethel's budget.

All her worries rushed forward, clamouring, beating upon her mind with painful blows. A new lodger. And who could she find? You read such awful things nowadays about men lodgers murdering their landladies and stealing their money; not that Ethel was fool enough to keep much in the house, but that didn't seem to prevent the murders. On the other hand, women lodgers were usually pernickety, wanting this or that and continually grumbling. Who could she find? Where could she look? Should she advertise? No; that was sure to bring one of those murdering thieving men down on her. Who could she consult? And there was that side of the house which really must be pointed before the winter rains. And the sink at Number 17 which was badly cracked, you couldn't say otherwise, and the shop which needed outside painting. There was her income tax and her Schedule A, and the ball tap upstairs which was behaving badly, and her bank balance which was lower than it ought to be. Dot's defection had hit her in her most sensitive spot. Her financial position was threatened.

She sighed and came to herself and found she was still standing at the foot of the stairs, just where Dot had left her. Vexed, she shook her head irritably and moved with ponderous steps towards the kitchen. On the way she caught sight of herself in the hall-stand mirror. Her large square face, usually so set and firm, looked weak and frightened. How thin and grey her hair was nowadays! She was growing old. Old and poor. Panic seized her. She sank heavily into the kitchen rocking chair, a horsehair relic of Fred's mother's days. Too dispirited to rock, she sat forward motionless, her hands spread on her knees, her shoulders hunched, brooding.

3

After a while she began to rally from the first shock of the blow. Well! She wasn't going to be knocked over by a chit of a girl giving notice. Not she. Not Ethel Eastwood. If she couldn't find another lodger to her liking, she'd have to make up the money in other ways. When this new Rent Act came in she'd be able to put up all her tenants' rents—not before it was time, either, thought Ethel virtuously. She stirred, and began to rock herself slowly backwards and forwards. Meanwhile . . . Was there anything she could do meanwhile? Anything to make up the loss of Dot's money?

Yes! She rather thought there was! Ethel smiled, and began to rock more vigorously. Tenants needn't think they could put her off with silly presents instead of paying their rent, thought Ethel with a virtuous sniff—for it was only a present, after all, whatever he might say. He *said* it would more than pay a month's rent, but that was nonsense. She'd take it back, and ask for her money in exchange. After all that was what she had meant in accepting it—simply to hold it as a kind of pledge, for him to redeem with the rent money when he was able. He'd better be able now. Because Mrs. Ethel Eastwood couldn't wait any longer for her rightful money, not with Dot leaving and everything. She'd go up there first thing to-morrow morning, you could bet on that.

But wait a minute. Why not go now? She wouldn't be able to sleep a wink all night unless she did something to offset Dot's notice. When money worries harassed her mind she was apt to toss and turn in a perfect stew for hours. So why not go to-night? It was a nice light evening. She could take the Hudley bus as far as Blackstalls Bridge, change there into the Blackstalls Brow bus, get off at Brow Lane and walk up to High Royd, get her money and come down the lane and catch the bus on its return journey, just as she had done before. (Though it was a shame to have to spend four bus fares to get her rightful rent, still, for the sake of peace of mind, she'd do it for this once, and teach that Freeman a lesson.) Of course it might take a little longer than it had before to get her money, with the present coming into it and all that. But not much longer.

She rather fancied she was a match for Mr. Francis Freeman. More than a match, she rather thought.

She laughed aloud, and rising from her chair began to bustle about the house making preparations. There was no sound from Dot's room as she passed the door.

"Probably sobbing her heart out beneath the bedclothes," thought Ethel, smiling. "Well, she needn't think I shall beg her to stay, because I shan't."

She took out Freeman's present from her wardrobe drawer and without troubling to wrap it up wedged it into her big shopping bag. (It was small enough to fit in fairly easily; that in itself showed you how little value the thing had, didn't it? Quite a small thing. She'd been a ninny ever to accept it, even as a mere pledge, a token; but she'd been feeling pretty well off at the time and the old man had a way with him.) She put on her good flowered print and her off-white coat and hat and her chamois gloves and black court shoes, and decided as she looked in the glass that although her hair was thinning and her bust swelling, she was still a smart good-looking woman, equal to anybody.

She caught the Hudley bus without any rush, made the transfer to the Blackstalls bus at Blackstalls Bridge successfully, secured a good front seat, and clasping her bag firmly in her ample lap, was borne away up and up among the hills that surrounded Ashworth and Hudley.

"It must be awkward driving up these hills in the winter," reflected Ethel, as she had done the last two months when she had visited Mr. Freeman. "I shouldn't like to be a driver on this route. But then, of course, they're paid for it."

At Brow Lane she dismounted. The bus rolled away along the flank of the hill.

Ethel stood considering. There were two routes up to High Royd. The main way led up Brow Lane, a steep cobbled causeway which curved round the slope of the overhanging brow from which its name was derived and brought you to the side of the farmstead before meeting a gate and degenerating into a mere bridle path over the moors to Blackstalls. (This was the old route to the upland township of Blackstalls, Ethel had heard say, but it was so steep and rough that later road-makers had rejected it with a shudder and taken the longer way round.) There was, however, another route to the house available for pedestrians which was even shorter and steeper than the lane; namely some steps through a stile in the wall and a flagged pathway straight up the rocky, grassy, heathery bank itself. This pathway was certainly much shorter, reflected Ethel; if she took the pathway, she would have more time in which to extract the rent money from Freeman. But it was really appallingly steep. And then again, possibly the fact that the interview must be very short because she must leave quickly to catch the bus might be useful in the interview with Freeman. She could perhaps more easily bustle him into it. She turned up Brow Lane.

Soon she came in sight of the old stone house. It was very old: stone lettering above the porch gave its date as 1672. Its twin-gabled roof was made of stone tiles. As she approached Ethel eyed these suspiciously; but apart from a little moss here and there they looked in good condition.

The appearance of High Royd vexed her. She had let it very cheaply because it was almost a ruin, but now it looked quite smart, "all poshed up," Ethel described it to herself, with glossy black and white paint, and old tubs painted black standing by the door with cheap flowers, nasturtiums and such, growing in them. Of course she ought to have been pleased because her property had certainly increased in value under Mr. Freeman's care, but somehow it annoyed her. She disliked all that arty, highbrow stuff. She felt at once snubbed and contemptuous in its presence. Who had ever authorised that expenditure on paint, anyway? Certainly not Ethel; as far as she knew she had ordered simply the minimum number of coats of a respectable drab. No doubt Freeman had painted it all himself—just like his cheek. The inside of the house was just as bad, too, she remembered sourly; some of the walls were painted different colours, and others had pictures actually painted on them. Such nonsense! There was one very long picture, for instance, a kind of panorama of what you could see from the front windows of the house, showing the hills and the valley and Ashworth and Hudley down at opposite sides in the distance, with mill chimneys smoking. As if mill chimneys were proper things to be put in pictures!

Hot and breathless from the climb, Ethel paused a minute before turning along the front of the house to the doorway. A large black cat, its paws tucked in, lay on the wall facing her in the evening sunshine. Motionless, it gazed at her stonily from gleaming yellow eyes. Ethel took a step forward. The cat leaped up and fled, with an effect of insult. Ethel tramped on angrily. She felt a trifle nervous, for Mr. Freeman was a rather overpowering sort of man—"his eyes stick out like chapel pegs," she remembered uneasily—but all the same she meant to stand no nonsense; she couldn't afford to stand any nonsense now that she was losing her lodger; she meant to have her rent.

VI

FRANCIS FREEMAN, STAGE DESIGNER

I

He was old, of course. His strong, solid body, once so magnificently robust, so instantly responsive, though still a powerful instrument now fell short of muscular perfection; his physical functions were beginning ever so slightly to falter— they were already something of a nuisance to himself, soon they would become a nuisance to others. The thick black hair which once sprang so vehemently from his great forehead, though still plentiful and wiry, was beginning to recede and whiten; the skin of his hands had begun to wrinkle, his bold blunt profile had blurred and roughened.

But all this was of no consequence if one accepted it with the dignity of full awareness. It was good to have a time, before the thought of death became too intrusive, of leisure in which to survey one's life, acknowledge one's defeats and commemorate one's victories, to repent of one's stupid blunders and unintentional cruelties, to savour the agonising, joyous, passionate, tender, angry, striving whirl of sensation which had been one's life.

And High Royd was a good place in which to perform this survey.

Of course it was strange, and sometimes struck him as unbearably ironic, that he, after his wide rangings over the capitals of Europe, his frequent excursions to New York and Hollywood, should be tucked away in this quiet, remote, almost barbaric spot. But from this lofty perch one saw on either hand great vistas of Pennines rolling away into the distance; while at one's feet, as one leaned against the low wall of the little garden, fields of long grass, moulding in intricate curves the contours of the hills, plunged headlong down to the road and thence to the valley and the invisible river far below. Far to the right down there, with the yellow evening light blazing here and there in sudden gold on its windows, lay the town of Hudley; to the left, more in shadow for some grey clouds were rising up the sky, lay the town of Ashworth. Both these teeming industrial cities, so important in their own eyes, looked at this distance like agreeable toys, their mill chimneys and water towers, their cinema domes and school blocks, their long terrace rows and concentric brick housing estates, taking on a playful, childlike quality; it was easy from here to compassionate them, to forgive what went on in their tiny neat little streets, to perceive the fundamental well-meaning innocence of human activity, the pathos of humanity caught in an externally imposed predicament. Freeman smiled at the towns benevolently now, and examined the wide landscape with the eye of an artist.

In the west a charming though not vivid sunset was developing in shades of pale gold and grey. The wind—there was always a wind at High Royd—rippled the fields; red sorrel, white hemlock, tall dandelion clocks in fluffy grey and branching golden buttercups bowed their heads rhythmically amongst the deep grasses, which as usual in the West Riding were of a somewhat muted green.

"A pretty landscape," decided Freeman. "A bright scene."

He smiled and began to hum that naïve but catchy tune from *Maritana* known as *Scenes that are Brightest*, inventing words of a suitably childish kind to fit the tune.

> *"Scenes that are brightest,*
> *Grass in wind blowing,*
> *Grass in wind blowing!*
> *Scenes that are brightest!*
> *Grass in wind blowing*
> *On a Pennine hillside."*

It was one of the jokes which he and Fiammetta had shared: when they saw an agreeable landscape together, to burst forth with adaptations of this verse—in English, German or Italian as the fancy took them—the sillier the better, and if the improvised lines proved sometimes a trifle obscene, they laughed all the more heartily. (There was one version, for instance, composed at the top of the Eiffel tower, which would probably have led to their arrest by the authorities had it been sung in French.) Freeman laughed as he remembered it, shook his massive head and began to think of Fiammetta. His whole life unrolled and lay before him for the viewing, like the landscape at his feet.

He had been born down there in the Hudley slums, and had

lived his first ten years in two rooms in Howgate Close, a dark filthy little court now cleared away. His father, Francis Freeman the elder, was an Irish labourer who had come over a few years before to work on the reservoirs then being constructed in the Pennine moors: a broad immensely strong man with black hair growing thickly over his arms and chest and down his low forehead almost into his sparkling, gleeful, slightly squinting black eyes. He was a Catholic, of course, though hardly a practising one, and would sometimes shout cheerful abuse at his wife because she was a black Protestant—indeed she had been brought up in some very strict obscure sect, Plymouth Brethren as far as the young Francis could make out, and still when challenged professed this faith. She had lived in one of the old remote hillside townships near which Freeman's reservoir was being constructed, and had married him secretly in the face of violent family opposition, Francis gathered. Whether his father's name was in fact Freeman, or whether this was his mother's name, taken by his father to avoid the consequences of some violation of the law, Francis was not sure —there was always a vague atmosphere of secrecy hanging over the house, any question about names from the authorities was received with uneasiness, and the police were ill regarded. Once when Francis, then a young child, was out shopping in Hudley with his mother, she suddenly seized his hand and jerked him round a corner into a draughty passage, and they stood there for some minutes pressed against the wall, his mother breathing deeply, her lips pursed, a strange look of mingled anger and amusement on her face. Clearly the Freemans were concealing themselves from someone, and it was Francis's guess that this someone was one of his mother's relations: a family feud seemed indicated, which probably had its origin in his parents' marriage. That they *were* married, however, was certain, for his father often joked about this, coarsely though not unkindly, with his mother, and she was apt to drawl out a tart response in her sardonic Yorkshire tones:

"Tha needn't go on so. We all know tha were fair capped to find thisen wed."

His mother was a strange woman, Francis often thought; tall and buxom, white-skinned, green-eyed, infinitely cleaner than anyone else he saw in those early days, with strong features and a great mane of straight red hair. This she usually wore tightly wound round her well-moulded head, and it was supposed to be a great favour to her husband and son, for which they were required to be respectfully grateful, when she let it loose so that it flowed down her shoulders to her waist. Francis was sometimes allowed on Saturday night to brush this river of hair, but his father when he came in, usually slightly drunk, would seize a great handful and wind it round his wrist, and draw his wife's head back and kiss her lips, laughing loudly.

The attachment between his father and his mother was indeed very strong; the little Francis, looking up at them, hands dirty, nose unwiped, realised that fully. Any quarrels they had sprang from his father's jealousy, which was violent, and directed, since his wife gave him no other cause, invariably against her family. The most terrible row which Francis remembered occurred because his mother gave him a cheap little box of paints for his seventh birthday. His father in a fury tore the little metal box apart and threw the six squares of paint all over the room—it seemed from his angry ravings that his wife's brother had dabbled with paints.

"Ye gave 'um up when ye married me and I won't have ye turn back to 'um!" he shouted.

"Have it thi own way. T'lad can do without a gift, I reckon," said his wife with calm indifference.

Her husband eyed her suspiciously, but roared with decreasing force and finally flung himself muttering out of the room. The moment he was gone his wife collected the scattered paints and pressed them back into their little sockets with her broad thumb. As she did this, she smiled—to herself, not at her son.

"Best not use them except when I'm here, Frankey," she said.

She was not at all discomposed, it was clear, by the preceding scene, and was quite prepared to endure more such scenes in the future. But Francis did not feel that his own happiness counted for much in the matter. He was a little perplexed and disappointed, but he played with the paints whenever he felt the wish to do so—he was not a child easily downcast.

The work on the reservoir had finished before Francis was born—or perhaps his father had left it at marriage; at any rate his father was now a labourer on the roads, sometimes wielding a pick with a fierce energy which Francis greatly admired, sometimes hardly raising a hand but entertaining his fellow labourers so well with story and song, keeping them in such good humour, that foremen turned a blind eye on his idleness. What foremen would not overlook, however, was a late arrival on the site. Unfortunately, for some months when Francis was about ten years old his father was employed on widening a hill road out of Hudley, at the foot of which stood an inn, the Ring o' Bells. In those days inns opened early in the morning, and some of the roadmakers caught the habit of dropping in to the Ring o' Bells for a drink of coffee laced with rum, on their way to work at six o'clock. It fell to Francis's lot to follow his father discreetly to the Ring and try to get him out after his first cup, before it was too late. His father was apt to resent this surveillance.

"Ah, get away with yez!" he roared, swiping Francis aside with his mighty arm. "Don't come bullocking here where ye're not wanted!"

Francis did not mind the physical blow—blows were customary in Howgate Close and the boys there were skilful in sidestepping them. He found himself harder hit by the suggestion that he came where he was not wanted. It seemed to touch into active pain some latent discomfort in his mind. Without quite knowing why he was very glad indeed when that section of road was finished and his father went to work in another direction.

Later, in his teens, when he understood the facts of procreation, he understood too that his earlier instinct had been sound. Only a mad physical passion for each other could have been strong enough to drag his mother from her respectability and his father from his footloose rovings into the bond of such unsuitable matrimony; they wanted only each other, children who came as a result of their intercourse were unwanted intruders. (Luckily they had but two more after Francis, who —perhaps also luckily—died of smallpox in infancy.) So though they were kind to Francis in an offhand manner and as Howgate Close understood the word, their son never really mattered greatly to either of them. Francis had too robust, too independent, a nature to brood over this lack of parental interest; it was only natural, he thought, he did not resent it, he just accepted it as a minor nuisance which it was no use grumbling about, like a crooked nose or a sore finger. (Still, it was a sore.) But it probably shaped his life. For one thing, it made it easy for him to leave home early when the chance offered.

In the winter and whenever the weather was bad his father was, in the manner of the times, "laid off" from road work, unemployed; then he took any work which offered itself. His great muscular strength stood him in good stead here. By this time his son's strength was also quite considerable; Francis was in his teens, strong, stocky and solid, his brief and sketchy schooling over, and father and son worked side by side. One day some chance or other—a scene-shifter was ill, Francis seemed to remember—led to their employment at the recently built theatre nearby, the Empire, where the millhands who crowded the slums on this side of Hudley roared their approval of the melodramas of the day. Some of the scenery they were hired to shift was still being painted when they arrived, and somehow—like so many crucial moments in life, this one was obscure, Francis could not recall it clearly though he tried—Francis found himself helping to paint it.

His foot was now on the ladder, and he climbed. At the end of the week the Empire offered him a regular job as scene-shifter, painter and general bottle-washer (the 1897 equivalent of dogsbody) for a few shillings a week. He took it. When he announced this to his parents, as he expected his father raged. The elder Francis had all the native fluency of the Irish, with a command of profane invective all his own. His son listened appreciatively until, exhausted, the older man subsided into less decorated English.

"Is it a painter ye'll be making of my son like ye're mealy-mouthed brother!"

He banged his fist on the table—an old round wooden one, uncertain in balance and long since bereft of varnish, Francis could see it now—till it shook beneath his blows, and thrust his flushed face menacingly into his wife's.

"The pay's good," said she in a considering tone.

This apparent defence of her son was in reality no such thing, as Francis well knew; it was spoken in order to exacerbate her husband's jealousy, which she enjoyed. It seemed time to end the scene.

"It's what I want to do and I shall do it," said Francis.

He spoke without malice or animus, but solid as a rock.

His parents looked at him with astonishment, even a little fear.

"Ah, ye're a bold boyo, no doubt of it," jeered his father.

"Lad knows his own mind, seemingly," said his mother in her sardonic drawl.

"I do," said Francis.

For the first time in his life he received a look from his father which held real interest.

"So ye mean to follow ye're fancy, do yez, my boy?"

"I'm your son," said Francis.

His father laughed and flung away, and on Sunday evening,

136

when the load of scenery and furnishings arrived by rail for the touring company which was to open next day, Francis entered the employ of the Empire.

Presently one of the better-class touring companies carried him off with them on a round of provincial bookings. His mother seemed a little taken aback when he announced his imminent departure. Her tone in talking of it was reproachful and almost tender; she washed her son's bits of underclothes without being asked to do so, and actually kissed him goodbye when the time came for him to leave. She also pressed into his hand a tiepin—a cheap poor thing enough, purchased no doubt at the pawnbroker's down the street, but even so it was a miracle how she had found the money for it—and said wistfully, looking up at him:

"Tha's grown a gradely lad nowadays, Frankey."

Francis, who felt his entrails move within him, said nothing, kissed her quietly and left the house. Outside the door a stone slab flanked by rusty iron railings, and five uneven stone stairs, led down over the windows of the "house" below to the broken muddy pavement of the close. Francis had reached the bottom of these stairs when his name was called. He turned. His father stood in the doorway, his great arms stretched up to jamb and lintel.

"Do ye mean to come back home after this tour, now?" said he.

"No," said Francis.

His father hesitated, then stepped on to the stone slab and held out his hand. Francis likewise hesitated. But this huge rough hand, scarred by labour, covered up to the top joints of the fingers in black hair, somehow could not be refused; Francis would not retrace his steps, but he stretched up his arm and father and son shook hands across the railings.

The Sunday morning train crawled out of Hudley station, crawled into the tunnel and after an interminable interval of sulphuric darkness, crawled out again. It had now left Hudley and entered the neighbouring township. Francis sprang to his feet, let down the window of the compartment, threw the tiepin as hard as he could at the adjacent hillside and jerked up the window again almost before his companions had begun to protest against the intrusion of smoke and smell. He sat down and folded his arms, well content; he hoped he was now free for ever from his parents, free from the humiliation of living with those who did not want him.

He was right; he never saw his parents again. Ten years later a letter from a Howgate Close neighbour, a scrawl on cheap paper, ill-written and ill-spelled, told him that his mother was dead. For a few days he felt sore and moody and he indulged in one or two of those explosions of temper, which were already becoming known in his profession. But he was in Milan at the time and there was nothing he could do except send a hypocritical letter and a money order.

"The old man won't last long without her," he thought.

Sure enough a few months later a letter in the same hand told him that his father had gone. There was enough, it seemed, from some of the money Francis had sent before, which the neighbours had prudently laid aside, guessing how things might go, to bury him decently. This had been done, and the neighbour would keep for his trouble the few shillings which the sale of the Freeman furniture had produced, if Francis agreed. Francis sent another money order. He drank rather more heavily than usual for a night or two and his temper was rough. But then suddenly he cheered up and came back to his usual robust and lively spirits; "all that"—by which he meant, not the Hudley slums but the biological jealousies— was safely over at last, he thought, and he was glad of it.

Looking back on it all now, he saw, of course, that he had not freed himself completely from his parent's influence either when he first left them or when they quitted life. It was not possible to eradicate any elements of one's experience; one could only learn to recognise them and control them. That strange affair with Freda, for example, had deep roots in the relations between his mother and himself.

For a year or two after he had left Hudley he was carried hither and thither about the provinces with various touring companies, setting up and striking scenery, painting it when he was allowed, looking after props, acting as assistant stage manager, while his ambition crystallised. At the end of one of the tours, when he had saved a few pounds, he took himself to London, and entered himself at the new Polytechnic Institute in Upper Regent Street to make good his deficiencies of knowledge in the arts of drawing and painting. When his money ran out he took a job as late-night-shift porter at Kings Cross, and managed to keep himself that way—his great physical strength made him useful and even popular, for he was always ready to tackle a heavy crate to help a friend.

At this time he was living in mean lodgings in a back street near the station, now cleared away. He would never forget the disagreeable *frisson* which ran down all his nerves when, a lad in his early twenties seeking the cheapest possible room near his work, he knocked on the cracked and filthy door and it flew open and revealed Freda. He backed away at once, for above her pale plump face and pale blue eyes rose those thick smooth swathings of hair which were for ever associated in his mind with his mother, only that Freda's massive coiffure was fair as lint—she was in fact of North Germany origin, twenty years older than Francis; large, strong and bosomy. She smiled— her lips were full and pale—at his discomfiture, and said in guttural but not unfriendly tones:

"You want room?"

"No. No," said Francis, unable all the same to take his eyes from her.

"Yes, you want cheap room. I have good cheap room empty," said Freda, and she ushered him up the odorous stairs into a miserable little garret, which was, however, not ill lit by a skylight.

"How much?" said Francis gruffly.

The woman looked at him and named a price within his range.

"Well," said Francis consideringly. He sat down on the narrow bed, which was covered with a thick red lumpy quilt, to test whether it was strong enough to bear his weight.

To his astonishment he felt a pair of massive arms come round his shoulders; his head was pulled back against Freda's breasts and her pale lips fastened avidly on his mouth. He was astonished and at first revolted, but then his mood changed. This was positively the first genuinely loving caress he had received in his life. Why not accept it? He threw himself back against Freda with such force that the woman, who had one knee on the bed, tumbled against the pillow, then turning over her he stretched up his hands and tore at her hair so that it came down in great yellow veils about his head and shoulders. He had never had a woman before but he took her with fierce enjoyment, and Freda's eyes gleamed and her pale mouth writhed with satisfied lust.

They remained lovers—the emotion between them could hardly be called love but there was no other term for their condition, reflected Francis, running his mind over translations in various languages—for some three months. Then he became aware that their embraces, though no less ardent, took place less frequently; and he began to guess that he was sharing Freda's favours with another man. He was not surprised; he did not need to be told the kind of woman Freda was, there were other men in the house and he had heard their gossip. He made Freda no reproaches, but simply refrained from asking her for meetings, though when she invited him he continued to accept; he had no claim on her fidelity; her lovers were her own affair; he would certainly never intrude where he was not wanted. He speculated occasionally with mild cynicism on the identity of his rival and was eventually assured of it by an old fellow-lodger: it was a young sailor, a fellow-countryman of Freda's, with fair curly hair, recently come to the house, who had succeeded him.

"Her old man being a sailor, she has a fancy for them, I daresay," said Francis's informant, sniggering.

"She really had a husband, then?" said Francis, who had imagined Freda's prefix to be a mere courtesy title.

"Still has, dearie," said the old Cockney. "He's sailing the Seven Seas somewhere at this very moment."

"Good luck to him," said Francis grimly.

"Ah, you may well say so," returned the old man. "He'll need it."

It was barely a fortnight after this that on approaching the house in the early morning after his night's work at the station, Francis saw a small crowd round the open door. A dark official-looking van stood in the street and a policeman was on guard at the top of the steps. This man civilly barred Francis from entering.

"I live here," said Francis. "Has something happened?"

"Only a double murder," replied the policeman sardonically.

He escorted Francis into the house and into the presence of a police officer of higher rank, not in uniform, who took down details of Francis's name and occupation. The bodies of Freda and her sailor lover were just being transferred to stretchers for conveyance to the police morgue, and Francis had a full view of them. Freda's pale face was frozen into a vicious beauty, a snarling tiger in marble, but the young sailor looked pitifully small and dishevelled. They had been stabbed repeatedly—the wounds showed a mad frenzy—in the act of intercourse, by the murderer, Freda's unexpectedly returned husband. (Francis saw his portrait afterwards in the newspapers; a most ordinary-looking man, short, solid and respectable, a bo'sun of hitherto unblemished reputation.)

Francis could not but reflect on his own good fortune. Had it been his night off duty, his life would now be over. He and the sailor had transgressed equally against Freda's husband. But the sailor lay horribly dead while Francis was vigorously alive. It was most unfair; Francis hated to benefit from such injustice, a burden of guilt seemed laid on his shoulders. The only relief was, and he accepted it with sober thankfulness, that no action of his own had placed the sailor in Freda's bed that night instead of himself. Had it been otherwise, had some change in plan, some convenience to himself, even some resentful cooling on his part towards Freda, caused the substitution, he would have felt morally responsible for the boy's death, and —as he had said to Peter only yesterday evening—such responsibility would be very hard to bear. As it was he could reject any direct feeling of responsibility; that the sailor had died instead of himself was a matter in which Francis had played no deliberate part. He pondered this, discovered the deep interconnection of all human activity, and never forgot this lesson; it was one of the formative experiences of his life.

The steps of his gradual advancement up the artistic ladder, from his first engagement as stage hand after the completion of his Polytechnic course to the position of one of the most sought-after scenic designers in London, though thrilling at the time, were (surprisingly) rather vague in his recollection. He remembered only the moment when a management had at last entrusted him with the designs of a stage production. They had given the job to him because—he had no illusions—he was unknown and therefore cheap; the play was a worthless little farce that he despised. Nevertheless the appointment was his chance, and as such he recognised it. He walked down the corridor from the theatre office at the close of the interview in his usual strong measured tread, but he raised his hands to shoulder height and snapped his fingers in exultation. Turning a corner he found himself face to face with a door-keeper, who gaped and seemed inclined to snigger.

"Laugh—why don't you?" said Francis, confronting him with hands uplifted.

142

The door-keeper lost his smile and shook his head.

"Discretion is the better part of valour," said he in his Cockney accents. (His striped shirt-sleeves rolled above his elbows, his unbuttoned drooping waistcoat, his pale bald head with the wisp of soft hair across it, were as vivid to Francis today as then, nearly fifty years ago.)

"Then come out and have a drink with me," said Francis, laughing and digging him in the ribs. "We'll celebrate together."

This story became part of the legend which presently grew round the name of Francis Freeman. So did the occasion a few years later when, a better-known artist having delayed and dallied and finally turned the commission down, and Francis been invited to provide designs in a hurry as a stopgap, he set to work and produced ground plans, elevation colour sketches and stiff-paper scale models for the three settings of the play, between Friday afternoon and Monday morning. They were good settings too, by the standards of the day, and Francis never lacked work thereafter.

But it was not till after the first world war that he became really famous. During the war, for which he volunteered immediately Belgian neutrality was violated, he declined to rise above the rank of private, and therefore had a very long experience of the trenches, a thorough training in all the wretched variations of blood and mud. He saw men live in reckless anticipation of death, become wounded, blinded, be torn to shreds and suffer agony, die; he saw men giving orders and receiving orders, he saw men carrying out stupid orders, he saw men failing from stupidity to carry out well-conceived plans. That deep acceptance of everything from the basest to the noblest of human activity as natural and to be expected, which was his innate attitude to life, was strongly confirmed; when he emerged from the Army in 1919, unscratched, perfectly sound in wind and limb and more muscular than ever, he felt that nothing ever could or would surprise him. His mind was now mature, his technical skill after a few months' practice appeared stronger and firmer than before; some grim and powerful settings for a war play brought him real fame.

Now he was no longer Francis Freeman, a promising young theatrical artist, but Freeman the celebrity, whose designs had box-office value, whose doings and sayings were the subject of countless anecdotes related in both the gossip and the serious columns of the press. *Scenery and Costumes by FREEMAN* appeared frequently, and always with prominence, on theatre, ballet and opera programmes; he was sought after; he had more commissions than he could execute; he had no time for leisure, only for swift and hectic pleasures. His designs were bold, flamboyant, sinister; the landscapes of his childhood—the interlocking hills, the soaring mill chimneys, the grim industrial terraces, of Hudley—influenced their form, while in colour they displayed strange, sometimes violent, but often strikingly beautiful juxtapositions. His work and his personality suited the new post-war world, he expressed it and moved at ease in it. Those tricks of the upper classes, clothes and manners, he picked up easily, without giving them much thought. His feeling for line and colour enabled him to dress well, in a colourful but never foolish style; while perhaps thanks to his Irish father, his English was always good and fluent, his accent, though not that of Oxford, neutral of dialect, his vowels pure. His deep strong voice could produce as required a warm caressing tenderness or a turbulent bellow.

In temper, he had learned with mild amusement, he was regarded during this period as difficult—a proud, strong, touchy man, who was apt to think himself insulted when nothing of the kind had been intended. His rage then was thunderous. Or sometimes his anger would show itself in another way: he was capable of the most prodigious sulks, declining to speak a word for several days. At such times his blunt swarthy face (which admirers likened to that of Beethoven) wore a scowl truly formidable. Or again, he might suddenly fling away from the theatre and vanish, under the mistaken impression that his work was not really respected. He had once been caught, on such an occasion, by the stage manager and leading man of the New York theatre concerned, climbing the gangway of a transatlantic liner. The resulting scene was quite terrific, even for the United States; the newspapers and press photographers had a field-day. The two New Yorkers besought Freeman almost with tears in their eyes to return to the theatre, making offers of quite large additional sums if he would do so. Freeman listened scowling at first, but gradually, as he came to believe no slight on his work had been intended, his expression softened and he melted into a childlike smile of pleasure. Finally they all walked down the dock slapping each other on the back, and the liner sailed without Freeman.

He had discovered in later years that the world of the theatre sometimes supposed his rages, his awful silences and his sudden disappearances to be calculated, "put on" in order to make himself valued and implored. This hurt him, for they were not in the least calculated, but as genuine as his talent. It was a fundamental tenet of his being never to stay where he was not wanted, never to presume on a welcome, never to expect or assume love. Not for him the weakness of trusting an affection which no longer, or perhaps never, existed; see things clearly, cut your losses, never ask for anything, for nothing is of value unless freely given. In money matters he was known as driving a hard bargain, and this too amused and slightly hurt him; the fact was, if he were offered insufficient reward for his designs, he believed at once that they were not really wanted. He was too proud a man to work under such conditions, and therefore, careless whether he needed the money or no, promptly turned the offer down.

It was the combination of these qualities—in fact it was the whole man, Francis Freeman himself—which won him Fiammetta.

Fiammetta had all the characteristics demanded of a prima donna: a magnificent voice well trained, an extremely beautiful person, a temperament passionate, fearless and headstrong. In body she was small, so that one marvelled such a superb volume of voice could pour out of such a fragile vessel—she was not in reality fragile, however, but brimming with a restless vitality, healthy, tough. Italian by birth, with an abundance of dark hair and huge dark eyes (grey or violet? Freeman never knew) which by some unusual coloration of iris and pupil had at times a silvery and starry appearance, Fiammetta dressed with the most exquisite taste; in ordinary life extremely neat, elegant, sophisticated, on the stage she could wear the flaunting costumes of operatic heroines with all the savage verve they required.

She was to sing the title-rôle in a production of *Carmen* for which Freeman was designing fresh costumes and scenery. Freeman considered this opera "old hat," but had been assured by those in charge that he was employed especially to give freshness and originality to a somewhat stale theme. He had accordingly let his imagination gallop; the glowing result pleased him, and when he heard Fiammetta sing at rehearsal, his pulses quickened with delight. It appeared, however, that Fiammetta wished to sing in yellow instead of the traditional scarlet. Freeman was summoned to a conference on stage and informed of this desired change in an imperious tone. A new design for the dress would of course be needed.

"It can be done if you postpone the opening night for a month or two," said Freeman with a smile.

"You require two months to design one dress?" said Fiammetta haughtily. (Her Italian-English, uttered in one of the finest contraltos of the century, was delicious.)

"By no means. But if the colour of Carmen's dress is changed, all the other costumes and the scenery must also be changed, or she will not appear the main character."

"That is nonsense. Never have I heard such nonsense."

"I think you're being a little unreasonable, Freeman," said the stage manager anxiously.

Freeman shrugged his shoulders.

"If the signora wishes to be a mere blur against the background, let it be so by all means, but take my name off the programme."

"Now, Freeman!"

"What is that, a blur? I do not understand this word," said Fiammetta, looking round the group angrily.

Nobody ventured to enlighten her, and there was an uncomfortable pause.

"Something so beautiful a Carmen should never be," said Freeman eventually, laughing.

Fiammetta gave him a glance in which, as Freeman clearly saw, disdain was mingled with calculation. He was not surprised therefore when she suggested that they should lunch together and talk over the matter, not surprised when he presently found himself alone with her in her suite at the hotel. He was not surprised, because her intention to use the power of her beauty to get her own way about the dress was throughout sufficiently obvious.

Sure enough, she began to flatter and soothe him, to gaze up into his eyes with that expression of admiring interest which is always so seductive, so apt to lead a man into those intimate confidences which place him in the power of their recipient. Freeman had had sufficient experience, in various preceding *amourettes*, of this enticing look, to know exactly what it meant; he therefore watched Fiammetta with a smile—he had no objection in the world to being seduced, but nothing would induce him to yield about the yellow dress. Fiammetta, it seemed, felt this, for she grew angry.

"You do not think me beautiful, Mr. Freeman?" said she, her wonderful eyes sparkling with rage.

(They really sparkled, thought Freeman, surveying them admiringly; in her case the *cliché* was literally true.)

"On the contrary, signora," he replied pleasantly: "I think you the most beautiful woman I have ever seen."

"Then why do you remain so cold? Come, kiss me! Do not be afraid."

"I am not afraid," said Freeman in an easy tone, laughing: "But it is only fair to tell you that I am capable of taking many kisses and yet not making you a yellow dress."

He rose and gave her a little bow, to take his leave.

"And yet you call yourself an honourable man?"

"No," said Freeman, pausing. "I have no such pretensions. I have come up out of the gutter and carry no sentimental luggage."

"And I too, you fool!" cried Fiammetta, springing to her feet. "I too am of the gutter. I am as relentless as you are yourself. I take what I want."

"Ah! Now we understand each other."

"Stay, then," said Fiammetta, stretching out to him her small hot hand, on which the diamonds glittered.

"No. It is the dress you want, not the man," said Freeman, turning away. He spoke soberly, but felt violence rising in him like fever.

She threw herself between him and the door.

"Are you so certain, Freeman?" she cried, panting.

"Don't try to lie to me!" shouted Freeman, plunging into rage.

For a moment they stood glaring at each other, furiously angry; then they both began to laugh.

"I shall not make you a yellow dress," said Freeman stubbornly.

"*Basta!* What do I care?"

"But I will design a beautiful new scarlet dress—the old one is too dull, too spiritless, for such a guttersnipe as you," concluded Freeman, laughing.

He took her in his arms; they strained each to each as if their embraces could never be close enough to express how near they were to each other, how separate from all the rest of the world.

A few days later Freeman said to Fiammetta, as she lay in his arms:

"Let us marry."

"Why?"

"We are more than lovers."

"That is true," said Fiammetta. "Luckily my first husband died."

"Who was he?"

"My first manager. A most kind, amiable, elderly man. But to me, nothing."

The wedding was turned by the company into a wild and riotous affair, typical of the stormy, gay, frenziedly restless life which Freeman now lived in all the world's capital cities. He had never had a real home and Fiammetta had long since left hers behind; they did not make a real home together now, but met when they could, dashing about Europe—to the furious alarm of the theatre managements with which they were respectively concerned—on preposterous schedules, in order to spend a few passionate hours in each other's company. Sometimes these hours were filled with ardent love-making, sometimes with quarrels which shook the theatrical world, but they were always immensely satisfying to Freeman and Fiammetta. Opera houses in Berlin, Milan, Naples, Vienna, New York; flower-decked suites in luxury hotels; flower-decked cabins in immense Atlantic liners; surging music, with Fiammetta's magnificent voice throbbing through it all; applauding crowds; bold designs in black and scarlet; hours of frenzied work; wine; books, plays, films, ballets, pictures; elaborate arrivals, hurried departures; the speech and currencies of many different countries; the emotions of many different peoples—all these were jumbled in his memory into a glittering pageant; a seething flux of colour and sound, in which the most brilliant colour, the most vibrant note, was always his feeling for Fiammetta. They both earned money in rich abundance and threw it away in lavish profusion, generous and open-handed to their friends, carelessly princely in their personal expenditure. Fiammetta's first husband, of a more cautious disposition than her second, had invested quite a pile of her earnings, but in some way Freeman did not trouble to understand all these savings were lost in the New York stock market debacle of 1929—they laughed together over this confirmation of the foolishness and meanness of trying to save.

Then, most unexpectedly and belatedly, long after they had abandoned any hope or even speculation on such a matter, Fiammetta found herself with child. They were astonished and disconcerted, and on account of Fiammetta's age, which by now was nearing the climacteric, somewhat alarmed. The alarm was justified, for Fiammetta's *accouchement*, which took place in Paris, was most painful and protracted, and the child, a daughter, appeared ailing and much underweight. But to Freeman's amusement and admiration, Fiammetta's peasant ancestry here asserted itself; shouting a vigorous stream of invective, she drove out doctors and nurses and tended the child herself with passionate care.

The little girl grew and thrived; the sweetest, gayest, darlingest child, as Freeman thought, in all the world, whenever he saw her. Gay was not a beauty like her mother, for she lacked Fiammetta's fine aquiline profile, and her dark hair was short and curly in a homely way, but the same wonderfully starry eyes shone in her round, merry little face, the expression of which was always most singularly loving, intelligent and tender. She lived chiefly in Freeman's flat in London, with excursions at first all over Europe to accompany her mother—her parents were always intending to take a cottage in the country somewhere and give her a settled life, but somehow they were never settled anywhere themselves long enough to bring this plan to fruition. Heaven knew, thought Freeman ruefully, looking back at it all now, how the child had contrived to be fed and clothed and educated, but somehow she had managed it—herself; smiling and happy, observing everything with those beautiful eyes and storing it all behind her broad white forehead, she made arrangements of the most admirable kind for herself, quietly and without any tears or fuss. This was all the more necessary because Hitler's war suddenly cut the Freeman family in half.

Fiammetta was in Germany when it began. Freeman did not believe in Hitler's promises for a moment and considered Chamberlain a deluded ass for doing so; he rang Berlin repeatedly and implored Fiammetta to return to England while there was time. But Fiammetta had a contract to keep and a rôle to sing; besides, Germany and Italy were allies; if war should break out, what of it? Her next engagement was in America and Freeman and Gay could meet her there.

War broke out and Fiammetta simply disappeared; in spite of Freeman's frantic string-pulling he could get no news of her. Had she perhaps returned to Italy? He hoped so. Was she regarded as Italian by the Germans because of her birth, or as English because of her marriage? He could not discover. He found himself busily employed in the matter of camouflage, and tried to still his anxiety by overwork, but at times the misery of uncertainty flooded his mind and drove out every other thought. He tried to send his little Gay away to America, but she would not go; when the matter was broached to her she said nothing, but clasping his arm with all her strength, she gazed up at him with such terrible though silent reproach that he simply could not say another word about it. Accordingly they went through all the vicissitudes of the war together and came to disregard them as most Londoners did at the time. In the absence of her mother Freeman loved Gay with all his heart but without knowing her very well; one could not force a daughter's confidence.

The war was over. The Red Cross found Fiammetta in a concentration camp, whither some stormy resentment of police regulation, or some indiscreet championship of her husband's country—Freeman could never discover quite which—had sent her. She returned to England—to die, as she bitterly said. Freeman and his daughter, now in her teens, stood on the station platform as the hospital train rolled smoothly in. Racked by an anguished expectancy, Freeman ran heavily up and down, seeking for his wife. It was Gay who found her; exclaiming "Mother!" she threw herself down beside a stretcher on which lay a small figure with a yellow, wizened face.

"No, no!" stammered Freeman, embarrassed, pulling at Gay's shoulder. "Some mistake—we are looking for my wife."

"You don't recognise me, Freeman?" said the woman, smiling. "But I know you, my dear. You are not changed."

The sardonic droop of her lip was Fiammetta's. But her once beautiful body was merely skin and bone, her face deeply wrinkled, her eyes lustreless and sunk into her head. Worst of all, her voice, that once superb instrument, now sounded shrill, uncertain.

Or rather, reflected Freeman, that was not the worst. The worst was that she was simply too exhausted to take any further interest in life. The once superabundant vitality was now flickering to extinction. Occasionally for a few moments her eyes would brighten and she would show her husband and her daughter the love which a wife and mother should, laying her hand on Freeman's, or putting the curls back from Gay's face, as the pair bent over her bed. But soon the flicker of interest died, the hand dropped, the look of almost peevish weariness returned. Fiammetta withdrew into herself, far away from Gay or Freeman, and lay silent, brooding. Eventually she slipped away from them. They wept together for her loss, not as she was now but as they wished to remember her. Then life began again for them.

In the great burst of theatrical activity which followed the close of the war Freeman participated at first joyously. He noticed that his commissions were slightly less frequent than of old, but attributed this to the dislocation caused by the war—as peace settled in, he thought, the world of the theatre would steady. He noticed too that his name seemed unfamiliar to most of the promising young men who were now beginning to make their appearance, and that there was a general tendency on the part of any who did know him, to regard him as the "grand old man" of scenic design. This amused him; he was in his late sixties, of course, but tremendously strong physically and as powerful as ever in his art. Indeed he thought himself more powerful; his war experience with Fiammetta had, he knew, deepened his sense of the ironies of human existence, and that should surely increase his feeling for beauty and truth.

Television came. Ever ready to attack a new problem, Freeman made an attempt or two to adapt his style to the requirements of this fresh medium. But he abandoned them impatiently. He felt like a bull in a small china shop. There was no colour yet, and his bold lines looked simply an untidy mess on the tiny screen. Designing for television was clearly a job for smaller people than himself, people who devoted their whole professional lives to television, who worked within one or other of the great television corporations. Freeman observed with a shrewd eye the decay of the theatre in the provinces as the new medium flooded them; he was troubled, for he did not see how, in such conditions, young men of talent, such as he had been, could work their way up to the top as he had done. He mentioned this to Gay, who listened with her usual look of loving sympathy but could suggest no solution.

Indeed she seemed even more troubled than the situation demanded, thought Freeman; almost, indeed, as if she were personally involved. She was rising eighteen, now; not handsome, not (it seemed) particularly talented in any special direction and rather silent in general, but sweet and comely and loving, altogether a most darling person. No doubt she would marry soon, thought Freeman benevolently; in the course of her work as his secretary and general manager of his affairs, she met many young men. He could not help being glad that her choice of a partner was delayed, but of course he would not for a moment stand in the light of his darling daughter's happiness when she found her man.

In the early 1950's Freeman was asked to design settings for a new play, the first by its young author to receive London production. Uncomfortably penetrating, full of *angst*, its popular appeal was doubtful and Freeman had been called in to give it the support of his name. Its disillusioned tone appealed strongly to Freeman, and he thoroughly enjoyed the preparation of the sinister and macabre sets, in the course of which he once or twice overruled the inexperienced young writer, he was sure for the lad's own good. At the first night, he saw well enough that the reception of the play was luke-warm; the audience's response seemed muted and the critics, though they stood about in groups as usual, were decidedly not engaged in animated discussion; they looked sour and said little. Opening the newspapers next morning, Freeman, all unsuspecting, was struck as by a sledge-hammer between the eyes. It appeared that the play had been *ill served by its settings*, which were variously described as *Victorian Gothic, heavily baroque, stale whimsy,* and *quite out of tune with the contemporary theme and writing* of the play. Freeman was stunned. His thick powerful fingers trembled as he turned over the pages, vainly searching for some more favourable comment on his cherished settings.

"Gay! Gay!" he shouted.

Gay came in—he was in bed, reading the papers and drinking his morning coffee. She chanced to be wearing a house-gown of a thin blue silk which Freeman had bought before the war in Paris, at the time of one of his greatest triumphs. The remembrance of this was bitter to him now. He looked into his daughter's troubled eyes and saw that she was perfectly aware of the failure of his latest settings, that she had indeed expected it, been expecting such a failure for some time. Instantly his decision was taken.

"I shall retire from my profession, Gay," he said. "I shall leave London."

Gay said nothing, but seating herself on the bed by his side put her arms round him and rested her head on his shoulder.

"I've harmed that young man," said Freeman gruffly. "I've put an unnecessary obstacle in the way of his career. I mustn't do that again, Gay. I'm not wanted here. I'm a nuisance. I shall take myself off somewhere—get out of the way of the younger men."

"Nothing can rob you of your previous achievements," said Gay softly in his ear.

It was true and it was the right line to take; the acceptance, frank and uncomplaining, of the common human lot: rise, triumph, decline. He had been lucky in that his period of maturity had brought him more than ordinary success; he must not grumble now that his greater height brought him a correspondingly greater fall.

He held to his decision to leave London, for he did not wish to be tempted to take further commissions. For a time he wandered restlessly about, looking at seaside resorts and picturesque country villages, Gay in faithful attendance. Then, chancing to hear in a London street—it was the day of some great football match at Wembley—a voice speaking with a Yorkshire accent, he laughed and said half-jokingly to Gay:

"I think I'll return to the home of my ancestors."

"Why not?" said Gay.

So they came to Hudley, and searching the hills for some small house which would suit at once Freeman's sense of beauty and his wish not to impose too much housewifery on Gay, they discovered High Royd.

The tiny farmstead was in a shocking condition when they first came upon it, a mere ruin, with that dark desolate look which long untenanted houses acquire. They saw it from the hillside road below, up which the car Freeman had hired in Hudley was conducted rather reluctantly by its driver at the direction merely of one of Freeman's whims. (He never drove himself nowadays; he had long since discovered that the combination of dreamy preoccupation with thoughts of designs, and sudden bullish charges to make up the time thus dreamed away, which formed his driving, was dangerous to the public and must be given up.)

"Stop!" cried Freeman suddenly.

The driver, grinning, stopped.

Freeman threw himself out of the car, thrust his burly body through the stone stile and clambered vigorously up the overgrown path to the old farmhouse. Gay followed, and after a moment so did the driver.

The door stood askew, its top hinge perished, and grass had invaded the stone flags of the front room. But the gabled roof, as Freeman discovered by climbing up to it, was sound except for a few strayed stone tiles, the stone staircase was firm, the bedroom floors not unrepairable; while even the driver was impressed by the magnificence of the view. Freeman enquired the name of the house and locality; a bus driver passing in the road below told him that the village over the brow was Blackstalls.

The name seemed to strike a note in Freeman's memory. Could this possibly be the hillside township where his mother had been bred and courted? Was there a reservoir in the neighbourhood, he enquired? There was indeed; but moorland reservoirs, in the hills round Hudley, were not so unusual as to constitute a means of certain identification. Freeman was the last person in the world, he told himself, to entertain superstitions or romantic fancies, and he put away the belief in an ancestral connection on his part with Blackstalls, with a laugh. Nevertheless, there was no harm in it as a mere fancy, and certainly he felt very much at home in High Royd.

He decided on the spot to buy it and settle there. Gay, as usual, was pleased with what pleased her father.

That afternoon, having "looked over", as he said, two or three Hudley lawyers—that is, charged in and out of their offices with Gay at his side—he picked one to do the business for him. Freeman was a good judge of men—he had seen so many—and this one served him well. Somehow in the course of the preliminary negotiations for the house all his financial affairs came into the solicitor's knowledge—Freeman was only too glad to transfer all that tangle to somebody else's hands—and the man told him emphatically that he had not the money with which to buy High Royd, he must be content to rent it. Freeman was amazed.

"Not the *money?*" he exclaimed, incredulous.

The solicitor had prepared a lengthy statement which he proceeded to explain in a blunt and forthright style, tapping each item with a square Yorkshire forefinger.

"I don't want to know all these details," said Freeman impatiently—details always cluttered a design—"Tell me the essence of the matter in half a dozen words."

"In half a dozen words, then," said the solicitor: "You've very little capital and no income."

"Really?" said Freeman. "Well, that is a surprise!" He laughed heartily, so that the solicitor stared at him; then fell to ruminating. "No—after all it's not surprising," he said at length ruefully. "I've earned plenty but I've spent it as it came."

"You never had anything at the back of you," suggested the lawyer in an absolving tone.

Freeman, recognising a local phrase but not quite sure of its meaning, looked interrogative.

"No savings—nothing left to you by your parents," expanded the lawyer.

"No savings and nothing left to me by my parents," agreed Freeman with a rather grim smile.

His solicitor, after a prolonged haggle with the owner of High Royd, a Mrs. Eastwood, arranged that Freeman should rent the place on a monthly basis for what seemed to Freeman an amusingly small rent. The solicitor also disposed of the lease of Freeman's London flat, paid all outstanding bills, tidied everything up generally and wished to invest the sum which remained so as to bring his client a steady if small income. But the income thus secured would be so ludicrously small that Freeman roared with laughter at the sound of it.

"No, no—put the money in the bank and let me live on it. I'll earn more long before it's finished," said Freeman cheerfully.

The solicitor did all in his power to persuade his client against this course, but was eventually obliged to comply, shaking his head and uttering mournful prophecies as he did so.

Freeman enjoyed himself immensely moving into High Royd. He did a great many of the repairs and all the painting himself, so that the old house looked really charming—just like a Freeman stage-set for a romantic play, in fact, when his few treasured pieces—furniture, pictures, glass—were installed. (Few—Freeman had rolled too far and too fast round the world to gather much of the moss of possessions.) And he was happy there. He felt at home. He and Gay settled in and became domestic; they discussed curtains and acquired a cat. The superb view was a continual inspiration; he painted the landscape from all angles, and felt his understanding of life clarified by its wide vision of human activity against the background of the uncaring hills.

On the material side, too, in spite of its remote situation the little farmstead was not too uncomfortable. Pure water from the Blackstalls reservoir gushed from the kitchen tap and the Hudley Corporation gas which lighted the sparse lamps in the road below had been brought up the slope to High Royd at some past time—the pressure was apt to be fitful, but the convenience for lighting and cooking great. A bus ran along the road up to Blackstalls once an hour and thence returned down to Blackstalls Bridge, where one could catch a bus either to Ashworth or Hudley. In the winter the Blackstalls bus sometimes stopped its journey much lower down the hill, daunted by the snow and ice above, and this was inconvenient; but then where in the West Riding were buses not sometimes in the winter daunted by ice and snow? In a word, as Freeman and Gay often said to each other in congratulatory tones, High Royd had all the advantages of the top of the hill and lacked few of those at the foot. A telephone would have been a boon, and a supply of electricity an improvement, of course. But the Hudley Corporation was adamant about the possibility of a telephone—the nearest wires were a couple of miles away down the hillside—and Freeman's lawyer was adamant about the impossibility of installing an electric plant, producing such huge estimates of the expenditure necessary that even Freeman was convinced and abandoned the scheme.

Not that money was in short supply at first. The articles Freeman had previously scorned to write for lack of time, he now gladly composed—or rather, he talked about the selected subject to Gay, who put down a draft which he then corrected and illustrated. He was also invited to give a course of lectures at the Hudley Technical College; the fees were amusingly meagre, of course, but when one was living so very quietly, really they were quite astonishingly useful.

It was during these lectures that he came to know Peter Trahier—an event of which he was never certain whether it was more boon or bane.

The course was entitled *Art and Civilisation*. It was not within Freeman's power to give a formal, logically constructed lecture on some well-defined aspect of any subject; his method was to stand up and, beginning with some well-known characterisation of the period he was supposed to be discussing, roam up and down the centuries saying whatever came into his head.

He did not care in the least whether he "stuck" or not, and freed from this inhibiting anxiety he never seemed to lack material; he strode up and down with his hands in his pockets, enjoying himself immensely, while his deep strong voice rolled along, discoursing of the theatre, the arts, and life in general. His anecdotes were always spicy and often highly contemporary, introducing familiarly great figures whose names were a source of awe to his young hearers. His generalisations were stimulating, and he was always on the side of the anarchic against the authoritative, the free as against the established. In a word, he was just what the more intelligent and public-spirited of the Hudley Technical College students wanted, and his lectures, after the first, were crowded. Peter was studying economics, civics, statistics, the law of meetings and such dull matters in preparation for the political career he hoped to make, and (as he admitted frankly later) he dropped into old man Freeman's art course rather contemptuously—it would probably have little to offer to a keen, well-informed young Marxist like himself, but it was free, extra-curricular, had caused a lot of talk; one might as well see what was going on.

Freeman noticed him at once. The lad was good-looking, almost striking indeed in appearance; tallish, with thick well-brushed sandy hair, and very lively grey eyes. The eyes were full of intelligence, decided Freeman as he strolled up and down the dais and observed Peter's quick response to his jokes and provocative paradoxes—Peter laughed always just a second before any other student, his reactions were just so much quicker than those of anyone else in the room. At the close of the lecture the lad asked some really admirable questions, well worded and spoken in a pleasant voice, and when the chairman closed the meeting, Peter came up to Freeman and continued the discussion ardently, admiration beaming from every feature of his agreeable young face. This admiration, this understanding, this ease of expression, were very

160

warming to Freeman, who discovered that the provincialism of his native town had been really rather chilling to his heart. Peter had to be driven away from Freeman almost by force by the chairman, and it was only natural that Freeman, laughing heartily, had called out to Peter over the intervening heads as they parted:

"Come and see me, my boy!"

"When?" shouted Peter.

"Oh, any time—Sunday afternoon."

Sure enough on Sunday afternoon Peter turned up, though the rain was pouring and the wind blowing as only on Blackstalls Brow could rain pour and wind blow. The young man's cheap raincoat was extremely wet, his sandy hair dark and ruffled, his cheeks bright red, when after a struggle with the elements and the criss-crossing lanes he eventually reached High Royd; it seemed he had walked from Hudley. He declined the offer of dry clothes from Freeman—probably, thought Freeman shrewdly, because clothes tailored for the burly Freeman would make the slender Peter Trahier look foolish—but accepted the kitchen towel from Gay to dry his face and hair.

Before the towel was handed back they were in love. Freeman could see them now, the bright rough stripes in blue and white tumbled between them, Gay's eyes downcast, Peter's wide, filled with surprised yearning. Less than six months later they married, and now their first child was on its way.

Yes, it was difficult to decide whether Peter was boon or bane. It was good that Gay should marry. But Freeman could not rid himself of the uncomfortable certainty that her chosen husband was inferior, to, unworthy of, his daughter. Since Freeman himself had come up from the gutter, naturally —though he laughed at himself for saying this: jealousy and pride were more natural than tolerance, he knew well— naturally he had no objection to Peter's birth, which was modest, to his education, which was elementary, or to his resources, which were meagre. Peter belonged to the "lower middle class"; he had lived before his marriage in a small house in a respectable little terrace in Hudley with a widowed mother and an elder sister, both in Freeman's opinion persons of stubborn dreariness; he earned his living as some kind of clerk in Ashworth Town Hall—Ashworth, not Hudley, because Peter wished to be elected to the Hudley Town Council and therefore must not be one of its employees lest he make himself ineligible. The Hudley Town Council was to be merely a stepping-stone towards Peter's political career, of course; he meant to enter Parliament and end up as a Cabinet Minister. And he might well do so, thought Freeman, laughing again ruefully; Peter was just the kind of man one met in high, though usually not the highest, political place. He had fixed plans of sociological reform, to which he was able to devote a quick intelligence, a good memory, a considerable fluency and a great capacity for work; he was conscientious in detail, and studied the relevant subjects with care and attention. But there was a soft spot somewhere in his character, a spot of decay, which would spread under the pressure of a political career. Was it conceit? Partly. The lad was young, of course, jejune indeed, with that kind of naïveté which consists in aping sophistication; but he would grow out of that. Self-interest? To be fair: not quite. No: the soft spot—or perhaps it was a hard spot, a calloused spot; at any rate it was diseased tissue, a centre of corruption—consisted in Peter's belief that the end justified the means. (He had said as much in that argument they had had yesterday evening.) Peter believed in the deliberate acquisition of power, he admired the use of "clever" tactics to acquire it, and to further its acquisition thought a certain lack of scruple justifiable—thus, though genuinely dedicated to serving humanity in the mass, he was apt in the process to override individual human rights and think this proper.

At the time of the marriage Freeman and the young couple

had agreed, on Freeman's suggestion, to divide High Royd between them. Freeman had made the proposal partly to keep Gay at his side, partly to keep her from the dreary little house in Hudley, belonging to Peter's mother who disapproved the match, which was all Peter had as yet to offer his wife, and partly because Freeman thought the pooling of household expenses would prove an advantage to Gay and Peter. The gable arrangement made the division of the house easy, and both parties promised to keep scrupulously to their own rooms unless invited, merely eating their meals together in the kitchen. But in practice, of course, among people anxious not to hurt each other's feelings, it did not work out quite like that, and the three saw a good deal of each other.

Fortunately Peter was out all day on weekdays, and often in the evenings too, pursuing his studies or attending political meetings. (Tonight, for instance, the day being Tuesday, he had gone straight from work to the Hudley Technical College, so that Gay and Freeman had eaten their evening meal alone together.) But even so, the frequent contacts with his son-in-law were often a trial to Freeman. On Peter's glib fluency, his resonant voice, his naïvely expressed "advanced" views, his cocky, sandy crest, Freeman felt he could have managed to look with fatherly tenderness; as for Peter's sensual love for Gay, Freeman knew his Freud and was on his guard against his own sexual jealousy. But the blemish in Peter's character, his cheerful casuistry, angered him. He hated to think that Peter would guide his daughter's life; hated too to think that on Peter and his like would rest the responsibility of steering the world through the problems created by nuclear fission. A fine mess they'd make of it! Moreover, Freeman had been humiliated recently to discover that the advantage of the pooled household expenses was mutual; it seemed his lawyer was right and he was really temporarily hard up.

With characteristic honesty he had at once imparted this discovery to Peter. At this Peter, his fresh face colouring, exclaimed that it was an honour to be of any—any—for once he stumbled amongst words, rejecting *assistance* and *advantage* and not immediately finding a less patronising substitute.

"It is an honour to live under the same roof with you, sir," he finished at length emphatically.

"Perhaps he's a good lad at heart, after all," thought Freeman.

But all the same Freeman did not feel he was as much master of his house as when the conferring of benefits had been all on his side, and he thought he discerned on Peter's part a continually diminishing deference to Freeman's views, an increasing stubbornness in upholding his own.

So it would be idle to deny that since Freeman's retirement, and especially since Gay's marriage, Freeman had experienced some moments of deep and bitter depression. But that was only to be expected. The right behaviour towards such depressions was to use them in one's art, and Freeman was using them thus at present; he was designing—solely for his own pleasure, he told himself, though secretly he believed his designs would be used some day and used with triumph— some magnificent stormy sets for *King Lear*. He cheered up now at the thought of them; whistled in a preoccupied style; jingled the coins in the pocket of his handsome loose brown suit; winked at the cat Simon which passed him in a cool but not unfriendly fashion on its way to the last ray of sunshine on the wall; and regarded once more the vast wild prospect which he had grown to love.

> "*How fearful,*
> *And dizzy 'tis to cast one's eyes so low!*"

The wind was rising; clouds in the west were beginning to obscure the setting sun. Rain might be on its way. It was perhaps appropriate, thought Freeman with a smile, that at this rather chilling moment when the golden glory of the sky was sinking to grey, he should see his landlady laboriously climbing the curve of Brow Lane, a stout, cross figure. Yes, even at this distance, decided Freeman, who did not like Mrs. Eastwood, she looked cross.

> *"O fat white woman whom nobody loves,*
> *Why do you walk through the fields in gloves?"*

A vulgar, disagreeable, narrow-minded woman. She had twice sprung upon him like a tigress, just because he was a few days late in sending his monthly cheque for the rent, and her behaviour at High Royd, though perhaps meant to be civil, had been as disagreeable as her errand. She had a way of setting her mouth, the heavy lips slightly awry, which gave her a contemptuous, sardonic look, as a prelude to the utterance of some piece of coarse disparagement in the guise of praise. (For example, on seeing Gay in her flowered red skirt, she set her lips and gibed: "A lot of people like those bright clothes nowadays.") But what had she come for this time? She was out of sight now, but had reached the side of the house no doubt, for Simon with a look of disgust in every limb came leaping round the corner to avoid her. Yes, here she was, exuding Philistinism from every fleshy pore. With a sigh Freeman stepped up the little flagged path to meet her.

2

"Have a drink, Mrs. Eastwood?" said Freeman after she was seated, turning towards his rather "amusing" little bar—a scarlet and white painted trolley.

"No, thank you," said Mrs. Eastwood in her gibing tone. "A cellarette on a tea trolley; that's a new idea."

"What can I do for you, then?" said Freeman.

He turned a chair round, seated himself astride and leaned against the back; he also put on the kindliest smile he could manage and tried to feel in charity with all men. It was a difficult exercise to include Mrs. Eastwood, but for a moment he managed it by considering the tones of her hair and coat as a problem of the palette.

"Well—I've come about the rent, you see," said Mrs. Eastwood.

"The rent! I paid you three months' rent last week," exclaimed Freeman, surprised.

"Three months!" exclaimed Mrs. Eastwood, surprised in her turn. "Well, that's not the point," she added. "You didn't really pay at all, now did you, Mr. Freeman?"

"I don't understand you," said Freeman stiffly. "I gave you the equivalent of three months' rent at least."

"I don't want any equivalent," said Mrs. Eastwood, setting her lips. "I want my money. I've brought that back, what you gave me I mean."

She fumbled in her shopping bag and drew out a small white-framed painting. It was in fact one of the most famous of Freeman's designs: a superbly dramatic backcloth for a play of northern industrial life, showing mill chimneys soaring black behind mean streets, against a deep blue evening sky. Fiammetta had had it framed because it was such a treasured possession, and Freeman had parted from it with great reluctance. But at the time of Mrs. Eastwood's last call to demand the rent he had really very little money handy, and not much immediate hope of gaining more. (The idea of an appeal to his son-in-law just crossed his mind but was of course at once dismissed: Peter might imagine Freeman was really embarrassed for money; he would tell Gay and she would be distressed.) So, as the local subject of the Northern Night picture would make it particularly acceptable, he took it down from the wall and gave it to his landlady in lieu of rent. He now saw this cherished sketch, unglazed as it was, drawn carelessly, unwrapped, from a shopping bag. Mrs. Eastwood held it out to him.

"I don't really care for it, not really," she said. "Those ugly

mill chimneys and that. Besides, the blue's not right, you see
—it doesn't go with the eiderdown in my bedroom."

Freeman perforce took the picture from her outstretched
hand. He made a great effort, perhaps the greatest in his
life, to keep his temper, though the blood beat in his temples.

"Will you have another picture instead? One with the
right blue this time?" he said, smiling.

"I'm not bothered," said Mrs. Eastwood.

Freeman was well aware that in the West Riding nowadays
this form of words indicated a blunt refusal. Suddenly and
completely he lost his temper; it swirled away on a wild blast
of rage. He sprang to his feet.

"Damn your mean ignorant little soul!" he shouted. "You
know nothing of art, and what you don't know you despise.
It's such people as you who destroy all that's good and beautiful."

"There's no call for you to shout at me, Mr. Freeman," said
Mrs. Eastwood, her heavy jowls flushing crimson. "I just
want what's owing to me, that's all. I want my rent."

"The picture was worth a year of your rent."

"That's what *you* say," returned Mrs. Eastwood coarsely.
"I'd rather have the money."

Freeman began to tremble.

"*Wearing worry about money like a hair shirt, I lie down in my
bed and wrestle with my angel*," he quoted hoarsely. "That's you,
Mrs. Eastwood, except that you wouldn't know an angel if
you saw one."

"I know I don't want a twopenny-ha'penny picture when I
see one," cried Mrs. Eastwood. "I want my rent."

"Very well. You'll lose by it. I'll send you a cheque."

"I'd rather have the money if you don't mind," said Mrs.
Eastwood smugly. "If you'd money in the bank to pay me
with you'd have sent a cheque before."

Freeman with a violent movement threw down the picture
on the settee and flung out of the room. Outside the door, with

angry fingers he plucked out his wallet and counted the notes it contained. They were not enough to satisfy Mrs. Eastwood. Exclaiming with rage, he ran up the stairs to his painting room, and crossing to a chest of drawers which stood there, began to ruffle up their contents—he knew he had a small *cache* of money somewhere. He was well aware that the imperfect old floor would betray every movement of his heavy frame to Mrs. Eastwood below, but would not demean himself by trying to act quietly. Ah, here was the money! He counted it. There was still not quite enough. By raking all the silver out of his pockets Freeman at length made up the exact sum. He descended.

He simply could not bring himself to lay the money in Mrs. Eastwood's hand, so he threw it down on the table beside her. Mrs. Eastwood laid down her bag and counted it carefully. The spectacle of her thick fingers smoothing out the notes and telling the silver coins aroused in Freeman a furious impatience amounting to physical nausea. She finished and put the money carefully away in her bag. She rose.

"Well, thank you, Mr. Freeman," she said in a tone of satisfaction. "I'm glad we're on a straight edge again. It's always better, isn't it? Of course it'll be May in a couple of weeks and the rent will be due again, but meanwhile we're on a straight edge, aren't we."

Freeman in silence flung open the door which led into the little garden. Mrs. Eastwood sailed cheerfully through.

"Well, good evening," she said, triumphant.

"Goodbye, madam," said Freeman, bowing.

3

Freeman slammed the door behind Mrs. Eastwood and stood there motionless.

For a moment rage seemed to course furiously through his whole body, setting it ablaze. Then the rage sank, succeeded by a searing humiliation. Everything in his life that made him particularly vulnerable—his mother's lack of love for him in childhood, Freda's rejection, his loss of Fiammetta, Gay's marriage, the failure of his last set of designs, his loneliness, the physical oncoming of old age—everything he had tried to forget or to anæsthetize by courage—had been excoriated by the rough fingers of Mrs. Eastwood; every sensitive spot in his mind had been pricked into quivering pain. As a man he was no longer wanted: he was no longer a husband or a lover, his protective function as father had been superseded by Gay's husband; his physical frame was beginning to decay. As an artist, though not in full activity he had hoped still to maintain himself honourably, but if he was so utterly rejected by the people—by the people of his own county—if what he had regarded as one of his best achievements on their behalf was coarsely laughed at by the West Riding—then it was useless to work any more. Perhaps even his lectures at the Hudley Technical College, it struck him in a scorching flash, had been a failure too; he had not been invited to give a second course. His financial embarrassment was not temporary and super-ficial, but deep and permanent. He was useless. Despised, rejected, totally unwanted; a bore, a nuisance, a liability; a drag on Gay.

If that was the case, he was far too proud a man—had always been too proud a man—to remain in such a position. He would remove himself immediately, as he had often done before.

He stepped through the room to the foot of the staircase, and shouted:

"Gay! Gay!"

His daughter appeared at the door of her bedroom. Her sweet plain face in its frame of dusky hair looked a trifle pale and weary; and no wonder, Freeman chided himself fiercely, since she had all the housework to do, two men to feed and care for—one quite useless—and a baby only a few weeks away.

"I'm going to put a wash on a sketch—don't disturb me, Gay," said Freeman.

"No, father," said Gay dutifully.

She was familiar, as Freeman well knew, with the tyranny of the washing-in of a background, and was not surprised by his request. She blew him a kiss and withdrew.

Freeman went into the kitchen. Never in his life had he been slow in action, and he was not slow now. He slammed about the little room, closing the small hinged windows, throwing out the shelves and grids from the gas oven, tearing down the blue towel from its roller and stuffing it along the foot of the door. (If he had been in any doubt—but he was not—this strip of rough fabric, reminding him of the day Gay and Peter fell in love, would have confirmed him in his resolution.) He looked around for a cushion, but finding none tore off his brown coat, folded it and threw it into the oven.

He lay down prone, crossed his arms over the coat and bowed his great head sideways. Yes, that would do nicely. He stretched up one hand and turned the gas on at full.

PART THREE
COUNTER-IMPULSE

GAY

EVERY HOUR OF the day had its own beauty, thought Gay, lowering herself carefully to the broad window-seat, but this evening hour, this hour of soft twilight, of *crépuscule*, was perhaps the one she loved the best.

Soon dark would fall, and the long ropes of lights which marked the roads, the modest knots of the hillside townships, the great clusters of Hudley and Ashworth far below, would become diamonds on black velvet, bold and coruscating, exciting and somehow restless, calling to gaiety and action. The dark would bring her husband. The homely one-decker bus, which was now standing at the Blackstalls terminus and would soon pass down the road towards Blackstalls Bridge, would presently return; she would see it from afar, a tiny jewelled insect in the dark, laboriously but staunchly tackling the ascent of the long steep hill, vanishing and reappearing along the winding curves, growing larger with every turn, till suddenly it roared into sight at the foot of the High Royd bank, full size, panting but triumphant. Peter would come springing up this bank, and one's own personal life, with all its tumultuous demands, would resume its thrilling, headlong course.

But now, in this hour, half day, half dusk, there was a pause. Her body, so heavy with child, was at rest after the toils and fatigues of the day; her spirit likewise rested. In this soft twilight the man-made lights were all still a lovely calm pale yellow, wistful, ethereal; one felt that by their utterly clear, pure light one saw the whole of life in all its depth, its richness and its complexity.

Gay had often been amused in the past by her own understanding of life in general and other people's problems in particular. She thought it came perhaps because her own life was so simple, so devoid of any personal participation in the feverish whirl.

Her parents were the most wonderful people in the world: famous, brilliant, loving, strong. Above all strong. Gay knew well the terribly severe, the almost savage discipline of study and practice which her mother had to impose on herself in order that her gorgeous voice should glow through every corner of a huge opera house, or soften to a dropping cadence of single grief-stricken notes, every one of which wrung the listener's heart. Gay knew well too the fierce rush of ideas which sometimes filled her father's mind, and the meticulous accuracy of execution which had to be employed to translate these ideas into reality. Yes, her mother and father were strong, powerful people, forceful in their passions as in their art. She loved them deeply and they loved her deeply, but they did not need her help to live.

Gay herself had no artistic talent of any kind: neither voice, nor design, nor beauty, as she often thought. But it was not this which troubled her. She had coursed about all over the world in her parents' entourage: she knew all the glitter, all the excitement, all the famous people, she had watched terrific back-stage scenes, she had listened to confidences from highly placed personages in at least four languages; she knew how little all that mattered compared with the feelings of the heart, compared with love.

So what she wanted above all was someone who needed her. When her mother returned, a physical wreck, from the concentration camp, Gay had joyously offered her fresh young strength to support her; but though Fiammetta accepted her daughter's ministrations with a kindly smile, she did not really need them; broken in body, she was to the last firm, strong, resolved and reserved, in mind. When the bombs fell, when Freeman's career began to dwindle, Gay was at his side,

174

yearning to help, to reassure. But again, her father did not seem to need her. He had disregarded the bombs, and when failure struck him he seemed equally unconcerned; he left London, he came to Hudley, he rented High Royd, in his usual strong decided fashion. Only when he occasionally wrote for the press did he seem to need his daughter, and these were the happiest, most fulfilled moments of Gay's life—until she met Peter.

As soon as she saw Peter she loved him. Of course there was a strong physical attraction between them—Gay had listened to the love-stories of too many despairing tenors and weeping corps-de-ballet girls not to be very familiar with the facts of physical love. Peter was good-looking, one might say comely, in his way: tallish, with very clean fair skin, bright eyes and a winning smile. But it was more than these physical graces— she had seen many handsomer men—which made Gay's heart turn over when she looked at Peter. He won her love because he was weak, because he needed her. He did not know it consciously, but his need of her showed in every action, every word he spoke, every turn of the head. Beneath his brash assurance, his fluency and argumentativeness, lay a soul afraid, timid and loving, quivering with pain.

> *Vain as thou wert, and weak as vain,*
> *The slave of falsehood, pride and pain . . .*

Yes, thought Gay, all her heart rushing out to her husband, that was Peter. He railed against the world, despised almost everybody, used long words about economics, discussed biology, history and philosophy in a knowing fashion, but was capable of secret anguish over the smallest personal failure: some fancied slight, a sharp retort on him in debate, even a word accidentally mispronounced. Any kind of rebuff almost killed him, he sank to the ground, he suffered agonies, before on some slight reassurance he resiliently bounded up again to his usual apparently conceited self-assertion. Well! Gay would be at his side through life; she would soothe and calm and support and if possible steer; she loved him, he needed her, she was his wife.

And now this wonderful fruition, this supreme fulfilment, was to be granted to her. She was to bear a child. A child of her very own, who would depend on her for every necessary of life for many years. Of course when the child grows up I must be careful not to chain her to me, thought Gay soberly; I mustn't be too protective, too maternal; one must serve the mind as well as the body; it is the last and greatest duty of mothers to set their children free. But even so, at the thought of this long service, this long devotion, her whole being glowed with love and joy.

"I shall be a mother," thought Gay with a happy smile.

Now it was almost dusk. A little wind rose and blew about the house, waving the branches of the ash-tree in the corner of the garden, and suddenly a spatter of rain rattled sharply on the windows.

"Poor Peter," thought Gay with concern, stretching out a hand to close the tiny window: "He didn't take his coat."

Down in the garden she saw Simon the cat running rapidly for shelter. The angle of his tail, held stiff and low, seemed to express an angry disgust at the change of weather. Gay smiled; the cat's fierce pride, its independent personality, its air of taking life on its own terms or not at all, always reminded her of her father. She watched the rain strengthen into a heavy shower, wondered whether it would be over before Peter left the Technical College, peered at her watch, looked out again and judged that the rain was not a mere shower but had come to stay; the fine summer's day had sunk into a wet evening. Simon was now standing in the middle of the garden with one paw uplifted, gazing up at her and mewing crossly.

"Father will let you in, Simon," she said, shaking her head at him.

She waited a moment or two to see this happen. No sound

came from the house, and Simon remained poised as before; the wind was ruffling up his fur, the rain poured on his sleek head, his angry gaze at her had become piteous, reproachful. Evidently for some reason Freeman had not noticed the cat or did not mean to admit him. Gay was surprised. A lack of observation or of consideration was equally unlike her father.

"Surely he must have finished the wash on his sketch by now? However—all right, Simon," said Gay with a sigh, nodding down to the cat. "I'm coming."

She rose reluctantly; she was decidedly tired and her body felt most decidedly heavy. But of course she could not leave poor Simon out in the rain. She went carefully down the stairs and opened the front door and took a few steps into the garden beyond the gables, and called Simon. As the cat darted past her she saw that there was no light in her father's painting-room. There was no light, indeed, anywhere in the house.

Gay was surprised, again. It was much too dark by now to work on a sketch, so what was Freeman about? She opened the door of the big room, the former house-body, downstairs, but her father was not there. She climbed slowly to Freeman's painting-room and stood at the door listening. There was no sound from within. After a moment she turned the knob and pushed open the door—very quietly; if her father were thinking out some design, he did not like to be intruded upon. The room was empty.

"Father!" called Gay. "Father!"

There was no reply.

Suddenly Gay felt uneasy. She remembered now that it was Mrs. Eastwood whom she had seen a few moments ago leaving High Royd—the landlady must have entered the house and had an interview with Freeman, while Gay was in the kitchen, washing up. Freeman disliked Mrs. Eastwood. Why had she come? Where was her father now? Gay hurried into all the rooms in Freeman's part of the house, one by one, throwing open the doors in sharp gestures, unlike her usual

177

placid movements, which reflected her growing fear. Her father was not to be found.

"He must have finished the sketch and gone out," thought Gay. "But it's strange he didn't tell me. It's strange I didn't hear the door."

She paused, irresolute, then entered in turn the two rooms which belonged to herself and Peter. As was to be expected, her father was not in either of these.

The only room unvisited was now the kitchen, so with a sigh Gay went carefully down the stairs again and along the back passage which led to the little room. Simon, who was lying at the foot of the stairs in an involved attitude, vigorously cleaning his damp fur, rolled to his feet and followed her with an air of expectancy, and this encouraged her to think that her father was within.

She opened the kitchen door; it seemed to move heavily as though encountering some impediment. She gave it an impatient push and the smell of gas struck her like a blow. In the half-darkness she gazed around, bewildered, while Simon fled over her feet. Then she saw her father lying prone on the floor.

"Oh, no! No!" cried Gay.

She ran to the gas oven, turned off the tap and tried to pull Freeman away, but his heavy, burly body defeated her. She ran to the windows and opened them, to the outer door and pulled it wide, then back to Freeman. Kneeling beside him, she seized the clothes at his waist and tugged with all her strength, but could not stir him; pain stabbed her body as she strained. She gave up the attempt and, sobbing now, managed to clasp her arms about his broad shoulders. She heaved and struggled; suddenly the body yielded; there was vomit in the oven and her father's grey hair dragged through it; the sight was sickening and a wave of nausea almost overcame her, but now at last his head lay heavily in her lap. One of his elbows was wedged within the corner of the oven; she struggled to bend it down to his side. It was a great triumph when she succeeded. Now he was clear of the oven; she rose to her feet and turned him on his back and tried to raise him, but the pain in her own body was too great, was not to be borne; she crouched down again, and clasping her father beneath the armpits, she dragged herself and him together towards the door.

Once they were out in the blessed fresh air of the passage, and the kitchen door closed, she rested, and putting her face down to her father's, listened for his breath. It was so soft, so shallow, so infrequent, that she could not be sure she heard it at all. She remembered what she had read of artificial respiration; with infinite difficulty she released herself from beneath Freeman's body and turned him on his face, then raised herself to her knees and tried to apply the necessary pressures. Instantly pain struck fiercely through her womb, so that she clasped her arms about herself and rocked in agony.

When the spasm had passed she knew that she could not save her father alone; she must get help or he would die. She must get help. Peter too must be summoned; he would feel slighted and guilty if he were absent during this disaster. Yes, she must get help at once. Her own pain counted for nothing in this emergency.

Clambering to her feet by the aid of the handle of the kitchen door, she staggered along the passage, supporting herself against the wall; then jerked open the front door and ran headlong down the flagged pathway towards the road.

PART FOUR
DIMINUENDO

I

ETHEL EASTWOOD

i

Twenty minutes she had waited already, and there was a good five more to go before that bus would condescend to arrive, thought Ethel crossly, peering at her watch in the half-light. And here she was getting drenched in this wretched rain, which seemed to get colder and heavier every drop that fell. Fancy that nice summer day turning out like this! But it was only what you could expect, it was never safe to trust anything or anybody; they always let you down.

Thinking she had heard a sound, she poked her head out beyond the stile in the wall where she had taken shelter, but nothing was coming down the road, and raindrops splashed her face. She drew in her head sharply and crouched down on the step. Her best coat, too! Trailing on the ground! She gathered it about her knees—but what was the use? She would only crease it. For a moment she considered returning to High Royd, but decided against it as she had decided before. She dare not go back, and that was the truth of it. Old Freeman's eyes as he gave her the money had been terrifying, almost mad. Yes, mad; that was it, mad. All those artists and people like that were mad, when you really got down to it, reflected Ethel virtuously; they were not safe to be about, really. It was best to have nothing to do with them. She wished she'd never let the place to Freeman.

How the old man's hand had trembled when he took the picture!

But what of it? Her rent was due to her, she was within her rights.

2

There certainly was a noise of some kind beating through the pouring rain. It came from behind her. Footsteps. Fast, heavy footsteps, rushing down the flagged path from the house. They sounded so urgent, so headlong, that Ethel moved apprehensively out of the stile so as not to be in the runner's way. Now the runner came into sight; it was a girl; it was Freeman's daughter, Gay. Her eyes were wide and staring, her shoulders drenched. She was heavy with child.

"You shouldn't be running like that!" exclaimed Ethel involuntarily.

"My father, my father!" cried Gay, panting. "Gas! Gas! He has tried to gas himself! Telephone the hospital. Tell them to send a doctor. Go to the telephone kiosk halfway down the hill. Quick! Quick! Please telephone my husband as well, Mrs. Eastwood. Peter Trahier. He's at the Hudley Technical College. Tell him to come quickly. Please telephone quickly, Mrs. Eastwood, or my father will die."

"But why has your father—done it?" asked Ethel, stunned.

"I don't know. He must have been unhappy. Please telephone quickly, Mrs. Eastwood. I wouldn't trouble you, but I can't go myself. I can't leave him."

There's another reason why you can't go, my dear, thought Ethel coarsely. And indeed as Gay turned to climb the path she stopped abruptly and crossed her arms over her body and bowed in pain. Her untidy hair fell forward round her face so that Ethel could see the nape of her neck, very young and white and slender. A groan burst from the girl's lips.

Suddenly a fearful feeling of guilt filled Ethel from head to foot. It burned and throbbed, it seemed to tear her fiercely;

her tongue swelled, her throat contracted, her stout legs trembled, her entrails moved. He gassed himself because I gave him back his picture, she thought. I don't mind that so much, she thought defiantly, he's an old man and he's had the best of his life, but if this girl has a miscarriage I shan't be able to bear it. I simply shan't be able to bear it, she thought, and to her astonishment found that she was weeping. Why was she thinking, not only of this young Gay—a silly name at the best, she told herself crossly—but of Charlie Martin and his widow and those ill-clad children of his, and of her own stillborn child, cold and deformed and strangely dark in hue? Why think of them? She did not know; she only knew that if this girl, with her trusting look and her heavy body, should lose her baby, Ethel would have to admit that this misfortune and all the rest of Ethel's dreary, barren, angry life was Ethel's fault.

"I'll go, I'll go, don't worry," she cried thickly. "I'll telephone. You go back and—have you turned off the taps and opened the windows and that? You go back and rest." Her common sense reasserted itself at the sound of her own familiar voice. "I'll wait for the bus and go down in that—it'll be quicker in the long run."

"Yes—that will be best," whispered Gay. She straightened herself with an effort, and, one hand held to her body, stumbled up the path to High Royd.

3

The journey in the bus was pleasurable, for Ethel in a loud excited voice told the conductor the story of Freeman's attempted suicide, and both he and all the passengers were eager to help, so that Ethel found herself quite the heroine of the hour. The conductor thought of change for the telephone and provided a pile of pennies, and going up to the front drew back the communicating window and told the driver the need for haste, so that the bus plunged and rattled down the hill. Advice was offered by the passengers on the proper mode of dialling the hospital, and an argument broke out as to whether High Royd lay in fact in the borough of Hudley or of Ashworth, or even in the domain of the West Riding County Police.

"It won't matter, they'll come whichever," said an old man.

"Don't worry, missus. They'll be here in five minutes from when you telephone," said another. "That's their rule."

Other passengers opined that the police should be summoned as well, and one woman even pressed the claims of the Fire Brigade, who were the people most practised, she said, in artificial respiration. This was considered far-fetched by the other passengers, and Ethel did not accept either of these notions.

"I shall do what Mr. Freeman's daughter asked me," she said virtuously. "The hospital and her husband—that's what she said."

All this was reassuring and even pleasant, so that when the kiosk was reached and the driver drew up the bus with a jerk, Ethel dismounted in a confident frame of mind, and declined various offers of help without seriously considering them. The process of self-rehabilitation had begun; guilt was being pushed out of sight; Ethel wanted to be the one who had saved Freeman's life by her prompt action. But when the brightly lighted cheerful bus had rolled away, and Ethel was left in a dark country road, miles, as she felt, from anywhere, guilt and panic sprang up again together. Her heart was beating heavily as she entered the lighted box and dialled 999.

"What service do you want?" said a voice at once.

"Hospital—an accident," cried Ethel. "Quick, quick!"

There was a pause. Ethel suffered. It Freeman should die! If Gay should have a miscarriage! Oh, why don't they answer, she thought in anguish. How long can a man live after being gassed? It's disgraceful how these public institutions neglect their duty. We pay for them, don't we?

"Ambulance depot, Hudley General Hospital," said a male voice in her ear.

Ethel, surprised, stuttered a moment, then recovered and panted: "Mr. Freeman of High Royd has gassed himself. Please come quickly."

"Hold on a minute, madam!" cried the voice urgently. "*Where* did you say the casualty was?"

"High Royd. Hurry, hurry!"

"But where is High Royd?"

"Oh, it's on the bus route to Blackstalls. Almost at the top of the hill. Brow Lane," wailed Ethel.

"Very good, madam. We'll be there," said the voice, and the line went dead.

Ethel leaned against the side of the kiosk, exhausted by her emotions. After a moment or two her breathing slowed, she sighed and felt more normal, and tilting the telephone directory on its shelf towards her, began to search for the number of the Hudley Technical College. She tried *College* and *Technical* but it was not there; she turned to *Hudley* and saw three pages of entries which she felt really too tired to scan. Sighing, she painfully tracked down the T items among the Hudleys, but the one she wanted was not to be found there. She slammed the book down angrily, and for a moment gave the whole thing up. Why trouble further? After all, she had notified the hospital. Surely that was enough.

But no, it was not enough. Charlie's arm round her waist beneath the hawthorns, his shabby widow and those untidy children, the look on the eldest boy's face as he poured silver into her hand, the body of her own poor infant—no, when one remembered these things, what she had done was not enough. She must do everything that Gay had asked of her, or she would feel forever guilty. Her face brightened as a thought

187

struck her; she made the greatest moral effort of her life and pulled herself up towards the telephone; counting pennies and examining the table of instructions, she rang her own number in Ashworth.

II

DOROTHEA DEAN

1

It was now quite dark, and the lamp at the end of Naseby Terrace suddenly lighted and shone into the room. Feeling her privacy unbearably invaded, Dorothea sprang up from the bed and drew the curtains with an angry hand.

After having once returned thus to ordinary life from her private world of grief, it seemed childish (excessive and unworthy of a Dean) to cast herself down on the bed again; she stumbled across the room and put on a light. Her smooth bare arms now prickled with gooseflesh; she realised that she was cold, that rain was pouring down outside; angrily she tore off her bright thin frock and began to dress herself in the skirt and cardigan and high-necked blouse which she wore to work in the shop. The change from the hot colours and exciting pattern of the frock to this plain black and white attire seemed to Dorothea to match the change in her life: poetry had fled and she was left with colourless, chilly prose. As she dressed she decided, with a kind of despairing mockery, to examine all her possessions with a view to eliminating some before her departure for Scarborough—this practical and immensely dreary task, she told herself sardonically, suited her mood. She had just thrust her arms into the sombre wool when the telephone rang downstairs.

Could it be Richard? The colour rushed to her cheek at the thought. But no; she had told Richard she was going to bed with a headache, and Richard, who was familiar with the position of Mrs. Eastwood's telephone, was incapable of dragging a girl with a headache out of bed and down the stairs to answer a call from him. No; the call would prove to be some dreary business matter for Mrs. Eastwood. Dorothea listened casually for a moment, expecting to hear Mrs. Eastwood tread heavily along the hall to answer it. This did not happen, and it then struck Dorothea that she had, in fact, heard without noticing it through her first wild outburst of tears, the sound of the front door closing, so that probably her landlady had gone out. She sighed with exasperation, considered for a moment the possibility of letting the telephone ring but rejected it as altogether too irresponsible, and ran downstairs.

2

Nothing whatever could be heard at first when she put the receiver to her ear, but the practical Dorothea Dean was familiar with this situation and merely said: "Press Button A" in a weary tone. The coins fell and clicked, and Mrs. Eastwood's voice came through, panting and anxious as Dorothea had never heard it before, relating the story of her old tenant who had gassed himself, alone with his daughter, up Blackstalls Brow, no telephone, ambulance on its way.

"But she wants her husband and it's only natural, after all, and I'm afraid of a miscarriage, you see," said Mrs. Eastwood. "He's at a class at the Hudley Technical College, his name's Peter Trahay or something, you must get hold of him somehow, Dot."

"How do you spell it?"

"How should I know?" said Mrs. Eastwood irritably. "They'll know him at the Technical, surely. Get him up here quick. I'm afraid of a miscarriage, you see."

"You'll stay with her till her husband comes?" urged Dorothea.

"Well—I suppose I *had* better go back," said Mrs. Eastwood reluctantly. "But it's a mile or more up the road—the ambulance will be there before me, or at least I'm hoping so."

"You must go back to her, Mrs. Eastwood," said Dorothea firmly.

"You get her husband!" shouted Mrs. Eastwood.

Dorothea slammed down the receiver angrily. Of course she would find the poor girl's husband. Her heart went out to the girl. Recently married, expecting a first baby. Ah, what would not Dorothea give to be in such a situation! And now that wonderful, beautiful happiness was threatened by tragedy. She ruffled the pages of the local directory with a practised hand, found the Technical College quickly under the general heading of *Hudley Corporation* and dialled, and urged the toll-call operator to hasten, and waited. A female voice which Dorothea classified as teen-age answered, and Dorothea crisply told the story. The owner of the voice was clearly moved to sympathy and eager to help, but puzzled.

"Do you know which class he was attending?"

"I'm afraid I don't," said Dorothea. "But can't you visit all of them?"

"We've more than a thousand students here tonight," replied the teen-age clerk primly.

"It's a matter of life and death," said Dorothea.

"We'll do our very best," replied the clerk. "But some of the students have already left, you know."

"*Please* do your best," urged Dorothea.

"Oh, I will," replied the teen-ager earnestly.

3

Dorothea rang off and stood considering. From being cold and stiff she now found she was hot-cheeked and trembling;

she felt as if, having been stranded on an icy bank of loneliness and rejection, she had been thrown back into the warm pulsating current of life with all its passion and all its agony. She imagined the dark hillside, the lonely house, the dying man, the young daughter, perhaps already in physical pain, certainly in nervous anguish, longing for the love and protection of her husband as Dorothea longed now for Richard Cressey.

Dorothea's eyes filled with tears; she followed the deep impulse of her heart and telephoned to Richard.

III

RICHARD CRESSEY

I

"RICHARD CRESSEY SPEAKING," snapped Richard sharply.

"Forgive me for troubling you, Richard," began Dorothea.

There were tears in her voice, and Richard's bitter mood broke at once into tender distress.

"Dorothea! Is anything wrong, my dear?"

"Yes."

"Good heavens, what? I'll come round at once," said Richard. (A self-denying ordinance against attempting to marry a girl did not preclude helping her in time of trouble.)

"No, no. I'm not in difficulties myself. It's Mrs. Eastwood's tenant out at High Royd, just below Blackstalls Brow. His name is Francis Freeman."

"Is that Freeman the stage designer, the artist?"

"I don't know. He's an old man and he's tried to gas himself."

"The hospital. 999. I'll ring them," began Richard.

"Mrs. Eastwood's done that at a kiosk—they've no telephone themselves."

"They?"

"There's a daughter, Gay, married to a Peter Trahier. He's at a class at the Hudley Technical College. Mrs. Eastwood wants to get him to High Royd quickly, because she's afraid Gay may have a miscarriage."

Richard exclaimed.

"I tried to get Peter Trahier at the Tech, but I only spoke to a young clerk, and there are so many students, I don't feel sure she'll find him. It struck me that they would take a lot more notice of you because you're a schoolmaster, so I hope you don't mind me asking you to help, Richard."

"I'm honoured that you thought of me," said Richard sincerely.

"Will you try to trace Peter Trahier and tell him to hurry to High Royd?"

"Immediately," said Richard.

2

As Dorothea had suggested, it was easy for Richard Cressey to get into touch with more powerful authorities at the Hudley Technical College than she had reached—in fact he knew the Principal slightly, and was soon explaining the situation to him. The Principal's hand was strong, and Richard guessed that he caused staff members actually to spring about the corridors doing his bidding, for it was not many minutes before he was able to provide the necessary information.

"I'm sorry, Trahier's gone. Left some time ago. He slipped out just before the class finished, I'm told. But the lecturer who takes that economics course tells me Trahier usually goes straight down into town and catches a bus."

"So he's already on his way home?"

"Yes. But I'm afraid he'll be a long time before he gets

there. I understand he has to change buses at Blackstalls Bridge and catch a bus there which goes up the hill. It's quite a long way."

"How long does the whole journey take?"

There was a pause for consultation at the Principal's end.

"About an hour."

"An hour! Good lord!"

"My economics lecturer here volunteered to go down to the bus terminus in his car and find Trahier and tell him, and drive him out to High Royd."

"Good man."

"He set off at once. But I'm afraid it's only too likely that he'll miss him. Trahier's probably already in a bus travelling to Blackstalls Bridge. There's a frequent service from here to Ashworth which goes through the Bridge village."

"I see."

"There's nothing else we can do, I'm afraid," said the Principal. "You said the ambulance was already on its way?"

"Yes. I'll check it, just to make sure. Well, thanks very much."

"Not at all. Sorry we couldn't do more. But the ambulance men will probably give Mrs. Trahier advice if she requires it."

Richard rang off, and checked with the Hudley hospital that the ambulance had, in fact, departed.

"Though whether it'll have got there yet or not, is more than I can say," said the porter. "It's an awkward place to get at, is Blackstalls Brow, and the directions weren't very precise. But they won't be long, sir, you can rely on that."

3

Richard however felt thoroughly dissatisfied with what he had accomplished of Dorothea's request.

He limped impatiently up and down, banging one fist into

G

the palm of his other hand, considering. It seemed to him unlikely that the economics lecturer would catch young Trahier
at the bus terminus. He imagined the young wife waiting
alone in the dark at High Royd beside her dying father, while
the ambulance took wrong turnings and Mrs. Eastwood trailed
slowly up the hill on her puffy ankles. Would a girl in such a
situation mention her own condition to two bustling ambulance men? Richard doubted it. Would Mrs. Eastwood
(who on the other hand would have no such qualms of delicacy) reach High Royd while the ambulance was there?
Would the ambulance pick her up *en route*? It was all possible,
but all doubtful, and the thought that the life or death of this
unknown girl and her child might hang on such uncertainties
fretted Richard beyond endurance. He was only too familiar
with the protracted effects that one moment's uncertainty might
produce—if his own foot hovering on the cellar step had been
halted by a look, a word, a gesture, how different would his life
have been! And this unknown girl who was in danger, this
Gay—a charming name, thought Richard—had become in his
imagination Dorothea; she had Dorothea's face as he had seen
it tonight, pale, sad and wistful.

Imagination was one of Richard's strong suits, and he had
only too clear a picture of Dorothea racked by pain, her crisp
dark curls damp with the sweat of agony. Oh no, this Gay
could not be left in that condition; he could not leave the matter so; it was intolerable. Something must be done. But what?

That wretched husband, too, thought Richard—a note in
the Principal's voice had somehow conveyed the impression
that the Principal did not very much care for Peter Trahier,
but what of that? Common humanity overrode such considera-
tions in times of trouble. Richard imagined the young man
sitting at ease in the lumbering bus, unaware of the tragic possi-
bilities which hung over him. He would reach his home, and
find it at best empty, with wife and father-in-law gone to hospital—which would drive him mad with anxiety, even if they

thought to leave an explanatory note—or at worst, with his father-in-law dead and his wife in premature labour. It really was not to be borne. One could not just sit back and leave one's fellow-humans to perish.

But what Richard Cressey, a slightly lame schoolmaster down in Ashworth, could do about a situation on a high hillside several Pennine miles away, Richard could not imagine. If only he had a car! A big, powerful car. Then he could dash along the valley to Blackstalls Bridge and drive slowly along the road thence towards Hudley and stop every bus and find Peter Trahier on one of them and pick him off and whisk him up to High Royd. A big, powerful car, driven by a skilled and spirited driver, a powerful authoritative man who would not hesitate to stop buses or race up hills in chase of ambulances: that was what was necessary in this situation. One had only to find such a man with such a car.

Richard laughed suddenly. He had remembered where he could find just such a man with just such a car. That the man was Richard's enemy was irrelevant; all that mattered was whether he would be willing to rush his precious car up and down narrow hillside lanes, on an unlikely humanitarian errand, through an unpleasantly wet dark night. Richard took up the telephone and in a somewhat sardonic tone, speaking with grim precision, asked the operator to connect him with Mr. Arnold Amos Janna Barraclough of Holmelea Hall.

IV

ARNOLD BARRACLOUGH

I

THE MOMENT THE telephone rang Jerry sprang up and went out to the extension in the hall.

"He hopes it's Chillie," thought Arnold bitterly.

The Barracloughs were sitting together in uneasy silence in the library. Meg had had a fire lighted, for the evening had become wet and cold. At one point Jerry had turned on the television, but almost immediately went off restlessly to do his packing—he was due back at school next day. Meg followed him to supervise the packing operation; Arnold turned off the instrument; for a few moments the voices of mother and son could be heard upstairs, giving an illusion of happy family life which made Arnold's heart ache. When they returned, Meg looked sad and perplexed, and Jerry looked cross and uneasy. Arnold, who was reading a rather uncomfortable discussion about proposed American tariffs against wool textile imports, in the columns of the morning newspaper, folded the newspaper and laid it down at once, with the air (he hoped) of a father eager to talk to his son on the last night of his half-term leave. No conversation, however, seemed to be forthcoming. His son was silent, and Arnold himself could think of nothing to say.

"Want the telly on again, Jerry?" he said after a moment.

Jerry shook his head. He stretched out a hand and took up a weekly from a nearby table, and began to turn its pages.

"He won't even speak to me," thought Arnold.

For a moment he felt hot and angry. He shook the newspaper open again viciously. Damn the Americans! Damn wool textiles! Damn Chillie! Damn everything! But presently his anger subsided into heartache. There they sat, the three of them, he thought: Meg knitting, Arnold and Jerry reading, feet stretched to the fire, clean, well dressed, well fed —the dinner, especially chosen by Meg no doubt for Jerry's last evening, had been excellent—the picture of a normal happy family; and yet they were all as wretched as could be. Arnold gave an exasperated sigh, and it was at this moment that the telephone rang.

Jerry returned looking disappointed.

"It's for you, father."

Father again, thought Arnold with a pang.

"Who was it?"

"I don't know," muttered Jerry. He seemed then to perceive that he had been lacking in initiative, and added rather less sulkily: "Man with an educated voice, who said it was urgent."

Arnold threw down his newspaper and strode out into the hall. More trouble, he thought; the mill's on fire I shouldn't wonder. That would just about match the rest of the day.

"Arnold Barraclough speaking."

"This is Richard Cressey. I don't know whether you remember me—I was one of the unsuccessful candidates for the Holmelea headmastership this afternoon."

"I remember you," said Arnold grimly. "My God," he thought, "is this smooth-tongued fellow trying to lobby for a change of decision about that appointment? If so he's come to the wrong man, and I shall enjoy telling him so."

"You may be surprised that I should telephone you."

"I am rather," said Arnold even more grimly.

"I'm applying to you because I noticed this afternoon you had a powerful car and were a skilful driver."

"What is all this leading up to?" said Arnold. He spoke roughly but with less contempt; he was now genuinely puzzled.

"An old artist named Francis Freeman, who lives up at the

top of Blackstalls Brow in a house without a telephone, has attempted to commit suicide."

"Suicide!" exclaimed Arnold.

At this word the whole wretched and sordid episode of his father's death, which had lain in his mind all day owing to his worry about his son, became vividly present to him. He was sorry for anyone who had anything to do with a suicide, and that was a fact.

"Suicide!" he repeated. "Well—is there something I can do, do you mean?"

"Freeman's young daughter, who is several months pregnant, is alone in the house with him. The Hudley ambulance has left for Blackstalls, but her husband, ignorant of what has happened, is returning home from the Hudley Technical College by bus. He'll be an hour on the way unless we can get hold of him."

"Jerry!" shouted Arnold. "Get out the car! Hurry! Now listen, Cressey," he said urgently: "Where are you, eh? Well, look; that's on my way to Ashworth. Come to the end of your road and I'll pick you up and you can tell me the rest of the story as we go. Hurry, now; I shall be there in two minutes."

He ran to the table in the hall and picked up a large electric torch which customarily lay there. The front door stood open, cold wet air pouring in.

"The boy's jumped to it," thought Arnold with satisfaction.

Meg came running to him, her kind face drawn with alarm. "Is it the mill, Arnold?"

"No, no. Nothing to do with us really. Man tried to suicide up by the moors, pregnant daughter alone with him, we must get hold of the husband who doesn't know."

"Oh," said Meg. Relief showed for a moment on her face, to be succeeded by pity. "Take your raincoat," she cried, throwing it after her husband as he ran down the steps.

Not to waste time, Arnold caught it, and threw it into the back of the car, which now leaped up to the steps with lights blazing, Jerry at the wheel. The boy slid over and Arnold took his place and they flew out of the Hall drive and down the hill at considerable speed.

"Is it the mill, father?" enquired Jerry.

Two aspects of this remark warred in Arnold's heart. On the one hand, he was still relegated to the icy fringe of fatherhood, apparently; on the other, it seemed that Jerry at least cared enough for Holmelea Mills to enquire about their safety. He sighed, perplexed. But the excitement of the chase had loosened his tongue, and as they raced along the road to Ashworth he told Jerry the object of their excursion as far as he knew it.

"Don't you know Francis Freeman at all, then?" said the boy in a tone of surprise.

"No. Never heard of him."

"*I* have," said Jerry unexpectedly. "He was quite a good stage designer in his day."

"That's not the point, however," said Arnold. "The point is, he's a man in trouble."

"Oh, quite. It was pretty cool of this Cressey type to expect you to go to the rescue of a complete stranger, though, wasn't it?"

"Not at all. He rang me because he knew I had a powerful car," said Arnold, pressing the accelerator.

"Especially when you practically lost him his job this afternoon," pursued Jerry. "I heard you telling mother. I mean, you're practically enemies."

"Well, that's England for you," said Arnold, dismissing the matter. "But what the dickens are you doing here, Jerry? I didn't intend you to come. You'd better get out when we stop for Cressey, and take a bus home."

"Oh, please let me come!" said Jerry.

They were now in the main road close to Ashworth, and in

the greenish-purple light of the overhead lamps Jerry's young face, turned towards his father, looked pale and earnest.

"Suicides are sordid and unpleasant affairs," said Arnold. "There's nothing exciting or glamorous about them, and don't you ever forget it."

"I might be useful to run messages, dad," pleaded Jerry.

It was really not possible for Arnold to refuse a request couched in such terms; to have risen to the status of *dad* again warmed him all over.

"Well, all right," he said gruffly. "But you'll have to ride in the back and keep out of the way. There's Cressey now; get out and get him in beside me as quick as you can, there's a good lad."

2

It proved a simple matter to find Peter Trahier. They reached Blackstalls Bridge and examined all the buses from Hudley which were clustered there, and the queue, already forming, of passengers for Blackstalls Brow. Trahier was not there, but they left messages everywhere in case they had missed him. Everyone they addressed was kind and helpful and promised their best service. They then drove along the valley road towards Hudley. Whenever they saw a bus approaching in the distance, its lights gleaming through the rain, they turned round and made speed to the nearest bus stop. Cressey dismounted and waited; the bus stopped for him; he climbed on and called out: "Is Peter Trahier on this bus?" in his resonant schoolmaster's tones. The third bus they accosted like this—it was about halfway to Hudley—contained Peter. He came pushing his way down the crowded aisle with a look of anguish on his agreeable face, and seizing Cressey by both arms, cried:

"Is it Gay? It's Gay, I know it is!"

"There's trouble at your home. We have a car here," said

Cressey. "We tried to catch you earlier, at the Technical College, but unluckily you had left."

The bus passengers looked on sympathetically, and the conductor held the young man's arm and helped him to alight, lest he should stumble, for indeed he seemed to have gone quite to pieces. He stood in the pouring rain, gesticulating and exclaiming, instead of getting into the car like a sensible man, thought Arnold impatiently, and when at last Cressey and Jerry between them had stowed him into the front seat, he still kept on exclaiming and had to be recalled by Arnold to the business of directing the car to Blackstalls.

"If only I hadn't left early! But why should he do it? He was quite happy with us. And Gay all alone with him! She'll be in the dark there, we haven't any electricity. Surely she won't forget and strike a match to light the gas!" cried Trahier in agony. "If only I hadn't left the Tech early, I should be there by now!"

"Right or left here?" said Arnold.

"Right, right. Across the bridge and then right. Oh no, left here, round this bend. *Now* right."

The car soon left the bus from which they had taken Trahier out of sight—clear proof, reflected Arnold, that Cressey's appeal to him was justified—flew along the valley road and turned up the hill across Blackstalls Bridge. The blue and white Jaguar was conspicuous, and several people who had a few minutes ago received Cressey's enquiries, pointed it out to their neighbours and nodded after it approvingly, knowing its errand. The feeling here was therefore one of hope and excitement, but as the car left the lighted village and mounted the dark hillside, the nocturnal landscape—trees rustling, wind sighing, rain pouring heavily, hills rising and falling in sombre folds, old cobbles gleaming in the light from the rare gaslamps—seemed to him to take on a more sinister and less hopeful air, so that Arnold's spirits sank. This unease was increased by Trahier's lack of control, for he poured the whole history of his admiration for Freeman, his love for Freeman's daughter, their courtship and marriage and hopes of a child, into the embarrassed ears of Arnold, who wondered uncomfortably what Jerry was making of all this—"Well, it's his own fault for coming and mine for allowing him to come, after all," he reflected —and also what use a fellow of this kind could be to a woman in a crisis. Trahier talked too much and expressed what he meant too clearly, for Arnold's liking; a more silent grief would have pleased his Yorkshire taste better, seemed more sincere.

"Here!" said Trahier suddenly.

The Jaguar's lights had already illuminated a large greyish van standing at the side of the road, its back doors open.

"The ambulance," said Cressey with satisfaction.

"But where's the house?" demanded Arnold.

"It's at the top of this bank—there's a lane at the side but it's too steep and rough for motor vehicles," replied Trahier, who was wrestling with the unfamiliar handle of the Jaguar's door.

"Oh, pooh!" said Arnold.

With a swing of the wheel he skirted the ambulance and put the Jaguar at Brow Lane. The car flew up, throwing its passengers about as it bounced over the rocky surface. Arnold swung it partly round to face High Royd. The headlamps poured light on the house side and figures were revealed through the sloping spears of rain: Gay leaning against the wall, a couple of men in uniform stooping over a stretcher which lay on the ground between them. Arnold leaned across Trahier and pressed the door catch so that the door swung open, and the young man scrambled out and rushed to his wife and put his arms round her.

"Gay! What's happened? Why did he do it? Are you all right? Surely he was happy with us? How is he?"

"Peter," sighed Gay. She staggered, and let her head drop to his shoulder.

"She's at the end of her tether," thought Arnold.

He got out of the car and strode up to the little group, taking his electric torch with him. Cressey and Jerry also dismounted, but stood by the car, not wishing to intrude.

"Is this Mr. Freeman, then?" said Arnold, looking at the crumpled bundle, covered by a grey hospital blanket, on the stretcher at his feet.

"Yes, sir. We can't get him round. We shall have to take him to the hospital—he needs oxygen," replied one of the ambulance men.

"Well, get on with it, then," said Arnold impatiently.

"He's a very heavy man, sir," said the other man on a note of apology. "We're doing our best."

"We'll give you a hand. Then there'll be six of us," said Arnold, looking round. "Cressey, you take this torch and walk ahead and light the way—it's no use wasting time trying to turn the car—the lamps won't shine round the bend in the lane. Trahier, you take that side with one of the ambulance men. The other man, take the head. My son and I will take this side. Jerry! Come on now, all; are you ready? Lift!"

The old man certainly is heavy, thought Arnold, as the little procession went slowly down the hill. But we couldn't have got him into the car without a lot of difficulty; it would have wasted time to try and we might have hurt him; besides, that gate gives no room to turn, I should have had to back down and that takes time. He noticed with satisfaction that his allotment of posts had been the right one; Cressey's slender physique and slight limp were no detriment to his task of lighting the path, which he performed with care and skill. Trahier was of very little use, as he kept exclaiming and jerking about to look at his wife, who followed the group in silence, so that it had been wise to put him beside the experienced ambulance man. Jerry had a strong grip and did as he was told, avoiding stones when his father warned him of them. The group accordingly reached the foot of the bank and slid the stretcher along the proper rails into the ambulance, without mishap. The ambulance driver leaped into the front and started the engine;

Trahier climbed hurriedly into the back; the second ambulance man began to close the doors.

"Mrs. Trahier must go too," said Arnold, gently pushing the young woman forward.

"No, no. You stay here and go to bed, Gay," said Trahier, leaning out of the ambulance.

"The house is pretty well clear of gas now, sir," said the ambulance man. "No real danger. No point in Mrs. Trahier coming down with her father."

He gave Arnold a significant glance and silently mouthed the words: "He's gone."

Arnold was sorry; in spite of the strange pink flush which marred Freeman's face, he had taken a liking to the old man.

"Mrs. Trahier requires medical attention herself," he said firmly. "My wife had a miscarriage once—we don't want anything like that to happen."

"Good God, no!" exclaimed Peter, leaping out of the ambulance.

At this moment Cressey very sensibly turned the light of the torch full on Gay. The ambulance man for the first time looked intently at her. His face changed—and no wonder, thought Arnold, for she appeared scarcely conscious, white, obviously pain-racked, swaying on her feet.

"Give me a hand, sir," said the ambulance man to Arnold.

Between them they lifted Gay into the van. Jerry gave Trahier an impatient shove up the steps; the man closed the doors from within; the van drove off.

Arnold became aware that the three members of the rescue party were standing in drenching rain; Cressey wore a raincoat but Jerry and himself lacked that protection. He turned and led the way briskly up Brow Lane towards the shelter of the car, remarking that the rain was growing heavier.

"You should have put on your raincoat, dad," said Jerry. "It's in the car."

"Never thought of it," said Arnold. "No time, anyway."

They climbed the lane in silence, feeling flat and cross now that the need for action was over, and settled into the car with sighs of relief. Jerry meekly sat in the back according to his father's previous instructions; Arnold threw open the front door for Cressey to sit beside him. Arnold backed down the lane—a tricky job, but there was no alternative—and headed towards Blackstalls Bridge.

"Well, it's a good thing we came," said Arnold.

"Yes," said Cressey.

"I didn't think much of the husband," remarked Jerry with youthful intolerance.

"He was under a great strain—perhaps it's hardly fair to judge him until we have experienced a similar strain ourselves," said Cressey.

"How did you get to hear about it, Cressey?" said Arnold.

"A friend of mine, Miss Dorothea Dean, has rooms in the house of a Mrs. Eastwood, who is Mr. Freeman's landlady. Mrs. Eastwood made the discovery of the attempted suicide, I don't know how, and came down this hill to telephone for the ambulance. She then telephoned Miss Dean and asked her to try to trace Peter Trahier."

"And Miss Dean telephoned you?"

"Yes."

"Good lord," thought Arnold, "the fellow's in love with the girl. I misjudged him badly this afternoon."

"It occurs to me," Cressey was saying, "that Mrs. Eastwood may very likely be somewhere along this road now. Surely her natural course would be to return to Mrs. Trahier at High Royd? It's a long pull up for an elderly woman in the rain. If you wouldn't mind going slowly, Mr. Barraclough, we can keep a look-out for her and pick her up?"

"Of course," said Arnold, slowing. "You watch this side of the road, Jerry."

"We didn't see her as we came up," said Jerry, peering out.

"We were in too much of a hurry then."

"Our minds were preoccupied with reaching High Royd."

"Will Mr. Freeman recover, dad?"

"No," said Arnold shortly.

"Really?" exclaimed Jerry, horrified.

"The ambulance man gave me to understand he was dead," said Arnold as before.

"I believe the flush we observed was a very bad sign," confirmed Cressey.

"I'm sorry. He was a fine-looking old chap," said Jerry.

"It was a cowardly act, however," said the schoolmaster.

"Yes—he should have thought of his daughter," said Arnold with feeling.

"But, Mr. Cressey," objected Jerry: "You said we shouldn't judge that Trahier chap, and now you're judging poor old Freeman."

"I'm not judging him, only his action."

"Well, I'm sorry for him," said Jerry warmly.

"So am I, extremely. But one is not always required to admire what one compassionates."

"There's something female tottering along this side, by the wall," said Jerry, not sorry perhaps, thought Arnold, to abandon the argument, for Cressey's voice had held a note of bitterness.

"Thinking of his own limp, I expect," judged Arnold.

He drew up the car at the woman's side.

"Mrs. Eastwood!" said Cressey, getting out promptly into the rain. "Richard Cressey here."

"Oh, Mr. Cressey, how you startled me!" exclaimed the woman. "What are *you* doing here?"

"We've taken Peter Trahier up to High Royd, and he and his wife have both accompanied old Mr. Freeman to the hospital—Mrs. Trahier will receive medical attention there. So there's no need for you to go up to High Royd. Mr. Barraclough will, I am sure——"

"I'll take you both home, of course," said Arnold cordially.

"Hop in, Mrs. Eastwood. Jerry, give Mrs. Eastwood a hand. Where do you live, Mrs. Eastwood?"

"I'm afraid I'm very wet," said Mrs. Eastwood, climbing in. "Naseby Terrace, please. Number 19. The end house. I saw the ambulance go by a while ago, but I thought Mr. Freeman's daughter might be left alone, you see. So I thought I ought to go back to her."

Jerry made appreciative noises, but Arnold noticed that Cressey did not participate in these. As for himself, he found too much smugness in Mrs. Eastwood's tone to please him. The Jaguar flew down the hill to Blackstalls Bridge and paused, the lights into the Ashworth road being against it.

"How do you come to be mixed up in this business, Mr. Cressey?" enquired Mrs. Eastwood.

"Miss Dean telephoned me and asked me to find Peter Trahier," said Cressey shortly.

"Ah, Dot thinks the world of you, Mr. Cressey," said the woman.

Her tone was unpleasantly fawning, and Arnold was not surprised that the schoolmaster moved impatiently beside him.

"How did *you* come to be in the affair, by the way, Mrs. Eastwood?" said Cressey in a cold tone as the car moved on.

Mrs. Eastwood cleared her throat.

"I was just standing at the bus-stop at the foot of Brow Lane," she said, "when Gay, that's Mr. Freeman's daughter you know, Mrs. Trahier, came running down and asked me to summon the ambulance."

"Had you just left High Royd, then?"

"Er—yes. About half an hour before."

"Did you see Mr. Freeman while you were there?"

"Oh yes. It was a business call, you know. He's my tenant."

"How did the old man seem when you left him?" put in Arnold.

"Oh, perfectly all right. Perfectly cheerful," said Mrs. Eastwood.

Cressey said no more, and Arnold respected this discretion.

"Here we are," called Mrs. Eastwood cheerfully.

Arnold swung into Naseby Terrace and drew up at Number 19, where light showed through the panels of the old-fashioned front door. All his passengers tumbled out promptly.

"Well, thank you very much, Mr. Barraclough, I'm sure." said Mrs. Eastwood. "It's your good deed for the month, eh?"

Her voice was cheerfully loud and she slammed the car door, so that their arrival was decisively announced to the neighbourhood, and Arnold was not surprised when the door of Number 19 opened while Mrs. Eastwood was still climbing the steps. The light from the street lamp fell clearly on a tall handsome girl who stood there; she gazed out into the rain with a look of anxious love.

"Is that Miss Dorothea Dean, I wonder," thought Arnold.

The tall girl's gaze fell on Cressey as he crossed the pavement; she smiled, and Arnold no longer doubted who she was. On an impulse he leaned out of the window.

"Cressey!" he called.

The schoolmaster turned towards him.

"I'm sorry we didn't choose you as headmaster for Holmelea this afternoon, Cressey," said Arnold. "I reckon we made a mistake. But it may turn out best for you in the end. If you'd become head of Holmelea you might have stuck there all your life, and it's a small school after all. As it is, you'll probably get a bigger school in a few years' time."

"That, however," said Cressey in an angry tone, looking down at him, "though very complimentary and reassuring, doesn't help me to get married *now*."

"My wife and I became engaged when I was practically bankrupt," said Arnold.

"This is a cul-de-sac. You can't get out this end, you'll have to turn," said Cressey, looking aside. His change of colour showed, however, that he had heard Arnold's remark and understood its implications.

208

"Richard?" said the tall girl in the doorway. She sounded diffident and uncertain.

"You'll come in for a moment, Mr. Cressey, won't you?" called Mrs. Eastwood from behind her shoulder in a fulsome tone. "Dot wants a word with you."

"In my view, the sooner you take your girl away from that old harridan the better," said Arnold quickly.

"I couldn't agree with you more. All right, Dorothea, I'm coming," called Cressey.

He ran up the house steps and, taking the girl gently by the elbow, turned her into the house. The door closed behind them.

"Don't let me back the car into that street lamp, Jerry," said Arnold.

3

Father and son drove away together.

"Well, that was quite an adventure, wasn't it?" said Arnold, feeling the warm well-being which follows the performance of a kindness.

"Yes. Good thing we had the Jag. I'm sorry we didn't save the old man," said Jerry. "What did you think of them all, dad?" he asked after a pause.

"Cressey is a very fine fellow," said Arnold. "Intelligent and kind, and reliable in a crisis. The two girls are good and pretty, a combination which is not as frequent as could be desired. Old man Freeman I took a fancy to. Mr. Peter Trahier I have no use for whatever, and Mrs. Eastwood is a selfish old hag."

"But, dad! She trailed off through all that rain to the telephone and was trailing back again," expostulated Jerry. "She started the rescue really."

"Perhaps she started the need for it too," said Arnold. "You noticed, I suppose, that she was probably the last person to see old Freeman alive?"

"No, I hadn't realised that," said Jerry, surprised.

"Cressey soon picked it out. That's why he stopped questioning her. What was she doing at High Royd? She's Freeman's landlord, and she said it was a business call, so at a guess, I should say she was making herself disagreeable about the rent. Nothing legally wrong in that, of course, but it will be an uncomfortable experience for her when she has to tell the police about it."

"Will she have to tell the police?" said Jerry, awed.

"Since she saw the old man before he gassed himself, I reckon she may have to give evidence at the inquest. She won't feel very comfortable, telling about it in front of his daughter, and that's a fact."

"No."

"Well, it may teach her to mend her ways, but I doubt it."

"I thought you came out of it the best of the bunch, dad," said Jerry in an embarrassed offhand mumble, looking aside.

Arnold gave a deprecating snort, but the sun of his world, which had gone in that morning, came out and he could have laughed aloud with joy.

"Of course Mrs. Eastwood didn't intend to make old Freeman kill himself," he said hurriedly, not wishing to acquire merit at the expense of the others concerned. "She's just nagged him a little too far, I expect. She made a mistake. But she's not the only person who makes mistakes," said Arnold—his own day had been full of mistakes, and now, he thought suddenly, was the time to repair them. He was so happy about Jerry that he could not bear the thought of remaining in anger with anyone.

He swung the car abruptly to the left up one of Ashworth's many hills.

"Where are we going, dad?"

"To see Ernest. Let not the sun go down upon your wrath, you know. I let fly at him pretty hard this morning—not that he didn't deserve it."

"But why were you so angry? I wondered at the time. Isn't damaged cloth, like that, insured?"

"No, it's not insurable."

"Chillie thought it would be."

"Ah, Chillie," said Arnold grimly. Now is my chance, he thought; by a stroke of luck I've got the boy's faith back; I'll never have a better opportunity. He drew the car up at the side of the road and turned off the engine. "I've been wanting to have a word with you about Chillie, Jerry," he said. "But I didn't want your mother to hear anything about it."

"Why not?" said Jerry, beginning to look sulky.

"Because it would upset her. Look, Jerry," began Arnold, carefully looking away from his son: "Of course if you want to live your life as a homosexual, I can't stop you. It's your life."

"What!" exclaimed Jerry angrily. "What are you talking about? Chillie's not a homo."

"I'm sure he is."

"I'm not a child, dad," said Jerry stiffly. "I've seen some of that sort of thing at school. Some of the prefects—with the junior school. Chillie isn't like the ones I know."

"Happen not," said Arnold. "But you see in this case, Jerry, you're seeing it from the other side. You're the junior."

"Oh, no!" exclaimed Jerry in a tone of extreme distaste. "No. You're wrong, dad, I know Chillie. I should have seen it if it were so."

"You didn't see that Mrs. Eastwood was the last person to see old Freeman alive and probably nagged him into the gas oven, though Mr. Cressey and I saw it at once," said Arnold. "Experience of life counts for something in good judgment, Jerry."

"Even if Chillie were—what you say, one needn't treat him as a pariah. One can be sorry for him."

"Quite," said Arnold. "But one is not necessarily required to admire what one compassionates, as Mr. Cressey remarked —I thought he was thinking of his own limp, did you, Jerry?"

he added, throwing in this neutral matter in an attempt to diminish the tension between them.

"I don't know," said the boy angrily. "And I don't know what you want me to do about Chillie."

"Just ask him the question straight out," said Arnold. "Is he or is he not, you know?"

"I'll do just that," said Jerry defiantly.

"You might also," added Arnold, "ask him how much private income he thinks I ought to allow you while you're living with him."

"You think too much about money, dad," said Jerry with a flash of spirit.

"That's because I've had to struggle so hard for it."

"Everybody isn't always thinking about it like you."

"You mean, Chillie isn't?"

"Well, yes."

"Did you post his suit-length to him?" said Arnold grimly.

Jerry looked aside and said nothing; the answer was too clearly in the affirmative, at Chillie's emphatic request. Arnold gave a quick glance towards the reflection of his son's face in the windscreen, and saw there pain and question and also a sudden remembrance of a host of small acts and words on Chillie's part which had meant nothing at the time but now showed as part of an all-over pattern in the sudden illumination of his father's words. Arnold sighed and started the engine.

"Well," he said, putting in the gear: "Don't let's say any more about it, Jerry, until you've asked the questions and made up your mind. I'm only asking you to make up your own mind for yourself, Jerry."

"I've made it up," said Jerry in a strangled tone.

"Oh?"

"I can see you're right," said Jerry as before, looking out of the far window.

"Good," said Arnold.

He was so afraid of saying this word too heartily, or too smugly, or too something-or-other—and that was the trouble, he thought sadly, a cloud for a moment dimming his relief and happiness; I shall never be quite as much at ease with Jerry again as I was before today—that it came out in a kind of strangled bellow. He cleared his throat.

"Only about Chillie, though," added Jerry with defiance. "I haven't made up my mind about my profession yet, you understand."

"I understand," said Arnold mildly.

They drove away uphill, turned on a long side street and halted.

"Now about Ernest," said Arnold in a confidential tone, descending from the car. "He's been with the firm more than thirty years and he's a first-rate foreman cropper and a thoroughly decent chap, but he's a bit apt to stand on his dignity, you know. I don't just know whether I ought to take you in with me or not."

"I'll wait here, dad," said Jerry, sounding rather forlorn.

"Perhaps you'd better. If things go well and they offer me a cuppa, I'll call you in."

He grinned at his son, ran up three steps and knocked on Ernest's door.

V

ERNEST ARMLEY

I

ERNEST SAT SILENT, looking into the fire, which was burning up nicely. Millie, in the old rocking-chair which had come from her aunt's, knitted away at a yellow pullover for Kenneth. The children were out: Kenneth at his evening class at

Ashworth Technical, Iris at some school activity, a play or something—"a lot of fancy work," Ernest was wont to grumble about these affairs, but tonight he said not a word against her going, for he was only too thankful to have the child out of the house; her pert chatter, which he usually heard with a kind of fond astonished pride, he could not have endured in his present condition.

At first stunned by the magnitude of the Bedford cords disaster and his employer's public rebuke, as the day went on Ernest had become more and more savage.

During the morning he felt simply numb. The men under him seemed also dazed; they moved about very quietly, and consulted Ernest over every smallest detail of their work, in low serious tones. He took a long time to consider their questions—his mind felt clogged—and replied slowly and gravely, repeating himself and pointing to parts of the machines, as if the questioners had never cropped a piece before. The output in the cropping department was very low that morning, everyone being in such a nervous and apprehensive state of mind, afraid of making mistakes.

The twelve-thirty buzzer startled Ernest. Surely the morning could not be over yet? Surely the ruin of the Bedford cords could not be now irrevocably in the past? Surely Mr. Arnold was not going to leave the matter like that, without another word? Not even telling Ernest what the customer, the owner of the ruined cords, had said? Ernest began to feel angry; his nerves awoke, and pain abruptly made its presence felt in his stomach. As he went towards his coat, which hung on the wall, to get out his sandwiches, his son-in-law came up to him with a hangdog air.

"It were me put them Bedford cords on," he said.

"We all know that," snapped Ernest.

Cliff coloured.

"Well—I'm sorry, Ernest," he said.

Mr. Arnold's words to Ernest came into Ernest's mind.

"A. & J. Barraclough have lost eight hundred pounds and a good customer, and you say you're sorry." Ernest could say them with equal truth to Cliff. But he scorned to do any such thing; he was a prouder man, he told himself, than any Barraclough. On the other hand, he could not bring himself to say anything comforting to his son-in-law. So he merely nodded his head crossly, without looking at the lad.

From that moment Ernest's fear and anger grew. He could eat nothing in the dinner-hour, and finding himself cold and sick in spite of the summer sunshine, he drank a cup of hot tea instead of milk, with bad results. The pain in his stomach increased till it seemed he wore a bar of red-hot iron there, and as the afternoon wore on and Mr. Arnold did not come up to have a word with him, his mind became similarly inflamed by resentful fear.

Cliff and Nora lived not far away from Walker Street, Nora having all her mother's liking for being near her kin, so Cliff and Ernest travelled home in the bus together. Ernest greatly wished that Cliff would not tell Nora anything about the damaged pieces—he wanted no family fuss—but he wouldn't demean himself by saying so. It wouldn't have been much use if he had, anyway, for as soon as he opened his own house door Millie, who was serving tea to Kenneth and Iris at the table, exclaimed:

"What's the matter, Ernest?"

Ernest, annoyed, went silently to the scullery to wash his hands. In doing so, however, he caught a glimpse of his face in a mirror which hung there, and was obliged to admit that his wife's concern was justified; his sallow face was livid and a deep vertical frown marked his forehead. He smoothed out the frown.

"Aren't you feeling so well?"

"I'm all right," said Ernest pettishly.

"Is there something wrong at the mill?" pursued Millie.

"Plenty," said Ernest grimly.

"Has Nora's Cliff happened an accident?" cried Millie.

"No, no. It's only some cloths got cropped wrong."

"That might happen to anyone," said Millie, relieved.

Ernest snorted and sat down at the table, where he drank a cup of milk with a great show of enjoying it and making a good meal. The children rushed off upstairs and rushed down again dressed to go out.

"Kenneth, did you renew your driving licence today like you promised? Eh?"

"Well, no, dad," began Kenneth. "I hadn't time, you see——"

"Then you don't go out on your cycle again till you have renewed it."

Kenneth sulked, but on receiving a warning look from his mother obediently set out on foot. Iris followed, hatless, in a flowered frock and white sandals, after an argument with her mother on the subject of taking a coat.

"The weather's not bound to keep up all evening," said Millie. "It's clouding a bit now."

"I shall look silly with a coat," pouted Iris.

"Do as your mother says, Iris," commanded Ernest.

Iris tossed her head but obeyed. It was clear that his family felt that Ernest was not to be trifled with tonight. (They were right for once, thought Ernest grimly.)

The house felt peaceful after the children had gone, but as Ernest had feared, the door was hardly closed behind them before Nora came hurrying in with baby Ernie in her arms and a look of alarm on her face, and with nods and eyebrow-raisings and other only too obvious signals drew her mother away into the scullery and shut the door.

Ernest lowered himself carefully into his armchair by the hearth and brooded. The scenes of the day enacted themselves over and over in his mind, grinding away round and round, lacerating and inflaming his feelings every time they passed. In such a state, a tearful scene with Nora would be more than he could stand, he decided; so when the two women came out of the scullery he closed his eyes and pretended to be asleep, opening them only when the house door closed behind his daughter.

"Nora wants to know if you're still mad with her Cliff about those pieces," said Millie, vigorously clearing the table.

"I'm not all that pleased with him, Millie," said Ernest sardonically.

"He's only young," said Millie in her comfortable voice.

Ernest snorted.

"Little Ernie was that disappointed you were asleep," continued Millie from the scullery. "He kept on calling for his grandpa. It was laughable, really."

Ernest knew that this was decidedly an exaggeration of the truth. He understood perfectly that Millie was trying to work on his feeling for his grandson, who bore his name, in order to make him feel friendlier towards his grandson's father. He had often smiled at such manoeuvres before, but tonight, with financial disaster hanging over all the family, he felt that it was all deeply pathetic, even tragic; more than he could bear. He closed his eyes again.

"If you're not feeling so well, Ernest, why don't you go up to bed, love?"

But Ernest did not want to go to bed. He was afraid of beginning another night of anguish like the last. If he sat quiet, kept very still, he did not feel too bad.

"Why should I go to bed?" he said with false cheerfulness.

"Do you want the telly on?"

"I'm not bothered. Where's the newspaper?"

He pretended to look at the evening newspaper for some time, while the events of the day laboured painfully through his mind again and again, as before. Millie got out her knitting. It grew dark; Millie rose and put on the light and drew the curtains.

"Why, it's raining!" she exclaimed, looking out. "Ken'll get wet, walking home."

"Serve him right," said Ernest. (He thought: "If I were to go on sickness benefit, Ken wouldn't be able to keep up the payments on that bike," and he felt sorry for his son, so unconscious of the disappointment hanging over his head.) "Good thing Iris took her coat." After a moment, because he was feeling chilled to the marrow except in his head, which felt very hot, he ventured to throw out in a casual tone: "It's turning cold, too."

"Would you like a bit of fire?" cried Millie.

"I reckon I would," said Ernest in a tone of surprise, as if he had never thought of a fire before in his life.

Millie bustled about and soon had a fire going. It was pleasant sitting there with the flames leaping up the chimney, and Millie opposite, smiling and knitting, and the ball of yellow wool rolling between. Or rather it would be pleasant, if this anger and fear were not gnawing continually at his heart.

"There's a car stopping at our door," said Millie.

Ernest's blood seemed to freeze.

"Who can it be?" wondered Millie. She went off into a brisk discussion of possible family visitors, concluding: "Perhaps it's not for us."

However, a knock came.

Millie went to open the door.

"Why, it's Mr. Barraclough, Ernest!" she said, surprised.

"I thought it might be," murmured Ernest grimly.

"Good evening, Mrs. Armley. May I come in? I just want a word with Ernest. Good evening, Ernest."

"Good evening, Mr. Arnold," said Ernest coldly, not stirring from his chair.

He nodded sideways at Millie who, understanding the signal, went away at once into the scullery, leaving the two men alone. Mr. Arnold sat down in the old rocking-chair.

"Here it comes," thought Ernest.

"I must apologise for intruding on you after working hours, Ernest," began Mr. Arnold.

"Humbug as per usual," thought Ernest. "He's in a better mood than he was this morning, though. Done a good stroke of business, I expect."

"But I was so vexed about those Bedford cords this morning, for one reason and another, that I'm afraid I spoke a bit sharp without getting to the bottom of the matter. What really happened, eh?"

"I wondered you didn't come up and have a word about them," said Ernest crossly.

"I've been away from the mill all afternoon. What really happened?"

"I missed my bus and was late, and the lads put those cords on to be cropped ordinary, in the absence of special instructions. Of course if I'd been there, I should have set the machines different."

"That's a bit of Cliff's work, I suppose," said Mr. Arnold grimly.

Ernest said nothing. He would not give away any fellow-worker to a boss, much less his own son-in-law.

"Well, it won't do young Cliff any harm to be taken down a peg; like all young men he's inclined to think too much of himself. But when you missed the bus you cost Holmelea a packet, Ernest, and that's a fact. Was your alarm clock wrong or something?"

Ernest cleared his throat. It grieved him to the heart to appear careless and irresponsible, but short of admitting his illness there was nothing else he could do. (*Finding the work a bit heavy, eh?*) He set his jaw.

"I missed the bus, that's all," he said gruffly. "It won't happen again. That's all there is to it."

There was a pause. Mr. Arnold looked put out and disappointed.

"In all the thirty years I've known you, Ernest, I've never known you late before."

Ernest remained silent and gazed obstinately at the fire.

"Nay, I'm losing my eyesight now on top of everything," he thought in despair, for a cloud of steam appeared to him to be rising on the hearth.

"I'm afraid I'm a bit wet," said Mr. Arnold apologetically, leaning forward and holding one of his trouser legs towards the fire. More steam poured out.

"But did you get as wet as that just coming up my steps?" exclaimed Ernest, astonished.

"No. I've been involved in a bit of an unpleasant affair," said Mr. Arnold in a reluctant tone. "Up Blackstalls Brow way. An old man gassed himself, alone in the house with a pregnant daughter. We had to help carry him down to the ambulance, and find her husband, and all that. No time to put on a raincoat."

"Why, you must be soaked!" exclaimed Ernest. "Millie!" he shouted.

Millie appeared in the doorway.

"Put the kettle on and make a cup of tea. Mr. Arnold's soaked."

Without thinking—for any man who was wet must be warmed and dried—Ernest bent forward to throw more coal on the fire. The swift movement brought an agonising stab of pain. Ernest involuntarily gave a sharp cry. He sat back, clutching at his stomach.

"Why, you're ill, Ernest!" exclaimed Mr. Arnold. "What's wrong, eh?"

"It's nothing," said Ernest, straightening up. "Make up the fire, Millie."

"He's been poorly for some time, Mr. Barraclough," burst out Millie on her knees before the fire, energetically piling on coal. "He's seemed better lately, so I haven't bothered, but yesterday he took a sharp turn for the worse. He was up most of last night, being sick and that. He thought I was asleep, but of course I wasn't. Me and Kenneth both told him this morning he wasn't fit to go to the mill, but he's that obstinate, you know. Right down stubborn when it's anything to do with his work."

"Have you been to the doctor, Ernest?"

"Aye, I've been."

"What does he say about you, then?"

Now that the catastrophe had happened and his illness was revealed, there was a certain grim satisfaction in admitting it at its worst.

"I've got myself a rich man's disease, seemingly," said Ernest. "A stomach ulcer."

"Oh, Ernest!" exclaimed Millie. She turned towards him, still on her knees, and tears came into her eyes. "You might have told me, you might indeed."

"Ulcers come from worry. You'll have to go to bed for six weeks or so and drink milk," said Mr. Arnold. "That's what my father-in-law, who was a doctor you may remember, used to prescribe."

Ernest was silent.

"Now I take a real look at you, I can see you're thin and a poor colour. I wonder you didn't keep him at home before this, Mrs. Armley," said Mr. Arnold in a tone of some reproach.

"He never told me a word of what it was till this minute," wailed Millie. "I never heard a word of an ulcer till tonight."

"Have you been to the doctor again this afternoon?"

"No—I didn't leave the mill," said Ernest, offended. Just because he was ill and missed a bus, was he to be suspected of a complete disregard of duty?

"Well, you'll have to stay away tomorrow and go to the doctor, that's certain," said Mr. Arnold. "And then see you do exactly what he says. See you look after him well, Mrs. Armley, for I can't do without him—the thought of young Cliff managing the cropping makes my hair stand on end."

"You'll have to look after it yourself," said Ernest slowly.

"Yes, I reckon that's what it'll come to," said Arnold with a sigh.

"Or get another foreman cropper," said Ernest. In spite of himself his voice quivered as he made this crucial suggestion.

"Oh, talk sense, Ernest," said Mr. Arnold irritably. "You'll be back in a few weeks. Now let's see. You'll draw your National Health sickness benefit, of course. How much will that be, now?"

"I've no idea," snapped Ernest untruthfully. "I've never had occasion to draw it."

"Well, they'll know in the mill office. We shall make up the difference between that and your usual wage, of course. That is, if I'm allowed by the insurance regulations. Heaven knows what we're allowed to do nowadays. I'll make enquiries. In any case, we can get round it one way or another—a lump sum out of the general account, if necessary. I'll manage it somehow. Clifford can bring it up for you—he lives nearby, I think?"

"It's very good of you, Mr. Arnold," began Ernest in an angry tone: "But I don't want anything but what's my rightful due."

"Oh, rubbish, man! It's customary. Well, I'm glad I came up tonight."

"So am I, Mr. Barraclough, because he'd never have told you if you hadn't found out," said Millie, getting up from the hearth. "He takes everything so much to heart, you know. As I always say, Ernest by name——"

"What about that tea, Millie?" snapped Ernest.

"Well, if you'll excuse me, Ernest," said Mr. Arnold: "It just occurs to me that my boy's out there in the car and he's as wet as I am."

222

"Will he come in and have a cup?" said Millie. "He could dry by the fire."

"That's very kind of you, Mrs. Armley. But he's got to go back to school at the crack of dawn tomorrow, so I'd better take him home quickly to his mother, or she'll be on my track."

"Well, that's only natural," agreed Millie, smiling.

She crossed the room and opened the door.

"Goodnight, Mrs. Armley. Goodnight, Ernest."

"Goodnight."

Ernest lay back in his chair and closed his eyes.

"How are you feeling, Ernest?" said Millie, hurrying anxiously to his side.

"Well, I can't say but what I feel relieved in a manner of speaking," said Ernest cautiously.

3

Ernest pushed open the heavy door of the Borough Treasurer's Office. There were a couple of chaps standing by the Driving Licences sign, but one of them moved off as he approached, so he hadn't long to wait. In any case, it didn't really matter if he had to stand a while; not after what the doctor had told him at the surgery this afternoon.

"You've done it now, Mr. Armley," said the doctor. "You've worried yourself properly sick this time. No more half measures; it's an operation for you as soon as I can get you a bed."

So a little standing wouldn't make much difference one way or the other, and Ernest had made up his mind to get Kenneth's driving licence and give that sandy-haired young clerk a piece of his mind at the same time. He'd made up his mind what he was going to say.

"You caused me a packet of trouble by leaving your work five minutes early yesterday"—that's what he had planned to tell him.

But unfortunately the sandy-haired clerk was not there this afternoon; a grizzled man, middle-aged, cheerful and competent, was there instead. It was disappointing.

"You aren't the one was here on Monday," said Ernest when his turn came to take his place at the counter.

"No. He's not here today. His father-in-law's killed himself and his wife's had her baby too soon, so he's in a bit of trouble like."

"Why, that must be the one Mr. Barraclough was telling me about last night! I hope the baby's all right," said Ernest, shocked.

"I believe it is, and the mother too, though naturally she's upset about her father," said the clerk, writing busily.

"Ah," said Ernest, thinking with compunction of the anger he had felt against the sandy-haired young man, and casting it aside: "We never know the whole story, do we."

"We don't at that," agreed the clerk, licking the gummed strip of the licence. "Perhaps it's just as well."

"Nay," said Ernest feelingly: "It's better to know."

THE END